In the autumn of 19... ...seven years old, his ...story that became the ... had just been appointed as a lecturer in Jewish Mythology, at the University of Leiden, and was deliberating on what area of research he should concentrate. The story that his grandfather told him helped him to decide to specialize in the Jewish oral tradition of folklore and legend. Eventually Isaac was to produce over six hundred cassettes of interviews with Ukrainian, Lithuanian and Polish Jews, containing stories of the Shoah – the period in history that gentiles generally refer to as the Holocaust. It was a valuable and unique archive. Most of the stories depicted miraculous interventions – how people had been saved from death and torture.

All of Isaac's background research was on audio cassette, mainly because it was the quickest and easiest method of collecting research material, but also because Isaac was blind.

*

I knew that the tape of Yehuda's story existed but it had not been catalogued in the university archive, and it was not until the spring of 1999, when Isaac was attending a conference in Milan, and I was clearing out his sock drawer, that I stumbled upon it. It was a few days before we were due to embark on our annual pilgrimage to Ukraine. That night I listened to the story, and the next day I completed the transcription of the tape and lodged the cassette in the university archive where, I presume, it still exists, waiting to be found by some curious research student who will probably never realize its true significance, and who will simply reference it as tape JL/20c/169/IG.

After I had listened to his story, I looked at the old photograph of Yehuda with his long white hair and the deep diagonal scar across his forehead and realized why Isaac had spent so much time sitting in front of the photograph talking to his grandfather, even though he couldn't see his face. Isaac had worshipped Yehuda. I had never met him, but I learnt from Isaac that he was an unusual man, and that something strange had happened to him during the war. I knew it was something out of the ordinary, and I had always been curious about it.

*

It is the first of five stories concerning five individuals, four men and a child, my own son, Aaron Goldmund. Their stories are quite different from each other, yet in one respect they are the same. It is a strange connection, and at first, when I began to recognize the connection, I was somewhat dubious about it – but as I became more acquainted with these stories, I began to realize that many people have experienced a deeply personal sense of divine intervention in their lives, which, for the most part, they tend to keep secret from the world. I count myself fortunate that I have been able to be witness to the testimony of these five individuals, and although their stories are likely to be viewed simply as fiction, I ask you to consider the possibility that they are not.

*

The first story is narrated by Isaac Goldmund. The other four stories are narrated by myself.

***

Johanna Klein, Spring 2007

regards.

John Smalley.

The author J. M. Smalley was born in Oldham, Lancashire, and studied Fine Art at Brighton and the Royal College of Art, London. He worked for fifteen years as an artist and lecturer in art and design, before training to become a Jungian Analyst at the C.G. Jung Institute, Zurich. His paintings, prints and sculptures are in museum collections and private collections in Europe and U.S.A.

He works as an analytical psychologist in Manchester and in West Yorkshire, where he currently lives, and where he enjoys spending much of his spare time writing, and hill walking with his three huskies.

The Serpent's Bride

J M Smalley

The Serpent's Bride

Vanguard Press

VANGUARD PAPERBACK

© Copyright 2007
J M Smalley

A CIP catalogue record for this title is
available from the British Library.

The characters of Otto and Liselotte Hassenstein are historical persons who lived
and worked in the Ukraine and aided the Jewish people during the Shoah. I have
intended to portray them as accurately as possible, and trust that reference to
them in the fictional context of this book, will not offend their relatives.
Otherwise all characters in this book are fictional.

Cover illustration. 'The Shekhinah' by the author, J. M. Smalley.

ISBN-978 1 84386 403 5

*Vanguard Press is an imprint of
Pegasus Elliot MacKenzie Publishers Ltd.*
www.pegasuspublishers.com

First Published in 2007

**Vanguard Press
Sheraton House Castle Park
Cambridge England**

Printed & Bound in Great Britain

YEHUDA'S ORDEAL

Tape JL/20c/169/IG. 'Grandfather'.
Narrator – Isaac Goldmund.

When I was twenty-seven years old, six years before my grandfather died, he bought a small bottle of Polish spirit, a bottle of French wine, a half box of rather expensive Belgian chocolates and some bread and cheese from the delicatessen. He purchased a few logs and kindling from the ironmonger next to the synagogue, and a dozen small schnapps glasses from the novelty gift shop just around the corner from the apartment. I was with him at the time and I recall that he had asked the shopkeeper if it would be possible to redeem part of his money by returning some of the glasses intact. She made a rather blunt comparison with the likelihood of pigs flying and the miraculous restitution of her hymen, which at the time we both considered was a fairly definite refusal to his request.

When we arrived home, Yehuda lit a fire in the hearth, and we squatted on the rug in front of the fire, drinking the wine and Polish spirit and eating the bread, cheese and truffles. We had never before had an open fire in the hearth. We hadn't needed one, the flat was adequately heated by electricity. It was my first taste of Polish spirit or, to give it a more appropriate name, "fire water", but it was a suitable accompaniment to my grandfather's story.

It was unusual for Yehuda to splash out like that. We were not poor, by any standards, but he normally kept his purse strings well tied.

I popped a truffle into my mouth. 'Grandfather, I know it is my birthday today, but it's not particularly a special birthday. It is also *Rosh Hashanah*, but you don't normally go to all this trouble and expense. I can only remember the time when I first came to live with you that we celebrated in such a manner. We ate apples dipped in honey and raisin bread, and listened to the sound of the *Shofar*. So what's the big occasion this year, Grandfather?'

'We are not just celebrating your birthday and *Rosh Hashanah*. We are honouring my meeting with Grossmann. This year is the first year that I can share and enjoy the occasion openly with you, Isaac.'

'Who is Grossmann?' I asked.

'All will become clear in a while,' he whispered, 'but don't you remember that a few months after you came to live with me I promised that some day I would tell you the tale of how I cunningly evaded the Nazis, and after many days of mental strife and intense physical endeavour, I overcame my fear of death and the conflict within me, and eventually arrived in Sweden as a free man?'

'I do Grandfather,' I replied. 'I remember distinctly that I was mesmerized by what you said, and I remember begging you to tell me the whole story there and then.'

'Did I not promise you at that time my little *boychik* that one day I would reveal the details of my ordeal? Details that no soul has ever heard before today?'

'Yes, of course I remember. I have asked you every year to tell me the story, but you have always refused.'

'That's true,' he said, 'and each time I stressed that when you heard it you would be amazed to the extent that it would change your life, and that if and when my secret was revealed to the outside world, my exploits would go down in the annals of Jewish history and my name would be as famous as such legendary heroes as young King David, Joshua and Samson.'

I coughed to clear my throat. 'Leave it out, Grandfather,' I said, 'I'm twenty-seven years old now, and I'm not so easy to impress as I was when I was six. I am a lecturer in Jewish mythology at the University of Leiden. I'm not a little boy any longer, or hadn't you noticed. I appreciate the trouble you have gone to, but you have probably missed your chance. You should have told me when I was six, when I was more impressionable. Legends don't amaze me to that extent now.'

'Oh really, well, today one will,' he announced with great authority and gently placed a glass of Polish spirit in my hand. 'To Grossmann!' he said.

I stood up. I felt his glass touch mine, and heard them tinkle. 'To Grossmann,' I responded and threw the Polish spirit down my throat. It was a mistake. I might as well have been drinking volcanic lava. I heard his glass crash into the fireplace, and I threw mine in the same direction, but I think it missed the hearth and rolled along the rug. I stumbled into the bathroom and put my throat under the cold water tap. I flushed the toilet and, after returning to the living room, resumed my position on the rug and apologized for needing to urinate at such an inappropriate time.

'Indeed,' he said and laughed, 'now listen carefully, Isaac. Today I am going to tell you of my ordeal. You must remember every word, and when your own son is old enough you must tell him exactly what I am about to tell you.'

'I think it is highly unlikely that I will ever have a son, Grandfather.'

'Pishtt, Isaac. Don't interrupt. Listen.'

He was gradually losing patience with me, and I realized that he considered this occasion to be of extreme importance. He then began to relate his story.

*

'First, before I tell you of my ordeal, Isaac, I will tell you what you have always wanted to know about your family. You will not like this, so stop me if you need to. Your father, Naphtali Goldmund, was one of the two hundred and fifty Jews who were executed by the *Einsatzgruppe*, the special S.S. taskforce, on the 7th July 1941 in the town of Brody, ten weeks before your birth. Your father was very brave, Isaac. He stood defiantly in front of the firing squad with his chest out as though he was mocking them by giving them a larger target to aim at. Some of the less brave clung to Naphtali as he laughed at the soldiers and accused them of being puppets of the fallen angel, Samael, by which he meant Adolf Hitler. He spoke to them in German so that his comments would be understood. I was so proud of your father, Isaac, and many times I have wished that I might have been blessed with such courage. Your father was twenty-seven years old when he died, the same age as you are now. It was a tragic waste of life. Do you want me continue, Isaac?'

I told him that I was alright, and that I had guessed that something like that had happened to my father. I had learnt enough about the Holocaust for it not to have been a surprise, and I was pleased that my father had been a hero. I told him to continue his story, though I was fighting back the tears.

Yehuda continued. 'Your mother Naomi, who had watched your father face the firing squad, gave birth to you on the eve of our New Year, *Rosh Hashanah.* Your mother and Naphtali had lived with us in Boznicza Street, in the south west quarter of Brody, fairly close to the synagogue, and just on the fringe of the ghetto. Your grandmother and I had both been born in Brody and had lived there all of our lives. I was a clerk in the town administration and many of my colleagues along with others were targeted for the executions of July 1941, but somehow I was spared. After the executions had taken place, I was asked to be part of the *Judenrat*, a small group of Jews who were ordered to control their own people in accordance with the requirements of the invading troops. For that I was promised special privileges.

'I declined the offer. I felt that my involvement with the town administration was endangering both myself and my family, and I was desperate to find a way to keep my family out of danger. We couldn't just leave the town; we would have been shot on the spot. We had to find a way to gradually ease ourselves from the ghetto to a place from which we might be able to escape. I approached Otto Hassenstein, a German forest administrator, and begged him for work. Otto was sympathetic to the plight of Jews and gave me a position as a clerk, to keep records of the planting of new trees and the felling of mature trees. We were moved into an apartment for forest workers. On the wall of the house Hassenstein placed a sign that read: *This house is under the protection of the Forest Master Hassenstein.*

'Then on September 19th 1942 three thousand Jews were taken from Brody in what is now known as the first deportation. They were herded into cattle trucks and transported to the death camp at Belzec. All of your mother's relatives were deported there, and every one of them perished in the camp, mostly in the gas chamber, but some by starvation and disease. For those left in Brody there seemed to be no apparent reason why certain people had been selected for deportation and others hadn't. It appeared to be a random cross-section of the Jewish population of the town – old people, children, the strong and the weak, the skilled and the unskilled, and in fact it was.

'That's what worried us most, Isaac. Those that were left in Brody had no way of assessing whether or not we would be deported to the death camps. There was no obvious reason for selection, until slowly inch by inch the truth crept up on us like a snake in the undergrowth. It gradually began to dawn on us that we were all going to be killed. It was not a question of who it was only a question of when. It was a lottery, and it was not determined by who we were or what we did. It was simply a matter of time. It didn't make any difference whether we were useful or not, criminal or pious, we were Jewish. That was the only criterion. We were all meant to die, every single one of us. The gradual realization of this fact struck fear into our hearts. Some people couldn't live with that degree of fear and committed suicide. I cannot describe the dread that I shared with the whole Jewish population of Brody during that time.

'Six weeks after the first deportation, the Nazis organized a second deportation to Belzec. Your mother was amongst those selected, as was my wife, Hester, your grandmother. When your mother arrived at Belzec, she was made a *capo*, one of those employed to work in the camp cleaning up excrement inside and outside the gas chambers and preparing the next victims by shaving their heads. Your mother may well have had to prepare Hester for the gas chamber, although it is more probable that Hester was selected for extermination as soon as she arrived in the camp. I have since learnt that Hester was gassed by hydrocyanic acid fumes (Zyklon-B pellets). She was one of six hundred thousand Jews to have been killed in the camp mostly by that method. Your mother also died there. She had been a witness to the atrocities and was not allowed to survive and testify about what she had seen. She was only twenty-three years old at the time of her death.'

I began to sob, and my grandfather heard me. He was quiet for a while and then told me that he was sorry that he had kept this information from me, but that he wanted me to understand it within a broader context. I didn't know what he meant by that, and I asked him what he meant. He said that he had felt that he needed to wait until I had gained a personal understanding of God and the meaning of human existence, and that I needed to have some faith or belief through which I could bear the senseless destruction of my family. He told me that perhaps the rest of his story might explain it better, and that he had promised not to reveal it to me until my twenty-seventh birthday. Then he asked if I wanted him to continue.

I requested a "time out". I went into the bedroom and cried for my parents. I said a prayer for them both. I was away for perhaps twenty minutes. When I returned he was still sitting patiently where I had left him. He said nothing apart from, 'So, I will continue, Isaac.'

I nodded my head and Yehuda continued.

✻

'I was working in the forest the day that my wife and daughter were deported. Otto Hassenstein had received news of what was happening in the town, and had informed me of the deportation. He had to physically restrain me from running into the town in what would have been a futile attempt to save my family. Otto persuaded me to continue working for him, which saved me from the appalling conditions of the ghetto.

'After the second deportation of three thousand Jews from Brody, when your mother and grandmother had been sent to the death camp at Belzec and had perished at the hands of the Nazis, news began to trickle back to Brody that those selected for the journey had in fact been killed. It did not come as such a shock, but for months I had been trying to convince myself that they were still alive. Now I decided that both my wife and daughter had been killed, and you along with them. I asked after you and searched everywhere, but I could not find you. I decided that I had to leave my home town of Brody. I began to realize that the situation there was not going to get any better. It was getting worse every day.

I had escaped the second deportation because I worked for Otto Hassenstein. The remaining Jewish people in the town were being held as prisoners in a closed ghetto, which was overcrowded and riddled with disease. The ghetto was surrounded by barbed wire, and most of the people there were starving. Some that I had known previously had committed suicide rather than face the prospect of being the victims of a third deportation to the death camps or even worse – the prospect of slow starvation.

'Only the members of the *Judenrat*, who confiscated the food that was being smuggled into the ghetto, had sufficient rations for themselves and their families. It had become a dog eat dog situation, which revealed the inherent weakness in human nature – that the veneer of civilization is not so strong, and that a significant fracturing of its surface will always allow the titanic instinctual behaviour to break through. Even so it is also difficult to blame anyone for wanting to preserve their own life.

I sensed that I was in imminent danger despite Otto's promise that he would be able to protect me from his countrymen. So, on the 10th September, 1943, I left the house of Otto Hassenstein. I couldn't stay with them forever. It would have been too dangerous for Otto and his wife, and also for me. They could have been shot for sheltering me. In fact a few days after I left, Otto and Liselotte Hassenstein were both arrested by the Gestapo. I learnt about this much later. Otto lost his position working for the German authorities and Liselotte was sentenced to death, but her sentence was eventually commuted to two years in prison.

*

'Somehow, unconsciously, I had anticipated what was to happen. I had decided that my best chance of survival was to leave and try to reach Sweden. I was forty-five years old and more than physically capable of undergoing the trek. I reckoned that my only real chance of freedom was to strike north in a line that ran between the German front and the Polish towns. The Germans were already deep into Russian territory. I could not go west into Czechoslovakia or Germany, or south into Moravia and Rumania, which were also German occupied territory. To the east, in Russia, the war was at its bloodiest, and rumours were rife that the Russians were being starved into surrender. I was surrounded on all sides. Eventually I decided to head for the Baltic Sea, from where, if I was lucky, I might be able to get to Sweden or possibly England. I knew a reasonable amount of Polish, though I realized that I couldn't pass as a Pole, and I had a rough knowledge of Lithuanian. I knew the forest trails for the first thirty kilometres of the route, and Otto had given me a hand drawn rudimentary map that covered the next fifty or sixty kilometres. After that I would have to navigate by the North Star and trust to luck.

'My plan was to stick to the forest trails as much as possible and make my way north to the Baltic port of Gdansk, where I would try to get passage on a boat to Malmo. I intended to skirt around the towns and villages along the route – Dubnow, Kovel, Brest, Siedlce, Mazowieka, Nidsica and Elblag. I had chosen the route nearest to the Russian border with Poland. The other route north would have meant getting too close to Warsaw, to the death camps of Treblinka and Sobibor. The German army was too far to my right to be a problem for me. But I had to be cautious crossing their supply lines and careful not to be spotted by Polish informers. It was a journey of over six hundred kilometres.

'Liselotte had given me a little food – bread and cheese wrapped in muslin, as well as potted meat and Polish sausage wrapped in grease-proof paper. She had also provided me with a bottle of water and a small bottle of Polish spirit. There was enough food for perhaps the first three or four days. I was wearing a vest, flannel shirt, waistcoat, cord jacket and trousers, and a cloth cap with flaps that covered my ears, and I hoped that I was suitably dressed to survive the trek. I didn't even have a change of clothes. Autumn had been early that year, and on most mornings there had been a harsh frost on the ground. So, in order to ensure that I would keep as warm as possible, I stuffed newspapers in between my vest and shirt, and around the lower half of my trousers, and tied rough jute sacking around my legs and shoes. My shoes were fairly sturdy and not that old. I reckoned that they would probably last the journey. I was ready for my adventure. I was ready for my ordeal.

*

'Leaving in darkness at nine in the evening, after thanking Otto and Liselotte for their generosity and bravery, I walked away from them with a heavy heart, not knowing what was to be my future. Liselotte shouted after me, "Yehuda, take care with the *grosse mensch*. If you meet one of them, keep still and don't run." What had she meant by that? Who were these big people – a Siberian Yeti, or perhaps a Polish Big Foot, or a Russian Mujik? It wasn't like her to indulge in fantasy and folk tales, so perhaps it was her name for the S.S. Perhaps she meant that if you run they will shoot you. I wasn't too accepting of her advice. I had already resolved that I was not going to die by starvation. I would rather have been shot than starve, and I was prepared for that eventuality.

*

'As I set off on my journey, I could not get the images of Hester and your mother from my mind. I tried singing and humming to myself, I tried reciting prayers and the *Kol-Nidre*, but the pictures would not go away. The overwhelming sadness and the feelings of guilt about abandoning my wife, daughter and you, Isaac, gnawed away at my resolve, and many times on each and every day of my

20

journey I almost turned back to give myself up to the Nazis. The intense conflict within me almost broke me in two. As I entered the blackness of the forest and tasted the pungent and slightly sweet scent of wild garlic, tears streamed down my face and froze in the tangled strands of my beard. On that first night and many of the other nights after that my beard was as stiff as a washboard. You could have used it as a drum.

'I made good progress during the first few nights. I had sharp eyes in those days and I soon acclimatized to seeing quite well in the dark. There wasn't any moonlight on the first two nights but I was acquainted with that particular section of the forest, and I felt safer without the moonlight. My strategy was to walk through the night, through the coldest hours until about eight in the morning, when it was beginning to get light, and to try to find a place where I could conceal myself and sleep during the day. I knew how to make a rough raft bed from spruce branches and birch twigs, to keep my body away from the damp moss on the ground, and to cover myself with fern fronds.

A few times, when I felt that I was sufficiently distant from villages and roads, I lit a small fire. The days when I sat by a fire, gazing into the flames, and feeling my body gradually warm were the most sensual and comforting experiences of my whole life. I'm telling you, Isaac, when you are cold, wet and starving a fire is better than sex, better than alcohol and even better than food. Prometheus should have got a medal for stealing it from the gods. Why hasn't he been made an honorary Jew, already? Somebody should unchain the *goy* and shoot the eagle that's been dining out on his liver for far too long.'

I smiled and he laughed out loud. He had always been the more ardent fan of his own jokes.

*

21

He placed another glass of spirit into my hand and clinked his glass against mine. 'To Grossmann,' he shouted.

'To Grossmann,' I echoed. Our glasses hit the back of the fireplace almost simultaneously. 'Tell me about Grossmann,' I asked, feeling for the plate of chocolate truffles. 'Was he one of the *grosse mensch*?'

'Patience,' Yehuda snapped. 'So where was I – day three, I think? I had got about one hundred kilometres north of Brody, perhaps close to Kovel, and I was beginning to make my way north east. I felt good. My food had run out, but I replenished my water bottle a few times when I stumbled across clear springs. I had to be careful with drinking water, Isaac. Most of the water in the forest was stagnant, fetid and poisonous.

'On day four I had a near miss with a division of German troops that I heard approaching along a forest path, but fortunately the noise of their jackboots alerted me to them long before they came into view. The Germans didn't know the meaning of stealth. I dived into the undergrowth. They goose-stepped past me without noticing me, but my heart was pounding furiously. The next day I was spotted by a game warden. He approached me with a shotgun, pointing it at my head ready to shoot me. He probably thought that I was a poacher. He looked at me for about a minute, and I really thought that he was going to shoot me. So I lifted my cap and let my *payos* hang down. He nodded to show that he understood. He shook his head as if to inform me that I had no chance, but wished me good luck nevertheless. He walked away, still shaking his head.

'The next few days were uneventful. I was in a daze, and if anybody had spotted me I wouldn't have been able to run away. I was so desperately tired. I knew that I had managed to skirt around Brest, from the signposts on a road that I had crossed, and I knew then that I had completed about a third of my journey. It had taken me six or seven days to get so far. I had lost count. I was a little confused by then. Sometimes the forest paths were rocky and overgrown with bracken, which slowed me down and hindered my progress. I hadn't eaten for three days, and on the next day I caught two frogs. I considered eating them, but I wasn't yet desperate enough. I let them go.

During the first eight or nine days I was also feeling so guilty about Hester and Naomi. I would stop and cry for ten minutes or so every two or three hours, before carrying on. By then I must have looked like a wild man. I said my prayers every morning and every night. I prayed for my own deliverance but mostly I prayed for Hester, Naomi, and you, Isaac, and asked God to be merciful and to welcome you all into His arms. I was still racked with guilt but I knew by then that I must survive this ordeal for your sake, although it also seemed pointless. Many times I felt that Naomi and Hester were with me and sometimes when I started to feel sorry for myself and when I was about to abandon my expedition, I would hear Hester scolding me with her sharp tongue, and berating me. I tell you Isaac be thankful that you never experienced Hester in one of her moods.'

*

He paused for a while, and I could hear that he was sobbing.

'To Grossmann,' I called out.

He stood up and helped me stand up, so that I was facing him. He slid a glass into my hand. 'To Grossmann,' he replied.

I was pleased that I had managed to get a handle on this ritual by now. Both glasses smashed into the back of the fireplace simultaneously, and we sank down onto the rug again. I was concerned that we might run out of glasses at this rate. The drink tasted different, and I realized that we had finished the Polish spirit and had started on the wine.

'It's very good wine, Grandfather,' I said.

'I should hope so,' he muttered. 'It cost me an arm and a leg.'

He became quiet for a few minutes. I didn't quite know whether he was distraught or simply trying to remember the sequence of events. I kept silent. I could hear him breathing in air, as though he was about to embark on a sprint race and didn't want to breathe out again until it was over. I assumed that we were about to meet Grossmann, and my assumption was correct.

*

'On day nine I still hadn't eaten much, since my supplies had run out, but on that day I managed to catch a wood pigeon that I had stunned with a stone. It was a complete fluke. I grabbed the bird before it came to its senses. I plucked it and cooked it on a fire, but it had little flesh on it, and I was still ravenously hungry. It was two days before my meeting with Grossmann. I was still very much in need of food. I shivered all the time and my bones had become very cold.

'By day eleven my mind was beginning to play tricks on me, and my attention was poor. I would be thinking about something quite trivial, like the words of a folksong, and then find myself sprawled out on the forest floor. I must have tripped over tree roots ten or twelve times during that night. Sometimes it took an immense effort to pick myself up off the ground.

'Then I became aware of something or someone close to me. It was about four in the morning and I had been walking for about seven hours through the night. I felt a chill run down my spine. I shook it off. I had been used to such eerie feelings when I had been forced to sleep in the forest during my work shifts. Everyone has that experience, especially at night. It is as if you are being watched by something or someone. Your hair stands on end, your scalp tingles and you become acutely aware of the slightest noise. I must have walked for a couple of kilometres with this sense of something trailing me. Sometimes it seemed to be behind me, then to the left and then to the right.

'"There is definitely something there," I whispered to myself. I would have run, if I had been physically capable of running, but I wasn't. Suddenly a man was standing in front of me, blocking my path, perhaps fifteen metres away. I froze. He didn't speak, and neither did I. I stood looking at his silhouetted frame. He was a mountain of a man, perhaps two and a third metres high, and stocky with it. Eventually I plucked up enough courage to address him.

'"Good morning," I said in Polish. He didn't reply. He just looked at me. I tried again in Yiddish, in German and then in Ukrainian. Still he said nothing. The combination of his immense size and his silence scared me to death. I swear that, if there had anything in my bowels at the time, it would have been evacuated involuntarily. I watched him as he slowly dropped to the floor and started to crawl towards me, emitting growling noises. Oh, hell, I thought, it's a bloody bear. Excuse me, Isaac, I hope you don't mind me using such language.'

'Not at all, Grandfather,' I answered. I had never heard Yehuda swear before, but it didn't seem out of place on this particular occasion. 'That's fine,' I said.

'It was a bear,' he continued, 'a huge, full grown brown bear. I sank to my knees, made myself as small as possible and wrapped my arms over my head. People have since told me that it is the best response when confronted by a bear. But I didn't know that at the time. I was petrified, and I couldn't do anything else. I had worked in the forests for two years and I had never until that day come across a bear. Of course I knew that they were around in the forest. I had seen their tracks and the occasional mounds of bear shit and my reaction had always been the same – I wouldn't want to meet the beast that had left that behind. Now I had it confirmed. My trepidation had been justified.'

I don't know how Yehuda had felt at the time, but I was shaking like a leaf just hearing about it. 'So what happened then?' I asked.

'Well, it seemed like ages, but the bear gradually ambled up to me and started to sniff around me, particularly around my genitals and backside. Then it came around to the front of me, sniffed again and licked my ear. It would have been a pleasurable experience if it had been a Labrador dog, but having one's ear licked by a full grown brown bear, when you are completely alone at night in the middle of a forest is not so pleasurable. I almost passed out. I decided that whatever happened I wasn't going to move an inch, although I am not sure that this was such a conscious strategy. I couldn't do anything else. I was petrified, frozen to the spot and trembling like a rabbit caught in a trap.

'The bear placed a huge paw on my head and licked my ear again. Its tongue was warm and it seemed to be a friendly gesture, but there wasn't the slightest possibility that I was going to move and look up. I was playing possum, and there was no way on earth that I was going to inform the bear that I was a warm blooded creature. I was a rock or a tree stump or a rather large deposit of natural compost, but I was absolutely not a living being. I didn't have the guts that your father had, Isaac. I couldn't stand up and challenge the bear.

'Eventually it seemed to lose interest in me and walked away to sit perhaps fifty metres in front of me. From somewhere I gathered the courage to stand up, although I was still shaking. We must have eyed each other for thirty or forty minutes. I was hoping that the great oaf would move off into the forest. But it didn't. I was in a standoff. It wasn't going to move and I wasn't going to turn and run. I remembered Liselotte's advice and I also remembered that once, just outside of Brody, I had been confronted by three Russian soldiers who took great delight in informing me that they were going to whip me. I had decided at the time that if that was the case, they would have done it already. They wouldn't have given me notice if they had really meant to do it. They wouldn't have allowed me to be on guard and prepared to defend myself. So I simply walked past them. You see it dawned on me that if the bear had wanted to kill me it would have done so by now. Despite the fact that I was shaking so much, I decided to walk a few steps towards it. As I did, it got up and started to walk in the same direction, keeping the same distance between us, and every so often looking back to make sure I was still there.

'We walked along the forest path for two hours – the bear in front and I following him, a respectable distance behind. Then he turned off the path, and I thought that this was where we were to part. But he kept looking back at me. He wanted me to follow him. We walked through the bracken, weaving between birch saplings, until we came to a clearing, where a few roughly sawn tree trunks had been left to rot on the ground, and there in the middle of the clearing lay the body of another bear, slightly smaller than the one that I had been following. It was obviously dead. A few crows were already perched on its flank, pecking through the fur but they flew off as soon as we arrived, and I noticed that they had already taken the eyeballs.

'It must have been about nine in the morning by then. The sun was faint, and it was beginning to get foggy. I sat on a tree trunk staring at the dead bear. Grossmann (that was the name I had given the other bear) looked at me and suddenly bolted from the clearing into a dense area of the forest, roaring as it went. I realized that I was not expected to follow. I sat there for an hour or so waiting for Grossmann to return, but he didn't. I gathered some branches and started a small fire. There was no risk of being detected. The fog was quite thick by now, and I was deep into the forest. I sat by the fire naked, drying my clothes and trying to dry the sheaves of newspaper padding, but they had mostly disintegrated by then. They had been soggy for days and, instead of keeping me warm, they had contributed to my being bitterly cold through to my bones. I was in danger of becoming hypothermic. I rubbed myself and stomped around the fire like a Red Indian until my clothes were dry enough to put back on. "What are you doing here?" I asked myself. "How on earth are you going to find your way back to the path?" I started to weep and eventually fell asleep on the ground next to the fire with the dead bear lying on the far side of the fire. I slept for perhaps a couple of hours and dreamed that I was in Sol Goetschel's restaurant in L'Viv, ordering roast bear and potatoes with a wild garlic sauce, served on fern fronds.'

✻

Yehuda put another log onto our fire. 'More wine, Isaac?' he asked.

'No, Grandfather. Please carry on with the story. If I drink any more wine, I won't be able to remember all the details.'

He laughed. 'Well, if you can't, nobody can.'

He was right – I had an excellent memory. In my studies I had to remember everything when people read to me, since there were few books in Braille on my subject.

'Go on,' I said. 'You were dreaming that you were eating bear.'

'Yes. The dream woke me up. I looked at the dead bear, and went around to it and touched it. It was cold but not stiff.

I decided it had died perhaps ten hours ago. There was no gunshot wound or other obvious damage. There were some old scars on its muzzle. "She must have died of old age," I said to myself, and retreated. You know, Isaac, when you have been on your own for ten days you begin to speak your own thoughts.'

I smiled. He had done that all the time that I had known him, alone or not.

'Go on,' I said, 'what did you do?'

'Well, I decided that I was meant to eat the bear, or as much as I could. It was a bit large for one sitting. Sol Goetschel's restaurant was strictly *kosher*, so God must have given me permission to eat the bear, since in the dream I was eating it in Sol's place. I also concluded that it was the reason that Grossmann had led me to her. She had been his mate and he was offering her to me. I know it sounds ridiculous but that's what I thought at the time, and I still think the same.

'It took some time for me to pluck up enough courage to approach her again and begin the dissection. I cut her open with my forester's knife and took out as much flesh as I could, hanging the hunks of meat on branches in order to drain off as much blood as possible. The crows were hovering about and dive-bombing me, but I managed to beat them away with a stick. I then hung the meat over the fire on branches. The branches kept setting alight, but I replaced them when they appeared to be getting too weak to support the meat. I ate as much as I could, and what I couldn't eat I wrapped in sheets of the soggy newspaper that I had discarded. The paper was still strewn around the clearing, caught on the branches of trees. I stuffed the bundles of meat into my jacket pockets. I must have smelled like a butcher's shop in a heat-wave.

'I know it wasn't *kosher*, Isaac, but I was in a strange state of mind at the time. Is bear meat actually mentioned in Leviticus?'

'Not specifically, Grandfather. It's covered by whatsoever goeth upon his paws, among all manner of beasts that goeth on all fours, they are unclean.'

'Yes, of course you are right. I did know that, but when I first saw Grossmann he was standing on two legs. So I wondered if bears might be classified as bipeds rather than quadrupeds, and be considered an exception to the rule.'

I laughed and admired his uncanny ability to find loopholes in most situations. He should have been a barrister. 'Well, you also broke the law by eating the carcass of a beast that was already dead, Grandfather. You were supposed to wash your clothes, and even then you would have been considered unclean until the evening.'

'I had been unclean for eleven days already. I stank and I had all manner of things crawling on me, through me and up me. What more do you want?' he snapped. 'Anyway I did ask God for forgiveness.'

'Well, I'm sure He has forgiven you by now, Grandfather. Go on with your story.'

✻

'When I was eating the bear I was engulfed by huge waves of guilt. I cried out to God to stop me doing it, but my hunger, and my instinct for survival forced me to continue. I realized that I was also eating my own guilt! That probably sounds a strange thing to say, but as I was eating, my stomach was churning with the guilt for the bear that I was eating, for Hester and Naomi, and even for Grossmann who had led me to his dead mate. Yet I carried on eating. I continued to stuff my mouth with meat and to force it down my throat with my fingers I kept arguing with myself. I hadn't killed the bear. I was not responsible for its death.

'The phrase repeated itself in my mind,
I am not responsible for its death.
I am not responsible for its death.

30

I am not responsible for its death.

'Then I felt strangely different, as if something had shifted. It took me a while to realize what it was. The phrase that I had been chanting had changed.

I was not responsible for her death.

I was not responsible for their deaths.

'The guilt was lifting. I understood the reason for the bear's motive. His mate was dead too, and he had led me to her so that I might not die pointlessly. He had offered her to me and then run off to suffer his pain and his loneliness, as he was supposed to. Despite the sadness that I felt for Hester and Naomi, I could not continue feeling guilty about them. I was not responsible for their deaths. My guilt had been an avoidance of grief and a temptation to throw my life away. The Nazis had killed them, not me. Suddenly it became tremendously important that I shouldn't die as well by their hands. I didn't know why that was. I didn't consider that I had an important mission in life as such, but perhaps I had some purpose to fulfil, like Grossmann had done; and that sometime in the future I might be asked to help a soul who was as lost and as helpless as I was then.

'I was about to leave the clearing when a thought suddenly struck me. It seemed such a waste to leave a perfectly good coat to rot on the forest floor. I returned to the carcass and shooed away the crows. I skinned the bear, scraped the pelt clean, and rubbed wild garlic cloves all over it, to keep the flies off me. I cut a hole for my head and wore the pelt like a poncho. It was heavy but it was warm. As I stumbled through the forest and eventually got back to the track, I was tired and sweating profusely, and I knew that I was running a fever.

'I decided that I needed more sleep. I had only slept for two hours that day and the food in my stomach was being digested and making me feel even more tired. I found a secluded spot just out of sight of the path and fell into a deep sleep. I remember waking up or thinking that I had woken up. I was dreaming but it seemed so lucid. I swear to this day that what happened next was real. Grossmann's mate appeared – the one I had just eaten. She crawled up to me, placed a paw on my thorax and slit my sternum and my abdomen with a single stroke of her claw. She started to tear out my vital organs and eat them, stripping the flesh from my bones and leaving only my head intact. I had consumed her, now she was consuming me, slowly and methodically. After she had finished, she laid out my bones on the ground and ambled back into the forest. That is the shortened version, Isaac. The procedure was slow and protracted, and it seemed to take for ages – and all the while I was experiencing unbelievable terror.

'After it had ended, I slept for twenty-four hours or more. It was bright daylight when I regained consciousness. I lay there rigid and shaking, remembering what had happened. I had to feel my limbs to make sure I was still there. I noticed that there was a trickle of blood coming from a wound in my forehead – a long diagonal wound that could have been made by a bear's claw or a branch that I had possibly stumbled into. Eventually I got up with the intention of continuing my journey. A tall figure was standing in front of me. It was Grossmann, but he was half man and half bear. No, that's not quite right. He was a mixture of man and bear, or something in between, and was carrying a long birch staff.

'I did not think it then, but looking back, knowing what I do now, I think Grossmann was, or had become, a *Lamed-Vovnik*. He had a human face and looked so much like you do now, Isaac. I didn't know it then, but now I know it was you.'

'Please, Grandfather,' I said, 'you are stretching things a bit too far. I was only two years old at the time.'

'I know that, Isaac. I had met Grossman on the day of your second birthday, and I agree that the figure wasn't a two-year old child, but the figure could have been your *neshamah*, your spirit soul, and the bear could have been your *nefesh*, your animal soul, or perhaps my own. Don't ridicule me just yet. I have proof that somehow this meeting was connected to you.'

I was stunned into silence, and I thought it best that Yehuda continue with his story.

✻

'The figure greeted me and said, "I know the way to Gdansk, Yehuda. Allow me to travel with you, and show you the way. The rest of your journey will not be an ordeal, it will be *Halikhah*," I was not sure if I was still hallucinating, but I agreed to follow the figure. I thought that the hallucination would soon wear off, but it didn't. Was I crazy? Had I invented an imaginary friend? We walked for a couple of days through the forest, and all the while he was talking to me about the medicinal properties of the herbs and plants that grew in the forest, about the concept of *nefesh*, the animal soul, and about *gilgul*, the transmigration of souls. I had ceased to see him as a man or a bear. He was simply my companion, and it was good to have a companion.

'Eventually we came to a road and he said, "From now on we walk on the roads. It is much quicker."

'"But isn't it dangerous? We might be spotted," I asked, afraid that it might be a crazy part of myself trying to get me killed.

'"No, we won't be spotted; trust me," he said.

'We walked along the road and after about ten kilometres we approached a German checkpoint. I had not anticipated it. It was on the far side of a sharp bend in the road, and we were at the checkpoint before I realized it. We walked right through it unnoticed. There were about ten German guards standing in the road and we walked right past them. We almost touched them and they simply didn't see us.

'My companion laughed, "Well, did we get spotted, Yehuda?"

'I couldn't answer him. I was in shock.

'This situation recurred about ten times during the remainder of the journey, and on each occasion the Germans failed to see us. But occasionally we would encounter a Jew or a friendly Polish peasant, who evidently could see us. Sometimes they would stand dumbstruck, and sometimes greet us and offer us food. And so with my companion's help, eventually I managed to arrive at the outskirts of Gdansk. It had taken me twenty-four days to cover just over six hundred kilometres.

'The first building we came to was no more than a rough hut. Outside the hut a young woman of about seventeen years of age was sitting on a bench, throwing pieces of dry bread to some geese. My companion went over to her and talked to her for about five minutes. She was giggling and laughing. He came back and told me that the young woman would help me for the remainder of my journey. He gave me a small leather wallet, which he said contained enough money for the boat and a message for my grandson. I protested that I had no grandchildren; that my grandson was dead, or so I believed. He insisted that I take the message and told me to keep it until my grandson was twenty-seven years old. He forbade me to read the message until the day that I read it out for my grandson. As he left and walked back down the road, I wept at seeing him go and shouted my appreciation to him. I watched him slowly sink down on all fours and turn back into a bear, and I cried as he disappeared into the forest. I felt desperately sad at seeing my companion, whom I had begun to rely on so much, walk away from me.

'The young woman beckoned to me. She told me to strip naked and that she would wash me. There was something about her, Isaac, which I can only describe as a benign authority. I could not have done anything else but what she requested me to do. I did as she asked. I took off my clothes and she washed me from head to toe and presented me with a neat pile of clean clothes to wear. I put them on. They were clothes normally worn by Polish sailors. She placed a cap on my head and tucked my *payos* into the cap. By that time I was barely conscious of who I was or where I was going. My head was spinning. Inside the cap, which I only realized later, was a small embroidered label that read, *Yehuda Katz, son of Bracha Katz, Brody.*

'The young woman walked with me to the docks and found a boat that was heading for Malmo. We strolled past the German customs control as though she did it every day. The German soldiers nodded their heads and smiled at her. She had charmed them before and she was doing it again. She kissed my brow, as though I was her father or uncle, and I felt my forehead glowing with warmth and light. Then she walked away swishing her hips and waving at the German guards, who appeared to be completely mesmerized by her. By then I was safely on the boat to Malmo, and you know the rest, Isaac.'

*

I sat cross-legged on the rug, feeling slightly drunk with the wine and Polish spirit that I had consumed, but conscious that tears were rolling down my cheeks. I wanted to tell Yehuda that I knew who she was, and that she had also helped me. I couldn't speak, but I felt that Yehuda knew already. He took my hand, opened my palm and placed a small cloth label into it. I knew what it was.

'Is it the same as mine?' I asked. I had kept the label that had identified me when I was five years old.

'Yes,' he replied, 'they are identical – the same cloth and the same coloured thread.'

He took it back and placed a slip of paper in my hand.

'Is that the message?' I asked.

'Yes,' he said. 'I have just looked at it. I was right. I knew that my companion was you. It appears to be a message from you to yourself. It is signed Isaac Goldmund.'

I felt a chill run down my spine. I knew that Yehuda might exaggerate some things, but I had never known him to lie. 'Are you sure it is signed by me? Is it really my signature?'

'Yes. It is definitely your signature.'

'What does it say, Grandfather?'

'It says – *Join me at the Kloiz in Brody when you feel that you are prepared.*'

'Prepared for what?' I asked.

Yehuda laughed and said, 'If you don't know, Isaac, then you are probably not prepared.'

I sat for a long time wondering what he meant by that remark. Suddenly I heard the sound of the fluttering of wings and a familiar scent of wild columbine filled the room. I didn't ask what it was. I knew what it was. I had heard about it; but I also realized at that moment that I had experienced it once before when I was five years old. It was my most precious memory.

'Was that her? Has she been in the room?' I asked.

'Yes,' he replied.

***

That was the transcript of the tape that I listened to when Isaac was attending the conference in Milan, a few days before we left for Ukraine. It helped me to understand so much more about Isaac's life and why he had venerated his grandfather so much.

The tape was to grow in significance over the next few years. I already knew that Isaac had also experienced the Shekhinah helping him when he was most in need of help, but I wasn't to know that her presence was to affect three other people whom I knew, one of whom was not born yet, but was already in this world.

Isaac returned from Italy and I think that he suspected that I had listened to the tape. He probably realized that something had changed. I had always been a little in awe of Isaac, but now I was running round the apartment treating him as though he was royalty. It didn't last long. Soon we were back to bickering at each other again. It was impossible to have an unruffled relationship with Isaac. He was a walking contradiction. I think that's why he had acquired the nickname The Blessed Grizzly which is something of an oxymoron. Even though Yehuda claimed that Grossman was a manifestation of Isaac's animal soul, which is hard to believe in the sense that it contravenes most people's normal view of physical reality, at another level it makes perfect sense.

✻✻✻

THE BLESSED GRIZZLY

Most people who were acquainted with Isaac Goldmund would confirm that he was incorrigible, and could never be relied upon to behave in the slightest way like a *zaddik*. He preferred to present a negative image of himself to the world, displaying such traits as stubbornness, irritability and gruffness, which aren't exactly the qualities that you would expect from a righteous man – more the characteristics of a bear, I suppose. But that was exactly what Isaac intended. He wanted to be mistaken for a bear, or at least he wished not to be viewed as a *zaddik*. It was part of a strategy that had been constructed over the years, and there was a good reason for it. Most of the time it enabled him to avoid being consumed by hubris, which as he often testified is the most dangerous of all sins, and most likely the root cause of all the others. For some years he had been aware of the danger of spiritual pride, and had decided that it was safer to serve God incognito. So he had adopted the persona of a bear in order to save himself from the unwanted prospect of being publicly venerated as a holy man. It was a conscious deception that didn't need too much rehearsing. There had always been a good deal of the bear in his nature.

I don't wish to disparage the ursine population of the earth, especially after having listened to Isaac's tape about his grandfather's meeting with Grossman. I am sure that in proportion to their number there are as many virtuous bears as there are humans, if not more. But when faced by a bear most of us wouldn't hang around long enough to establish its disposition or its moral inclination. And the same can be said about people who were unexpectedly confronted by Isaac Goldmund. So it is hardly surprising that most people were cautious when approaching him, and generally gave him a fairly wide berth.

The most obvious component of Isaac's bear disguise was a full-length moth eaten fur coat that he had picked up from a Berlin flea market in the winter of seventy-one, and which came with the seller's assurance that there had only been one previous owner. It wasn't like the overcoats normally worn by Hasids. It wasn't a garment that particularly flattered him. It made him look even more intimidating and it didn't even appear to have been tailored to fit the human frame. In fact it seemed more than likely that the one and only previous owner of the coat had actually been a bear, not someone masquerading as a bear!

Isaac once told me that it had smelled so much of wild garlic that he simply had to buy it. I had failed to see the logic in that remark until I listened to the tape about his grandfather and realized that there was another reason why Isaac was so fond of the coat. Still, the purchasing of the coat had been a masterstroke in Isaac's overall plan to keep his spiritual ranking a secret, for it is hard to imagine that anyone who had actually met Isaac in the flesh, or indeed in the fur, could be persuaded to believe that he was destined to enter into the hallowed company of Jewish saints. If they could accept the idea, they would most likely conclude that holy men are in fairly short supply nowadays and that God had felt the need to drastically reduce the entry requirements. But I know that this wasn't the case. I knew Isaac better than anyone. He deserved some acknowledgement of his spiritual attainment, even though he didn't desire it.

Of course he would never admit to his strategy. Whenever I mentioned it, he would laugh and call me a fanciful girl, or some such derogatory term. But you can't sleep with a person for five years and not discover their deepest secrets, especially when they are constantly talking in their sleep.

*

'What are you writing about, Johanna? I can't sleep. You keep giggling and shuffling about. It's very annoying. Are you writing about Yehuda?'

'Why should I be doing that?'

'My tape has mysteriously disappeared from the sock drawer. So I presume that you have listened to it recently.'

'Yes, do you mind?'

'No, not really, I was thinking that it was high time you knew about our secret. So what are you writing about?'

'Actually, I'm writing about you, Izzy.'

'For God's sake, Johanna, you are supposed to be writing about Wilton. Why the hell are you writing about me?'

'Wilton mistook you for Philip Grimes. So I need to establish who you are, in order to prove who you are not. Is that alright? I am introducing you into Wilton's story, and I was just about to set the scene of your childhood.'

'My childhood, I didn't have one,' he barked. 'Leave me out of it. You know how much I detest biographies of childhood. They are mostly inaccurate and always far too sentimental. Even if I could remember having one, I would prefer to forget it. You will probably stereotype me as some blind wandering Jew looking for Jerusalem. I've spent years trying to shake off that projection.'

'Alright, keep your hair on. I'll just say you grew up in the dark, Izzy. Is that alright?'

'Fine, at least it can be verified. Now, turn the light off.'

'Why do I need to turn the light off? You're blind. Or am I stereotyping you?'

'The bulb is buzzing. Just turn the light off, Johanna.'

*

Isaac's dismissal of childhood biographies was mostly influenced by the fact that he didn't have a history of his own, at least not until he was five. He remembers a few fragments from his infancy – different sounds, tastes, some names and voices, but no coherent story and no images. Isaac was blind from birth, and, to make matters worse, there is no record of his existence between the ages of fourteen months and five years. Nobody, not even Isaac, knows what happened to him during his early life, since on the 2nd November 1942, at the age of fourteen months, Isaac Goldmund disappeared off the face of the earth and only emerged again in 1946 at a camp for displaced persons in Hagen.

He arrived at the camp in the care of a seventeen-year-old girl who told the nurses that she had been asked to look after him by an old woman who was dying. The girl gave no further information about Isaac, and disappeared as mysteriously as she had appeared. The only clue to Isaac's identity was a small embroidered cloth patch that had been stitched to the inside of his ragged trousers. It read – *Isaac Goldmund, son of Naomi Goldmund, Brody, Ukraine.* It was little to go on, but the existence of this small label eventually enabled Isaac to be reunited with the only other surviving member of his family, his maternal grandfather, Yehuda Katz.

*

After Yehuda's ordeal, when he had also miraculously survived the war thanks to the assistance of Grossman, he lived for a short time in Sweden, and eventually settled in Den Haag, where there was a small Hasidic community, and where he managed to secure employment as a postman. When he was informed of the fact that his grandson was still alive, he welcomed him with open arms. From then on they lived together in a tiny one-bedroomed apartment. Isaac was six years old when he went to live with his grandfather. He arrived on the eve of *Rosh Hashanah*, which, Yehuda informed him, was also Isaac's birthday. Since Isaac had been born on the eve of *Rosh Hashanah*, Yehuda insisted he celebrate his birthday on that day every year, even though it was a different date each year. It was a moveable feast, but at least is didn't get forgotten.

During the first few years together, Yehuda considered that Isaac was too young to be exposed to the full impact of his family's suffering. He informed him that his parents had been killed in the war, but declined to give any further details. Isaac would often plead with his grandfather for more information about his parents, and Yehuda would describe how they had been as children, how they met, how they had fallen in love, but nothing about how they had died. One year when Isaac had been pressing him more than usual, Yehuda said that he didn't know how they had died. It was a lie and it was the only lie that he ever told his grandson. I can understand that it must have been frustrating for Isaac that the truth should be hidden for so long, but as it turned out his grandfather had his reasons. Of course Isaac eventually learnt about the Holocaust, and assumed that his father and mother had both died in a concentration camp. Isaac eventually learned the truth about his parents, when Yehuda told him the story and it only confirmed what he had already guessed.

*

Yehuda and Isaac had both survived the *Shoah*, and had found each other, but behind them hung a dark and depressing backdrop. Yet they managed to find joy and to laugh again. I never knew Isaac then, when Yehuda was alive, but he told me of the hilarious times that they had together. It wasn't all happiness though. In his youth Isaac had rebelled in the only way he could. He couldn't rebel like most adolescents. He couldn't play truant from school, and go off on his own somewhere. He could only rebel from within. His frustration at the restraints that his blindness caused him broke out in episodes of intense rage, when he would go berserk in the apartment breaking furniture and harming himself. When that happened, Yehuda knew that Isaac wasn't simply being fractious, but that somehow his earlier suffering was being exorcised. He sat with Isaac during those times until he became calm, and gradually the episodes became less frequent and less intense, and Isaac began to feel better about himself. He was bright and did well at school and later he studied at the local university.

In those days books in Braille were fairly limited, but Yehuda read printed books to him and helped Isaac memorize what he needed from them. It was not a chore for Yehuda. He shared Isaac's interests and enjoyed the subjects that he had chosen.

After Yehuda died, Isaac continued to live in the tiny apartment that he and his grandfather had shared for twenty years. He was a respected member of the Hasidic community, where he was known as Professor Goldmund. I called him Izzy, but generally referred to him as Isaac. At the university he was known affectionately as The Blessed Grizzly.

*

Amongst the numerous legends and folktales that Isaac collected for his work at the university, there was one that he preferred above all others, and which he would relate whenever an opportunity arose. It originated in Ukraine, and concerned a young woman, dressed in a Jewish bridal dress, who jumped from a crowded train in order to escape the death camp. She disappeared into the forest, holding an infant in her arms. It is generally accepted that the legend refers to an incident that actually happened during the second deportation of Jews from the town of Brody to Belzec concentration camp, though there are many variations of the tale that cite Treblinka, Dachau or Belsen as being the destination. Still, whatever the historical basis for the legend, there were numerous reports that this young bride was spotted in different locations around Ukraine and Poland, even as far north as Gdansk. After the war a belief gradually developed amongst the survivors of the Holocaust that the young woman was the *Shekhinah*, the Bride of God, who was saving the soul of a good man. Some people, uncertain of their parentage, claimed to have been that child, and a few incorporated it into the delusion that they were the Messiah.

Isaac's fondness for the story had always intrigued me, and I began to suspect that his concern with it went beyond professional interest. But whenever I asked him if he had ever considered that he could have been that child, he groaned like a demented walrus.

'Don't be so fanciful, Johanna,' he would say, tugging at his beard. 'Jewish legend is my subject. I am not the subject of Jewish legend. There is a difference. You should know better. Anyway, even if I had been that child, I would hardly want the world to know about it.'

I was always a little suspicious when Isaac denounced anything so vehemently. There was usually more than a grain of truth in it. Of course Isaac had chosen to study myths and legends, but it was not just an arbitrary choice. It is not coincidental that a boy without a history should grow up to be fascinated by mythology, and would choose it as his area of research. For Isaac, mythology was always preferable to history.

*

I watched him sleeping and recollected the times in the park when I had been living rough, and Isaac occasionally brought me food. I remembered when he first told me of his childhood and the miracle of his surviving the Holocaust. It was a turning point in my own life, as though my problems had suddenly dissolved and my feelings of anger and resentment regarding the accident of my own birth, my attitude to my parents and my rebellion against my own destiny had lifted, and I had felt for the first time an indescribable sadness for another human being.

I think Isaac told me his story because he knew it would help to cleanse the anger in my heart. He put his arm around my shoulder and said, 'Do not be sad for me Johanna. When my sight is returned to me and I can see for the very first time, I will be gazing into the Face of God, and in that moment I will see everything that has been kept from me during my lifetime; and much more, so much more. Do not be too concerned about my childhood. I have already received enough compensation for what happened then. If you wish to cry, then cry for my family, but do not ever picture me as the helpless child that I was then.'

I promised that I wouldn't.

It is hard to keep a promise when it goes against the tide of your deepest feelings; when you are caught in a vortex of emotions that easily overrides your strongest resolutions. As I watched him sleeping, I thought about the problems that he had faced at such an early age, and how for some children sleep must be the only respite from anguish. For some children sleep is the only mother. Isaac was fifty-eight years old at that time, but I often saw him as the five-year-old boy who had arrived at a refugee camp in Hagen, tired and bewildered.

***

2.

I was twenty-two years old when I first met Isaac in the park in Den Haag where I sat begging for food and cigarettes. I would like to say that I had run away from home, but that's not really credible when you are twenty-two, and anyway I didn't run away. I didn't run anywhere. I sleepwalked aimlessly from one limbo to another, perhaps in the vain hope that I was more visible sitting on the wooden bench in the park than I was in that small bedroom in Scheveningen, and that there was more chance that ultimately I would be found; that some divine messenger would tap me on the shoulder and announce, *'Johanna Klein, thank God I've found you. You are supposed to be in New York working for UNESCO. They need you. You are irreplaceable. We have all been waiting for you at the airport. Hurry there is still time.'*

It didn't happen quite like that. It wasn't so sudden and the messenger wasn't so obviously divine. In fact he was in his full disguise. He would wander into the park three or four times a week wearing his bear coat, shuffle up to the bench next to mine, sigh, recite his prayers with his head nodding like a metronome and then leave without any acknowledgment of my presence at all, though I was aware that he knew that I was sitting within earshot of him. Then one day he suddenly decided to speak to me.

'You want a bagel?' he muttered.

'I'm sorry, are you speaking to me?' I asked.

'Who else would I be talking to? Do you want a bagel or not? You look like you could do with a bagel.'

'How would you know what I look like? You are blind, aren't you?'

He groaned and turned his head to the sky. 'So why is the world always such hard work, Lord? Is it not time yet? What's with a few years? Can't you just beam me up now?'

I smiled. 'I'm sorry. I didn't mean to upset you. Yes, I would like a bagel. Shall we share it?'

He laughed and tossed the bagel in my direction. I caught it.

'Fine, we will share it. You have the bread. Leave me the hole. It's usually the best bit.'

We talked for a while then he shuffled off. He seemed so lonely. But I knew nothing about him. Perhaps I was projecting my own loneliness onto him. After that day he often brought me food and cigarettes and we would chat about all sorts of things. It was then that he told me about his childhood.

*

One afternoon it was raining hard and I was soaking wet and feeling even more miserable than usual. I asked him if it was possible for me to stay at his place for a night and dry my clothes. He said that he only had a one-bedroomed apartment, but I could sleep on the living room floor for one night. He stressed the word <u>one</u>. I knew that since Isaac was blind I would have sufficient privacy, and that I would be safe. I didn't reckon on his snoring, which resounded through the walls of the apartment, and sounded like an elephant with a migraine. I hardly got a wink of sleep all night. One night led to two and then to three, and by then I had managed to find some cotton wool for my ears, so I slept a lot better. I did errands for him and cleaned the apartment. It had been in a real mess when I first arrived.

After a week he said, 'I see that you have become one of Rilke's habits.'

'What do you mean by that?' I asked.

'"*The perverse loyalty of some habit that pleased us, and then moved in for good,*" It's a quote from Rilke, a German poet. Have you ever read Rilke, Johanna?'

'No, I don't think so.'

'Well, there's a copy of the *Duino Elegies* on one of the shelves. It's in German. Do you read German?'

That was a bit of an insult to a Dutch woman. 'Of course I read sodding German. I'm Dutch,' I snapped.

'Ah, yes,' he replied, 'a slack jaw, a foul mouth and a number of tongues. Isn't that what they say about Dutch women?'

I ignored him. I found the book and devoured it in one go. It was exquisite. I hadn't realized how hungry I was for something, and I hadn't realized that it was knowledge that I craved, not bagels. I said to Isaac, 'Isn't it wonderful how she managed to describe human feelings in such a profound way?'

'She's a man, Johanna,' he replied.

'Rainer Maria Rilke is a man? I don't believe it. How can he describe feelings like he does? My father was really bad with feelings and he never ever talked about them.'

'Well, that must have been a blessing for you,' Isaac said and smiled.

'What do you mean?'

'I mean that if he was so bad with his feelings, it must have been a blessing that he didn't talk about them.'

I hadn't thought about it like that. My esteem for my father had suddenly lifted a notch. Well, okay, perhaps half a notch.

*

I read another book that night, *Stories of God* also by Rilke, and in the morning I started on Baudelaire. I was hooked. I felt like I was in Aladdin's cave, and the treasures were all around me, stacked on bookshelves. They had been Yehuda's books. I read every day, and hardly went out that second week. Isaac bought me a futon, so I knew I was welcome to stay longer, and then he helped me study for the examinations that I had flunked at school. A year later I passed them and enrolled as a student in world religions at

Leiden University, the course that Isaac taught. I didn't hide my past, or conceal the fact that Isaac had encouraged me to apply, and Isaac wasn't involved in the selection process so nobody disapproved, or so I thought. At that time I had no romantic interest in him, and he had less in me. But that changed when I was in the first year of my course, and I fell in love with him.

＊

Five years later, Professor Kuntz, my tutor in the Department of Gnosticism, was reviewing my application to do a doctorate thesis on Simon Magus. He pointed his biro at me, and told me that he was slightly concerned that my obsessive interest with Simon Magus and Helen was perhaps a little too influenced by my own relationship with Isaac. He told me that I wouldn't be able to sustain a high enough level of objectivity, and that I was an extremely confused young woman. I told him that I was twenty-seven years old and not a schoolgirl, and to stop pointing his biro at me. In fact I told him where to stick it, and to get his nose out of my affairs and back into the book he had open on his lap, *Pistis Sophia*, which was probably the only thing he knew anything about.

It wasn't the most political strategy, but then I have never been particularly good at politics. He hadn't the slightest idea about life or love – as though my love for Isaac was a bastardization of some mystical allegory. It wasn't at all like that. Anyway why shouldn't Simon Magus and Helen have loved each other? Why couldn't Helen have been his lover at the same time as performing the role of *Soror Mystica*, the mystical sister and accomplice of alchemists?

Fortunately Kuntz, despite his outrage at my offensive remarks, was outvoted on my thesis proposal. I'm sure that at the time Professor Weissel and Professor Kemel were also concerned about my motivations. They had assumed because Isaac had never said anything to them or anyone else, that I was his secret concubine, and that he was ashamed of our relationship. Fortunately they both changed their minds about it. But Kuntz still shook his head when he saw us together. Quite frankly Isaac didn't care what anyone thought, but sometimes I felt like walking through the university with a placard, telling everyone the truth.

I AM NOT BLIND – IT'S ISAAC WHO IS BLIND!
HE IS NOT A REPLACEMENT FATHER FIGURE.
I AM NOT ENTHRALLED BY HIS ERUDITION.
I LOVE HIM OKAY.

＊

Isaac advised me against it. He said that it might start a craze and snowball. He thought that eighty or so students walking down corridors all wearing sandwich boards proclaiming their undying love for some tutor or other could create a log jam. Anyway, does anyone fall in love, without being unconscious to some degree? The Greeks used to say "*Eros possesses me*," and Isaac called falling in love a pleasurable insanity.

It took me two years to seduce Isaac. He was a hard nut to crack. We occupied the same apartment for those years, and sometimes I felt that I was going mad. Eventually I knew that he shared the same feelings that I had, but he wouldn't give in to them. Sometimes I felt that he was so besotted with the *Shekhinah* that he could not love a mortal woman, and to some extent my concerns were well founded. He did acknowledge that point; and when eventually I did sleep with him, he said, 'Now, my little dove, I am in heaven, but if this has been a disappointment for you, fly away, fly away,' – as though he was addressing the *Shekhinah*! I felt like flying away, I can tell you, but I didn't. Men are so inept after intercourse, and some are pretty inept during it.

＊

Isaac was an academic, but he did very little research that the university deemed appropriate for someone who held the Chair of Jewish Mythology. Still he managed to survive in the university largely through a mixture of his understanding of the predictability of people and his ability to pre-empt their criticism of him and ultimately avoid it. This allowed him to focus on his real work, which he described as being in the service of the *Shekhinah*. Even though Isaac was blind he was not one to stay at home and indulge in the contemplative life. His mission was to seek out where the *Shekhinah* had manifested herself in human history, and this involved travelling from place to place, practising the Hasidic ritual of *Halikhah*, which is sort of equivalent to the Christian and Islamic practice of pilgrimage. During the years that we were together Isaac visited most of the places where Jews had settled after the diaspora, though his favourite journey was to Ukraine.

I can't remember exactly how many years I accompanied Isaac on his annual pilgrimage to Ukraine. I think it is five or possibly six. I always enjoyed the trek from Brody to Medzybiz, and meeting the other members of Isaac's secret group, but I can't remember that any of those trips were more notable or memorable than any of the others, except for this particular year, when we encountered a British psychiatrist who appeared to be in dire need of his own professional services. His name was Dr James Wilton, but he preferred to be called Jim. Isaac had asked me to make a record of our meeting with Wilton. He seemed to think that it was important, although at the time I couldn't imagine why. I could understand why Isaac would consider our meeting with him to be unusual or even bizarre, but I couldn't understand why he considered it important enough to commit to paper. Isaac was reluctant to commit anything to paper, especially when required to do so by the university.

***

3

We were returning from our annual pilgrimage to Ukraine which, except for the cities of Kiev and L'Viv, looks, tastes and smells differently from most European countries. There is less traffic and the people seem less frantic, less concerned with hurrying all the time. But there is something else about Ukraine that is different. It is as though the old culture of the country is being slowly strangled, and because of that, throughout the thickly forested landscape of that remote region of Eastern Europe, there is a mood that hangs in the air, that clings to the spruce trees and lingers like mist in the valleys. It is fused with the poisonous sulphur from the steelworks and the nuclear fallout from Chernobyl, and it smells of death. It is slowly suffocating the people that live in that land. They have come to realize that it is pointless to protest against the death of their old traditions, and they also suspect that their eventual rebirth, if one can call it that, will be as part of a soulless collective Europe. The deeply unconscious mood of Ukraine is mourning the imminent death of its own soul. Isaac felt this. I know he did, but he rarely talked about it. Each year, when we visited the home of his ancestors, this feeling seemed to get stronger, and it was difficult for Isaac to accept the changes that were occurring in his homeland.

He pretended that it was his interest in the Baal Shem Tov, the founder of the Hasidic movement in Carpathia that drew him back to Ukraine each year. But there was more to it than that. He was in the stage of mourning which is ruled by anger, and he was refusing to let go of his anger and cry for the loss of his family, and for the land and the culture that he loved. I think that is why he was always so crotchety on the journey home. Even though he had only lived in Ukraine as an infant, perhaps for a couple of years at the most, Isaac could not break the tie with the land of his birth, where so many of his relatives had suffered and had been so cruelly killed.

*

During the return flight I had been jotting down a few facts about Jim Wilton, when quite by chance I glanced across at Isaac. I was totally astonished at what I saw. He had suddenly acquired a halo. The aircraft had banked into a turn, and the window where Isaac was sitting was filled with an eiderdown of billowing clouds. Rays of sunlight reflecting from the aircraft's wing pierced the porthole and radiated outwards. A nimbus formed around the dark silhouette of Isaac's head, a dazzling aura of scintillating colour and light. It appeared out of the blue, hovered around his head for about eight seconds then vanished as suddenly as it had appeared. If I had been looking from a different angle or if Isaac had moved his head slightly then it might not have been so noticeable. But fortunately I was in the exact position to witness it and fortunately he didn't move! The halo did appear. Of course you may argue that it was probably created by a rare combination of natural phenomena. The window may have acted as a prism. But one is still left with the question – why did the halo encircle Isaac's head so perfectly? Was it a coincidence, or was it a sign from God?

I already knew the answer to that question. I had always hoped that one day I might witness Isaac's sanctification, but it still came as something of a shock. You read about such strange occurrences, but it's different when you experience them for yourself. Your emotions are all mixed up and your reactions aren't as expected. Well, mine weren't. As soon as the halo appeared I shrieked with laughter. I didn't mean to laugh, and fortunately Isaac didn't appear to be too bothered about it.

For a few minutes I kept trying to detect the slightest sign that he had also been affected by the event. I looked for a

53

wry smile of pleasure, an expression of awe, some evidence of rapture, a seizure or even sudden death. But there was no indication that he had found the experience to be either agreeable or disagreeable. He broke wind, shuffled around in his seat and sat with his head bowed over his knees and his chin in his hands. This had the effect of returning me to the mundane world rather sooner than I would have preferred.

*

I bent down to pick up my notebook.

'Read the page again, Johanna,' he said, tugging at his beard.

'Just a minute, Izzy, I'm preoccupied at the moment. I need some time to collect my thoughts.'

'Yes, I heard you laughing. What was it that amused you? Was it about Wilton?'

'I'd rather not say. It's not easy to explain. I need time to reflect on it. Have you been praying since we boarded the aircraft?' I enquired as casually as I could, so as not to raise his suspicions. It didn't work.

'Why do you want to know?' he growled.

'Just answer the question. Have you been praying?'

'I might have been. Why do you want to know?'

'Oh, for goodness sake, Izzy, stop being so perverse. Tell me what you were praying about.' I pinched his leg and he winced.

'That's between Him and me,' he whined. 'It's really none of your business, Johanna. Why are you being so aggressive?'

'I need to know. It's important. I think it might have caused something to happen. Tell me what you were praying about.'

'I can't see what it has got to do with you, but if you must know I was asking God to ensure that there would be a minimum of turbulence on the flight and that my luggage wouldn't be sent to Moscow, like last year, if you remember.

Is that alright? Does that help with whatever it is that's worrying you?'

'Yes, that's fine, Izzy. It doesn't help me though. Let's hope God comes up trumps with the luggage request. He's already let you down on the turbulence deal.'

'Why do you say that? There hasn't been any turbulence.'

'Forget it, Izzy. I'm just off to the loo.'

As I walked towards the rear of the aircraft, I glanced back to see if the halo had returned. It hadn't.

✻

I know that most people will think that I have read far too much into the event. I certainly can't imagine that any of Isaac's friends and colleagues would consider it even faintly possible that he was a candidate for sanctification. They would be more likely to dismiss the idea out of hand and be rather more concerned about my sanity than Isaac's supposed sanctity, which is probably the reason why I have kept it a secret for so long.

I had always felt that Isaac was different in some way, but now I suspected that he had entered the ranks of the *Lamed-Vovniks*, those holy men of whom so little is known. It is written that they walk alone at midnight at the very edge of the world wearing only rough coats and carrying birch staffs. They are searching for the scattered sparks of lost souls, helping them to return to God, and to restore the holy vessels which at the moment of the creation of the world were smashed into billions of tiny shards. Some kabbalists believe that before this momentous event occurred, all God's creatures were unified in one great soul. I have also read somewhere that on the Day of Doom, when the *Lamed-Vovniks* are cold and weary of their work and of their isolation, they will gather together and approach the Throne of Glory to warm themselves in the Holy Gaze of the Face of God.

As I returned to my seat the image that confronted me was not that of a saint but more like Saturn in Durer's engraving of the hapless god, (who incidentally also suffered from turbulence.) It might have seemed that Isaac was depressed, but he wasn't. He was simply thinking and he was making more of a meal of it than was warranted, grinding his teeth and tugging his beard, which invariably signalled that he was bothered about something.

✻

'Good, so you are back. Now read the page again.'

'It was only a few lines, Izzy. Can't you just tell me what you think?'

'No. I need to hear it again, Johanna.'

My head was still reeling from the vision of the halo, but I opened my notebook and began to read out loud the opening page of my story about Jim Wilton. I had almost reached the point where I had mentioned that Dr Wilton rarely coveted the possessions of his neighbours, when Isaac interrupted me, and launched himself into a diatribe about the dangers of covetousness. He brought up the example of King David falling in love with Bathsheba, who was already married to King Uriah, and how David coveted her so much that he put Uriah into the front line of the army in the fight against the Hittites, in order to have him killed.

But it wasn't David coveting Bathsheba, or even Dr Wilton coveting the wife of a colleague that was worrying Isaac – what got him riled was the fact that ever since I started at the university, Professor Kemel had been sniffing around me and was intent on seducing me and taking me away from Isaac. To make it worse, Kemel was Isaac's arch rival from the department of Islamic studies – his nemesis, or so he believed. Isaac could be so insecure sometimes.

✻

'So there we are, Johanna,' Isaac concluded. 'Kemel...I mean David, brought disrepute upon the house of Israel.'

'Yes, I know that. You have told me the story hundreds of times. I agree, but....'

'He invited her enemies to smear her name, and the Hittites were not slow to respond.'

'Izzy, why do you keep going on about the Hittites? Do you have some personal vendetta against them? That's the third time today that you have mentioned the Hittites. What on earth have they done to you? They haven't been in existence for thousands of years. They are more extinct than mammoths and dodos.'

He grunted.

'Tell me, Izzy, did I actually promise to write a book about Wilton?'

He nodded. 'I'm afraid so, in the taxi on the way to the airport.'

'Well, I hope you realize that I have neither the talent nor the energy to write it.'

'It's not so hard, Johanna. Everyone has at least one book inside of them.'

'I wouldn't necessarily argue with that,' I replied in a loud whisper, snapping my pencil in two. 'I am disputing why on earth mine has to be about Jim Wilton.'

Isaac smiled. 'Well you offered to write it, my love. And by the way, you can't be more extinct. It's like death. You're either dead or you're not.' He coughed and began to tug at his beard again.

*

Isaac could be infuriatingly picky. It had become an ingrained feature of his personality and probably stemmed from years of scholastic argument with Professor Kemel. He was trying to help me, but it had the effect of making me want to tear out the page of my notebook and start again. The teacher in him was his most irritating personality. He was different when he was dancing and when he told his wonderful stories about the Hasidim. Now he was sulking and I told him so.

The in-flight food arrived and we were soon attempting to bite through impregnable cellophane wrappings and trying to eat cold salt beef and potato salad with plastic cutlery. I looked to see if Isaac was still muttering to himself. He was. He turned his face towards the window and sighed. Eventually he fell asleep.

*

The remainder of the flight looked like it would be fairly uneventful, until Isaac woke up suddenly, turned in his seat and accidentally dropped his stick on the floor. It happened just as an air hostess was manoeuvring a trolley of tax-free goods down the aisle of the plane. It was an unfortunate blunder. She reacted instantly to the noise and swooped down on us. She was unusually tall and skinny with shiny black hair, cut in a severe pageboy style, and she had rather too much black mascara around her eyes. She wore a tight fitting black skirt with a matching jacket and dull grey tights, which wrinkled at the knees, making her legs look even scrawnier than they actually were. The cumulative effect of these minor features made her appear like an anorexic crow.

*

'Did you want to buy something, madam,' she squawked through her lip-gloss, 'perfume, Eau de Cologne?'

'No, thank you,' I said.

'Wine, spirits, cigarettes, a watch for the gentleman, calibrated to one hundredth of a second, functional at sixty fathoms, with eight time zones and a state of the art compass?'

'What do you think, Izzy? Would you like a watch like that?'

'What should I want with such a watch?' he sighed.

'It has a compass, eight time zones and works at sixty fathoms.'

Isaac coughed up a little phlegm and dribbled it into the plastic tray that still contained half of his lunch. 'Well I don't,' he growled.

'You don't what? You don't want me to buy it for you?'

'No, I don't work at sixty fathoms. In fact I can't imagine what in heaven's name I would want to do down there. And if I did have the misfortune to have to work at a depth of sixty fathoms I would hardly be concerned about what time it was in another part of the world. I'd be more concerned about getting the hell back up to the surface again, and I wouldn't need a compass to figure out which direction to take.'

'Izzy, there is no need to be rude.'

He grunted and spat a little more phlegm into the tray. 'I see. You would like me to be more polite, Johanna. Alright, if the young lady can guarantee that this plane is going to plummet to the bottom of the sea, to a depth of sixty fathoms, in the next forty minutes, I might be tempted to buy the damned watch, just to check whether the watchmaker's claims are correct, even though I can't see to use it! Is that a little more considerate?'

The air hostess looked slightly embarrassed and completely bemused.

'Was that a yes?' she asked as she recoiled from the sight of Isaac's phlegm.

'I think you should take it as a no,' I replied.

'Oh, right. Well, could I interest you in the Flying Dutchman?' she asked as she opened a large metal drawer in her trolley, pulled out a cuddly raccoon dressed in a pilot's uniform and held it aloft, first to one side of her body and then the other, in the manner of a magician's assistant. I smiled to myself. It looked like the raccoon had borrowed her mascara. He had a black ring around each eye, although his rings were not as heavily painted as hers.

'It's a raccoon, Isaac. It's very cute and so lifelike,' I said.

She hopped closer. 'It's one hundred per cent genuine rabbit fur. So you would like to buy it then? Will that be American Express, Visa or guilders, madam?'

'No, I'm sorry. We really don't want to buy anything, thanks. We weren't trying to attract your attention. My friend accidentally dropped his stick.'

'I see, well have a nice day.' She cawed as she minced down the aisle.

I waited until she was four or five rows away. 'Why did you have to drop that stick of yours? That hostess got herself into a fluster over nothing. I felt like carrion on a country road, the way she was flapping around me.'

'What on earth has it got to do with me, Johanna? Couldn't she see that I'm blind? Do I look like I would be interested in Flying Dutchmen or novelty watches that do everything but wipe your *tush*?'

'No, I suppose not.'

'And you wonder why I am *kvetchy*.'

'No. I have never wondered, Izzy. I have always known what upsets you. It's not that difficult to read. It's etched across your forehead like some hieroglyphic script on an Egyptian stele.'

'So tell me already. What have you deciphered?'

'That you are sad, Izzy; that you are grieving for your family, for your ancestors and for their culture. Ever since you discovered your roots you have been in mourning for your family. If truth were known, you would prefer to be amongst them. You believe that you were born a hundred years too late and that you are an anomaly in a world that is becoming more and more materialistic, more and more overwhelmed by trivia, and you are afraid that despite your best efforts you have little

60

influence over it all. You despair that everywhere people are turning their backs on God, on nature and on the wisdom of the past. You see yourself as a voice in the wilderness, like some twentieth century Elijah, and to some extent you are, but you are at your worst and least effective when you start wallowing in self-pity. So snap out of it, Isaac. It's no way for a *zaddik* to behave and certainly no way for a ...' I halted in midstream. It would not have been appropriate for me to say the words out loud – *Lamed-Vovnik*. Anyway, he pretended to have stopped listening to me. He grunted and turned his face towards the window. But he had heard what I said. I waited a few minutes for him to respond.

*

'Johanna.'

'What is it now, Izzy?'

'Let's play my game.'

'Do we have to?'

'Yes. That air hostess, what species is she?' he whispered.

'Which one do you mean?'

'What do you mean which one do I mean, already? You know – the one that smelled of rabbit and Chanel Number Five, with the watch and the raccoon, who else?'

'She was definitely a bird,' I replied, 'why are you whispering? She can't hear us.'

'What kind of bird?' he whispered.

'I would say that she is a *Corvus cornix*.'

'Ah, the hooded crow; make a note of it, Johanna. She's the first we have spotted this year.'

'Izzy, do we have to play this game all the time?'

He didn't reply. I scribbled a couple of lines in my notebook.

Spotted – one hooded crow in the company of a raccoon – 20,000 feet above Meissen.

*

I closed the notebook and began to look around the plane at the other passengers. To my left a family of rather obese orang-utans had already demolished the in flight food, numerous packets of crisps and a carrier bag full of sandwiches. They were asking the stewardess if there was any more food available. In the seat in front of them a pride of a solitary lioness was breastfeeding her cub.

'God, I am doing it again. You have started me off on it again, Izzy. I can't stop playing that animal game of yours.'

'What have you spotted? Tell me.'

'Don't get so excited. It's only five orangutans and a lioness.'

'Make a note of them,' he said.

'No, Izzy. This has got to stop. We are on a pilgrimage, not a safari.'

*

I didn't normally mind playing his game. It may appear to be dismissive of people to reduce them to type. But since Isaac was blind it helped him to get an idea of a person without me having to describe all the details. It's odd really. He had never seen an orang-utan or a hooded crow, or anything else for that matter, but it gave him some sort of reference point. Isaac said it was like the task that God had given to Adam, to name all the beasts. It was a way of becoming conscious of the separate qualities of beings, and without this reference point he was even more in the dark. I could understand that, but sometimes I had my reservations about the game, though I knew that Isaac was rarely dismissive of anybody. I suppose that the game increased my own tendency to categorize people and when I caught myself doing it, I realized how arrogant and intolerant I could be. But to be fair to Isaac, his typological classification of human personality traits was about as broad as you could get, especially when you compare it to Kretschmer's categorization of physique and character, to Jung's typology or the Myers Briggs test. But it was also more specific. You know where you are with a hooded crow.

✻

Isaac slept for a while, whilst I continued to write down the story that Dr Wilton had related to us. It was a little complicated and I was content to remember the major incidents. It had been Isaac's idea that I should write about Wilton and the strange events of that week. As usual, I had taken up his suggestion and then found myself floundering about like a flatfish, wishing I had never taken the bait. Isaac had a knack of getting other people to pursue his whims for him. Anyway, I was well and truly beached. I could have wriggled out of it, but I didn't. I was doing it for Isaac. He was an ideas broker and a good one at that, but he didn't like to get his hands dirty. He was only interested in the ideas. Other people were conned into doing the bricks and mortar part of the work. In fact Isaac managed to get through life without doing much work at all. On the rare occasions that I begged him to finish a paper, or prepare a lecture, he would always reply with the same argument. '*Zitsfleich* is the key to the path of enlightenment, Johanna. A man has to learn to put his hands under his *tush* and sit on them. He has to learn to be patient and do nothing, especially when every wise guy this side of *Sheol* is rushing around all over the place, trying to tamper with God's creation and making an unholy mess of things.'

✻

We landed at Schiphol Airport roughly on schedule, but Isaac's luggage had been sent to Helsinki by mistake, and then the train from Amsterdam to Den Haag was delayed for a couple of hours near Leiden. We weren't particularly bothered. We were too tired by then. Isaac slept and I wrote down some more of Wilton's story. It was well into the

63

evening when we arrived back at the apartment. Isaac didn't look at all well, but I thought that he was probably worn out by the journey. He hadn't been in the best of spirits on the train. Normally he would chatter away about his friends who had joined him on his annual pilgrimage to Ukraine. I enjoyed sharing the gossip that Isaac had to offer and his humorous comments on the "lost tribe", as he called them, but this year he seemed more involved with his most recent acquaintance, Dr James Wilton. At our initial meeting I had Wilton down as a stoat, but later I tended to agree with Isaac, who thought that he was probably a mongoose.

We arrived home and Isaac went to sleep as soon as his head touched the pillow. I sat up in bed and read through the first few pages that I had written about Jim Wilton.

***

As mongooses go, Dr Wilton was a fairly typical specimen – slim, of medium height with the look of an ageing pixie, gaunt but not menacing. His face was the shape of an almond, his nose thin and pointed, and his eyes were piercing and alert. He groomed himself meticulously, taking the trouble to shower and shave twice a day. Yet however close he shaved there was always a metallic tinge on his cheek and neck. His hair was short and neatly trimmed with a parting on the left, and his hands were soft, with long delicate fingers terminating in sharp manicured fingernails. His scent was a delicate hint of musk.

Despite his attempts to disguise the fact, it was fairly obvious to all who met him that he shared the mongoose's neurotic temperament. Nowadays it is becoming more and more accepted by zoologists that animals who are employed to attack and kill cobras and other deadly snakes do in fact suffer from a reasonable amount of work related stress and anxiety, and therefore are justifiably prone to the odd panic attack or even a full blown nervous breakdown. This of course cannot be cited as the reason for Wilton's neurotic temperament, though I suppose that there must be some equally understandable cause for his malaise.

＊

When Isaac and I met Wilton in Ukraine, he was at the pinnacle of his career – a consultant at Crompton Hospital for the criminally insane, with a small private practice in Harley Street. He had contributed chapters to most of the psychiatric primers currently in use at the training hospitals, and his particular expertise was on the influence of dietary deficiencies on mental illness. He told me that he had published two books already on this subject, and also informed me that he was researching a new topic. That was why he was in pursuit of a psychotic patient who was under the delusion that he was a wolf. Unfortunately the man wasn't Wilton's patient, but was in the care of an acquaintance of his, a Dr John Spencer. Wilton didn't normally covet the belongings of his neighbour; but this wasn't your everyday ox or ass, it was a wolf.

＊

Spring had arrived early that year. Squirrels, intoxicated by the prospect of summer, scurried across the hospital grounds and frolicked on the lawns, chasing their tails around trees, balancing precariously on the narrow rims of litter bins, falling into the bins and clambering out again, seemingly undeterred by his presence. They couldn't have cared less what the important looking man in the pinstriped suit was up to, as long as it didn't affect their fun and games. Wilton shared a little of their enthusiasm for the day but not their frivolity. He strode purposefully down the rutted tarmac of the hospital drive, taking care to avoid treading on the sleeping policemen that had been repainted that morning.

＊

I read it a few times and changed one or two words, all the time arguing with myself whether or not to wake up Isaac to ask him about the plural of mongoose. He would probably know the correct word. I was sure it wasn't mongeese. I seemed to remember it came from an Indian word *mongus*. Did it really matter? Perhaps Isaac had infected me with his pickiness.

'Shut up,' I said to my chattering brain. Eventually I fell asleep.

***

4.

We did nothing on the Sunday. We were both too tired. I tried to write a bit more of Wilton's story but tore up everything that I had written so far. It was too caustic. I needed some distance from it and decided I would start it again in a few days. The next morning I let Isaac sleep in, and left the apartment to visit Dr Diederik, the family doctor in Scheveningen. My periods had been going haywire for the past three months. I had been to the hospital for a few tests before leaving for Ukraine, and I thought I would pop in to the surgery to find out the results. I was worried that it might be ovarian cancer, since my grandmother had died from it. I was hoping that Dr Diederik would inform me that I had polyps in my womb, or that it was a recurrence of some infection that I had contracted during my prodigal adolescence.

My life wasn't as wanton as all that, but it's easier and more acceptable for men to admit to having sown a few wild oats. So let's just say that I reaped a few heads of barley before I settled down with Isaac. I had had two serious relationships both of which lasted about eighteen months; one with Jan, a student from Leiden University, when I was seventeen, and the other with Pieter, a grocery boy from my home village, when I was fifteen, and when I lost my virginity. Other involvements with men were fairly brief affairs, and I can't even remember their names. Despite my desperate situation from the age of nineteen, sleeping in the park and begging for food and cigarettes, I never had sex for money. I wasn't a prostitute. But I was pretty damn close to considering it before I met Isaac, before he pulled me out of the swamp that I was sinking into.

Dr Diederik's news came as something of a surprise. It also confirmed that I wasn't the *Shekhinah*, but a real woman.

The irregularities with my periods weren't polyps or an infection. I was pregnant.

✳

I didn't return to the apartment straight away. I needed some time for the news to sink in, and I wasn't really sure how I felt about it. I could feel how my body was responding. I felt more alive and excited, but these feelings were accompanied by a rather stoical voice that reminded me how this would change all my plans, change my lifestyle and change my relationship with Isaac. I wasn't sure how Isaac would take the news. It would be awful if we felt differently about it.

I spent a couple of hours with my parents in Scheveningen. At first I didn't tell them what the doctor had said. I skirted around it and used the anecdotes about Jim Wilton as a smoke screen. My parents were pleased to see me and were amused by the stories that I told them about Ukraine and my meeting with Jim Wilton. They had always considered the English to be somewhat strange and eccentric in their behaviour, so they didn't find it odd that Wilton had appeared in Ukraine wearing a pinstriped suit and no shoes.

My father was looking decidedly old. He wasn't that old, but the work on the trawlers was beginning to take its toll on him. He mentioned that he had recently made a few visits to Dr Diederik. I didn't ask why. I presumed that it was for his asthma. My mother was the same as always. She never seems to change. We sat in the kitchen drinking coffee and chatting together. My father stayed in the living room reading the newspaper. Eventually I decided to tell my mother what Dr Diederik had said. She took the news well. I think that she was secretly delighted with it, but she was never one to say so.

✳

My mother was Jewish, but my father was a bit confused about his family tree. One of his grandfathers was Dutch, but before that there was some confusion as to whether the great

68

grandfather on his father's side was German or Jewish, since Klein was a surname used by both. I had always assumed that he wasn't Jewish, since he had neither the facial characteristics nor the temperament, and he loved the sea. I think that his ancestors probably came from Schleswig-Holstein. When my father wasn't on the boat, up to his waist in fish guts, he would take my sisters and me sailing in a small craft that he had built himself. We hadn't done that for some time, since his asthma had got much worse.

✳

I once asked Isaac if he would like to go sailing, and he replied, 'Sailing to where?'

'Just sailing,' I answered, 'not to anywhere, just sailing.'

'What a ridiculous idea,' he said.

The truth was that Isaac didn't like sailing. He had been on a ferry once from the Hook of Holland to Harwich, when he was attending a conference in Cambridge. He swore he would never do it again, but he loved to tell the story of how he had gone to the cafeteria on board the ship and asked for another breakfast because he had lost the first one. The woman who was serving noticed that Isaac was blind and rushed off to look for the lost breakfast. Five minutes later she returned and said that she couldn't find it. She asked him if he knew roughly where he had lost it. Isaac replied that he knew exactly where he had lost it – over the starboard side of the ship, near the lifeboat assembly station. She laughed and gave him a free second breakfast and told him not to lose that one. I think that trip put him off sailing for good. He didn't even have the stomach for the return crossing. Someone gave him a lift to Stansted, and Isaac took a flight to Amsterdam. His luggage flew to Berlin.

✳

Later that morning, my mother and I walked in the woods and visited the Madurodam, where she used to take me when I was a child. I had always felt a strange fascination for the place, the tiny houses and the children milling around. I would go there whenever I was upset about something. Perhaps that's why she had suggested that we walk there. She told me that last week my father had had some disturbing news from the doctor. She hadn't wanted to tell me on the phone, so she had decided to wait until I returned from Ukraine and paid them a visit. It certainly eclipsed my news. My father had been diagnosed as having pancreatic cancer and it was fairly well developed and had moved to his liver. He was due to start treatment the next week. My mother was crying as she told me the news. We held each other close and I tried to tell her that maybe it wouldn't be terminal, but I didn't even believe my own words. I had recognized that look in my father's eyes. It was the same look that my grandfather had worn a month before he died. We walked home in silence.

*

When I returned to our apartment Isaac was still in bed, and he looked decidedly ill. I was not unduly worried about him, but he had undergone a strenuous pilgrimage even by his standards. I told him about my father's news, but decided to wait a while before telling him mine. He asked me if I had written anymore about Jim Wilton. I explained that I had done a rough draft of the first chapter, but that I had no idea where I was heading or what was coming next. This sort of writing was unfamiliar territory for me and I preferred the world of academic research. I had been intending to convert my thesis on Simon Magus into a book, and I was way behind schedule with it. It seemed a waste of time to be concentrating on Wilton in preference to Simon Magus. Isaac disagreed.

*

In the afternoon, P.S.V. Eindhoven was due to play an important match and Isaac had been looking forward to listening to the match commentary on the radio. It was probably the reason why he perked up a little during the afternoon, though he continued to look slightly weary. I still didn't tell him our news. I thought that I would wait until he had completely recovered. Not that Isaac ever needed pampering or treating with kid gloves. He was probably the most robust man that I had ever met, and fiercely independent in spite of his disability, or probably because of it. I had known him for ten years and during that time I had never experienced him being ill. Perhaps that is why I was hanging back a little, unsure of what to say and do. Anyway he wasn't making a drama out of it, so why should I?

I slipped out at two o' clock to get a bottle of wine and some bagels from the deli, and bumped into Wilma, a friend from university. We went for a coffee and a chat about old times. I told her that I might be pregnant. She was quite surprised that I was drinking coffee and red wine. She said that in the early stages of her pregnancy she couldn't abide coffee or red wine. They both made her feel sick, but she said that it wasn't the same for everyone. Then we talked about old times, and how Professor Kemel had been interested in her too. It was two hours before I got back to the apartment.

When I returned Isaac was standing by the window in his black fedora, vest and underpants, waving his football scarf above his head and listening to the match on the radio.

'Can't we have the curtains drawn, Izzy?' I asked.

'So why should the curtains be drawn, is it dark already?'

'No, but you can't see anything out of the window.'

'Exactly, so it makes no difference if they are drawn or not.'

'May I remind you of the nature of windows, Izzy? Lucidity is available from both sides, and because of that simple scientific fact, it does make a difference to Toybe Rosenberg and her three daughters, who live opposite. They are not blind, and the view from their balcony just happens to be one of you cavorting about in your Y-fronts. They are pointing at you and laughing, you big oaf.'

'So what is there to see? Mazeltov,' he shouted through the window, and waved for Toybe's benefit. The three daughters waved back and Toybe blew Isaac a kiss.

'She's blowing you kisses again. What is it with her, is she in love with you or what?'

'How the hell should I know?' he replied and blew her a kiss.

'Who are we playing?' I asked.

'The Hittites of course, shush.'

I smiled. 'Oh I see, and who are the Hittites this week?'

'Ajax Amsterdam – they have an Armenian striker, who is more than likely descended from the Hittites. Shush'

'Who's winning?'

'How the hell should I know? Five minutes ago we were losing two nil, and there is only ten minutes left to play. I've missed the last five minutes what with you nagging me to draw the curtains and going on about Toybe Rosenberg.'

'So what is your fascination with football, Isaac? You have never seen the game being played. Why do you get so excited?'

'It's tribal, Johanna. Am I not allowed to be part of a tribe?'

*

P.S.V. lost three nil. We had our evening meal, drank the bottle of wine and talked for an hour or so about how I should deal with writing the book about Wilton. Isaac warned me about being too flippant and impressed on me that, despite the improbable nature of the tale, the frivolous happenings and the ludicrous turn of events, the story was more important than I could possibly imagine. He urged me to look deeper beneath the surface and not get too tangled up in the humorous and often idiotic incidents that were connected to Wilton's version of events. He said that I should look up the twin motifs in Genesis, and suggested I get in touch with a man called Philip Grimes, who had written about this topic and who had access to the other half of the puzzle. I didn't take this up until much later, when I began an email correspondence with Philip.

✳

Isaac went to bed and I did as he had suggested. I looked up the stories in Genesis, but I couldn't find any connection to Wilton's predicament. I stayed up, intending to write about Simon Magus. I had been getting a bit bored with the Wilton saga. It all seemed a bit too silly for words, and I had wasted too much time on it. I was also worried about my mother and father. When I was younger I couldn't get away from home soon enough, but now I realized how precious they both were to me and how much I would miss my father if he died. I cried a little and then decided that I shouldn't be so pessimistic. My father was a fighter. He wasn't going to give up without one hell of a struggle. I phoned my mother. It was late but she hadn't been able to sleep either. I suppose I rang in order to be comforted by her, not to comfort her. My sisters, Susannah and Ruth, were still living at home, so my mother had someone there for comfort. She didn't mind that I had phoned. We talked for an hour and afterwards I went to bed. But I couldn't sleep. I decide to do a little work on the story.

I wrote a few pages and then began to wish that Isaac would wake up. He was talking to himself in his sleep again, and I needed to talk to him, to take my mind off my father's illness. I kept trying to think of a good reason to wake him, but eventually had to settle for one that was fairly trivial. I kicked him.

'Are you asleep, Izzy?'

'No, well, I was. What is it?' he groaned.

'You were talking in your sleep.'

'Was I?' he mumbled sarcastically. 'Well, thanks for interrupting me. You talk, why shouldn't I? What's the difference if I was asleep or awake?'

'It's called conversation, Izzy. It's pretty difficult to converse with someone who is talking in their sleep. It's a bit of a one way street. Look, I'm sorry that I woke you, but now that you are awake, what's the collective term for a group of orang-utans?'

'You woke me up to ask that?'

'Yes. I'm sorry, Izzy. It's been preying on my mind. I can't sleep for thinking about it. What is the word?'

'A bowlful, now go to sleep.'

'Not oranges,' I screamed, 'orang-utans!'

He turned over, grunted a few times and pulled the duvet off me.

'Well, Izzy?'

'Well, what? There's no need to shout. I'm not deaf.'

'Sorry, what's the collective term for orang-utans, Izzy?'

'How the hell should I know? A tree full. Now go to sleep.'

'Don't be silly. I can't say that a tree full of orang-utans was on the plane. I don't think it's a troop. That's monkeys. Shit, I don't know. Is it a colony, do you think? That would be close enough. Should I just say a group or a band?'

'How many of them were there?'

'Five.'

'Call it a quintet.'

'Oh, thank you, Isaac! Well done! You are a great help.'

'Good, now let me sleep, for God's sake, Johanna. What the hell are you writing about orang-utans for? You are supposed to be writing about Wilton.'

*

Isaac fell asleep again and I managed to write a couple of pages before I fell asleep beside him. I had called him Isaac to his face and he had let it pass. It was a lucky escape. I know that his real name is Isaac – *he who laughs* – but Isaac doesn't find it funny. He doesn't particularly like being called Isaac because it brings up comparisons to the biblical Isaac, whom God spared from being offered as a sacrifice. That is a bit close to the bone for Isaac, as is the comparison that some people make between him and Isaac the Blind, a Jewish scholar of the thirteenth century, who amongst other things wrote a discourse on God as *Deus Abscondus*. Isaac ridiculed this work by saying, 'If God is immanent in the whole of his own creation, where the hell is he going to abscond to? It's man that plays truant, not God.' But Isaac's real concern was that he didn't want his own disability to be so prominent in people's minds. He didn't wish to be stereotyped.

*

It was fairly late and I was tired, but I managed to do a little work on the story about Jim Wilton. I must admit that when Wilton first told me about the psychiatric patient whom he called the wolfman, I was fairly sceptical about it all. I asked Isaac if it was simply superstition. He assured me that such cases do in fact occur, although they are fairly uncommon. He told me the story of how the Baal Shem had been leading children to school through the forest when he encountered a woodcutter who had turned into a werewolf. But Isaac also informed me that humans who turn into wolves are not simply the stuff of folktales or horror movies. It is not only wolves. People have been known to believe that they are dogs, cats, tigers and even birds.

He told me to read Genesis and concentrate on the motif of two brothers, Cain and Abel, Isaac and Ishmael, and Jacob and Esau. How, after Jacob had faced his wild brother Esau, he had become Israel, the father of a nation. He said that

Cain, Ishmael and Esau were the sons that had not been accepted, that had not been loved. He sounded sad when he said this. I said that I understood that, but that Wilton was an only child. He didn't have a brother. Isaac smiled, shook his head and told me to look at the inner predicament, not the outer, and to look again at the delusional rantings in the file of the wolfman. I read the section to which Isaac had been referring -

*

Come children of Hecate, come Lilith's litter,
Come to Israel, come. Come to Israel Besht.
I am a wolf of the night. I am a wolf of the day.
I am what I am. I am Esau.
I have claws, teeth, and fangs, and anguish is my prey at night.
I will bite my brother Jacob and drink of the blood of his neck.
I will roam the earth after death, searching for salvation,
My punishment is greater than I can bear.
I shall be a fugitive and a wanderer on the earth.
Anyone who meets me may kill me.
My eye will avenge my other eye,
And I will find what I lack when the serpent is whole again.

5.

Isaac was supposed to be at the university that morning for a faculty meeting, but he didn't feel up to it. I was popping in to the university library to look up a reference for him, so I did a little detour and poked my head around the door of the meeting room. Ten chairs were spaced equally around the oval table. In front of each chair neatly arranged on the table was a set of papers, an agenda, a jug of water, an empty glass and a narrow rectangular sliver of folded paper with a different name on each. In the centre of the table were two flasks of coffee, a stack of cups and saucers, and two large plates of assorted biscuits.

Professor Weissel was in the room alone, precariously perched on the seatback of a chair, his feet on the seat cushion which was already covered in biscuit crumbs. He was twiddling his thumbs, alternately tutting and sucking through his teeth, and nodding his head sagaciously. It was a nervous tic, but along with his slightly balding head, and his tiny round glasses that magnified his eyes, he presented a convincing impersonation of a bird of prey. Isaac called him Wise Owl, which for Isaac was a fairly complimentary nickname.

I coughed to announce my presence. 'Good morning, Eli. You don't appear to have a quorum for your meeting.'

He twisted his head round 130 degrees, to both sides, just to check if at least one person might have sidled in unnoticed. 'So it would seem, Johanna. Do you think that I should take chairman's action and elect myself dictator? Democracy doesn't seem to appeal to my colleagues, or perhaps their togas are all in the wash?' He resumed nodding.

'Yes, it's a shame, Eli, I do sympathize with you. You must feel very disappointed with the turnout.'

'What turnout? There isn't a turnout at all, unless you are referring to me. Even my hair-brained secretary has forgotten. Have a biscuit. Have a handful.' He came down from his perch and slid the plate of biscuits across the table. 'Here, have a plateful.'

'Thank you, Eli,' I said, as I grabbed a handful of biscuits and sat in the seat reserved for Professor Kuntz. 'I can't stop long. I'm off to the library. Isaac isn't feeling too well. He sends his apologies,' I explained. 'He said that he would phone, but I thought that I would let you know just in case he forgot.'

'Thank you, Johanna,' Eli said calmly, and climbed back onto his perch. 'Sorry about the little outburst. How was Ukraine?'

'Fine, thanks.'

'I am pleased to hear it. Is Grizzly ever going to write that paper that he has been promising to write for the last ten years?'

'What paper is that?' I asked, although I knew what he meant.

'You know, the one on *Halikhah* – the paper that requires him to take a week off teaching and go on a pilgrimage to Ukraine every year with his girlfriend, Jesse.. Gemima...what is her name, Johanna?'

'Johanna,' I spluttered through the biscuit crumbs. 'Stop ribbing me, Eli.'

'Thank you, Johanna. Yes that's her name. Well, the faculty has paid for these trips for the last ten years, are you aware of that? You would think that Isaac has had sufficient practical experience by now. I mean *Halikhah* is only about walking; putting one foot in front of the other.'

I fell for the bait. 'You know that's not true,' I protested, 'you know the importance of *Halikhah* to the itinerant mystic. Walking is a sacred duty. Isaac is a member of the camp of the *Shekhinah* and it is his way of cleaving to God, just as your way is to sit at home and read the Talmud. And the paper is nearly finished, Eli. Isaac told me to tell you that it's nearly finished.'

'Did he now? You are a sweet young thing, Johanna, but you are a bad liar. It's not in your nature to lie. Just tell the itinerant misfit that I asked about it. In fact tell him that if the paper isn't presented within three months, the university honey pot will be well and truly sealed, which means there will be no research money available for him to get his paws on anymore – no more trips to Kiev or wherever it is he takes you for those little romantic holidays.'

'Yes, Professor Weissel, I will tell him. But could I ask your opinion on a different matter? Everyone says that you are something of an expert on miracles and weird happenings.'

'Yes, Johanna, I am. What is it you want to know?'

'Well, say, if you thought you had witnessed a miracle and it only lasted for eight seconds, would that sort of detract from it being considered authentic?'

He blinked four times and then stared at me with his sharp owl-like eyes as he reflected on my question. 'Absolutely not, Johanna, the duration of miracles has never been a significant factor in the consideration of their authenticity. In fact quite the opposite! Brevity is generally an advantage with most types of spiritual phenomena.'

'Oh really like what?'

'Well like the revelation of divine mysteries. They were usually completed within a split second. Total or partial kratophanies, theophanies and epiphanies were normally fairly brief affairs; and annunciations by angels, cherubim, seraphim, hosts and dominations were thankfully quite short and to the point, otherwise they wouldn't have fitted onto the speech ribbons in medieval altarpieces.'

'I see thank you, Eli. Well I must be....'

'Then there is a whole catalogue of paranormal events that you wouldn't wish to be anything other than brief.'

'Good. Well thank you, Eli.' I stood to leave.

'Apparitions of bogeymen, boggarts and banshees; visions of spirits, jinns and demons of practically any colour, creed, ilk or persuasion; not to mention evil sprites, imps and goblins – they were all restricted to nanoseconds.' He signalled for me to sit down again. He was in full flow, and I was expected to listen. I sat down.

'Then there are the more common instances of close encounters with aliens and abnormally large rabbits; the unexpected appearance of ghosts in general, including pranks by poltergeists, the haunting of houses, phantom pregnancies and unsolicited social visits from the recently deceased. Then we have the more unsavoury type of miracle – sightings of weeping, bleeding or perspiring statues, the inexplicable onset of stigmata or sore boils, and similar parasympathetic ailments, all of which one wouldn't wish to be long lived. Have I covered the one you were enquiring about, yet, Johanna?'

I laughed. 'Not yet, Eli, stop teasing me.'

'Well, what about the exorcism of people possessed by pigs or *dybbuks*; or psychical practices as exemplified by astral travel, speaking in tongues, and the receiving of messages from the beyond, without the assistance of Vodaphone or Orange.'

'No, it's not one of those.'

'Or uncanny natural aberrances such as burning bushes, cloven rocks and the parting of seas?'

I got up and began to shuffle backwards towards the door. 'No. I really don't think ...'

'Don't go yet, Johanna. What about the Greater Mysteries – the restoration of the dead, the healing of lepers, and the mystical transubstantiation of water into wine, rods into snakes, stone into bread, and milk into cheese?'

'No, sorry, it's not one of those. Look, you are beginning to upset me, Eli.'

'Or the Lesser Mysteries like the magical metamorphosis of frogs into princes, pumpkins into carriages, and ugly ducklings into swans?'

'Are you being serious, Eli?' I shouted.

'Not really. But I don't like to give up on a challenge. Perhaps it's one where a lengthy duration is important, like in endurance events such as walking on burning coals and sleeping on beds of nails; or the alchemical practice of producing gold from practically anything, which apparently took forever. Am I getting warmer?'

'No, you are getting colder. Let's just stop this game.'

'I give up, then.' He sighed and placed his hands on his head as a sign of submission. 'Tell me, what kind of miracle are you enquiring about, Johanna. Did you experience something in Ukraine?'

'No. It has nothing to do with me. It's just that a friend asked me to ask you.'

'Ask me what?'

'How long it normally takes to have sainthood conferred on someone, but it doesn't matter now.'

'Why didn't you say, Johanna? A few hundred years normally. It depends how much backlog of work they have on in the Vatican.'

'No, not like that, I mean someone being given the status of a *Lamed-Vovnik*, but as I said it doesn't matter now.'

'Your friend has seen a thirty-sixer?' He whistled and shook his head. 'That's highly unlikely, they aren't supposed to be recognized, Johanna. I don't like the sound of that. I assume that you are aware that *Lamed-Vovnik* comes from the Hebrew *lamed* (thirty) and *vav* (six). Traditionally there are always thirty six *zaddikim*, or righteous men, alive in the world at the same time, whose role is to support God's creation and to carry the suffering of the world. When one of them dies, a replacement is immediately chosen to take his place.'

'Yes. I know all that Eli. But my friend thinks that she witnessed her friend's sanctification. She saw the halo. It lasted for eight seconds. Would you say that was about right?'

'I haven't the slightest idea. There is no previous record of anyone witnessing the sanctification of a *Lamed-Vovnik*. If I were you, Johanna, I would advise your friend not to tell anyone else about it. It could cause all sorts of ructions amongst her friends and neighbours, not to mention her colleagues and students.' He raised his eyebrows and smiled.

I blushed. 'Oh, well, thank you, Eli,' I said, 'I must be going now. I will pass your message on to my friend, and the other one to Isaac.' I got as far as the door when he clucked loudly and a crooked finger beckoned me back.

'Just a minute, Johanna,' he said, 'did Isaac react at all to his supposed sanctification?'

I stood there in the doorway like a schoolgirl who had been caught with a sweet in her mouth trying to pretend there was nothing there. 'Errrrrr, who, who did you say?'

'I said Isaac, Johanna. We are both aware that you are talking about Isaac. Did he react to the event?' Eli blinked four times and his pupils narrowed as he stared at me.

I had to capitulate. Eli had always been able to see right through me. 'No, that was the extraordinary thing,' I blurted, 'he didn't seem to be aware of it at all. He didn't react at all.'

'In that case, Johanna, what you say might be true. He may have joined the *Lamed-Vovniks*. Even the *Lamed-Vovniks* are completely unaware of their position. They have been chosen to support the universe by taking on the suffering of all God's creatures. They perform the role unaware that they have been chosen to perform it. So, when and where did this miraculous event apparently take place?'

'Two days ago on the flight from L'Viv to Amsterdam, in a DC10, twenty thousand feet above Dresden.'

'A little lacking in ceremony, don't you think, cramped into one of those bucket seats. Couldn't God have chosen a more fitting venue?'

'Yes. I mean no. At first, yes, I thought of that. But then I thought no — since nobody was supposed to witness it, where better to do it. I wasn't supposed to see it. I just happened to glance across at him when it happened; I'm sure that no-one else saw it. My theory is that somewhere in the world, one of the thirty-six must have unexpectedly died, and Isaac was immediately called from the substitutes' bench and thrown into the fray.'

'Without being given any opportunity to stretch and warm up?'

'Exactly!'

Eli was chuckling to himself.

'You don't believe me, do you?' I said, 'You are making this sound like a farce. I'm being made to feel stupid. I know what I saw and I don't care if I appear stupid to you or anyone else. I know it may seem a little too fantastic, the odds are definitely against it, but somebody must be one of the thirty six, so why shouldn't Isaac be one.' I sank onto a chair and buried my face in my hands.

Eli came round the table and put a hand on my shoulder. 'Well, you do care, Johanna, and actually I do believe you. As I said, lying isn't in your nature. Of course you could have been confused, but I don't think so. I'm trying to understand the reason for it. It's a very poor argument to suggest that you weren't supposed to see it, but you did. Give God some credit. I suppose that you are aware of the fact that it goes against tradition that anyone can know the identity of one of the thirty six, but that wouldn't stop God breaking with tradition if He so desired. If God has deemed it necessary to reveal the identity of one of them, then there must be a reason for it. It cannot be for Isaac's sake. So it must be for yours.'

'What do you mean by that?' I asked, and lifted my head.

Eli sat in the chair next to me. 'I have always suspected that Isaac was a *Lamed-Vovnik*,' he said. 'I have always felt that he was probably born into this world as one of the thirty-six. After his family's suffering at the hands of the Nazis, he was kept alive in order to carry the sign of suffering of all those who died in the Holocaust for the benefit of those who didn't. He is a walking memorial to what happened, and he carries his burden with patience and tolerance. Grizzly is a man of compassion, Johanna.'

'I know, Eli, but it seems strange coming from you.'

'Why do you say that?'

'You always appear to be fairly contemptuous of Isaac.'

He smiled. 'Do you think that Isaac is the only person capable of keeping a secret? Do think that we would suffer him as we do, if it were not for the fact that he is held in such high esteem. Do you think that we would allow him to disregard the tiniest requirement that we automatically expect from every other member of staff, if it were not for an appreciation of his importance as a *mensch*.'

'I'm sorry, yes. I suppose that is quite obvious, but why did you say that the sanctification was for my benefit?'

'It is the only possible explanation, Johanna. I suspect that this glimpse of Isaac's true nature has been given to you to help you through a difficult ordeal that is awaiting you. It has been given to help sustain you in the face of immense difficulty. There can be no other possible explanation. Come and talk to me if you feel the need. Your secret is safe with me, Johanna.'

*

My heart sank on hearing those words. Eli must have thought that Isaac was going to die. He didn't say so, but I knew that's what he thought. It was stupid. Isaac was so robust, so full of life. I admit that he was a bit tired after our pilgrimage, but there was no way Isaac was going to die. Eli had interpreted the miraculous event as a sign that Isaac was going to die, and that I had witnessed the miracle in order to help me cope with this devastating fact. Eli had a reputation for his foresight, but this time his intuition was completely wide of the mark.

I laughed. 'Thank you, Eli, and I will tell Isaac that you enquired after his health.'

'Good,' he said. His tone had changed, perhaps in recognition of my unwillingness to accept his insight. His lecturing voice had returned. 'And would you also tell the Blessed Grizzly that Professor Kemel was very offended by his racist remarks at last month's meeting. Kemel wishes Isaac to know that the very latest research proves that people from the region once known as Anatolia, whilst they may be directly descended from the Hittites, were not Aryans. Apparently there is conclusive evidence that the Hittites and the Aryans did not intermarry. Professor Kemel also said that if his own ancestors hadn't been so kind as to allow Noah to park his ark on the top of Mount Ararat, then Grizzly wouldn't be around today to intimidate him, make racist comments and complain about his countrymen.'

'Of course, Eli, I'll pass on the message. By the way, thank you for your potted synopsis of unusual events. You have the unfortunate ability to make the miraculous appear somewhat commonplace. I was going to say uncanny ability, but that would have been something of a contradiction.'

'Indeed, Johanna. Don't judge me too harshly. I know that you consider me to be an old cynic. But cynicism doesn't come with age; it is caused by over-exposure.'

I nodded in deference to my academic superior, and left the room.

After I had left Professor Weissel's office I scurried to the library. It was almost deserted. I thought it was odd, but then I remembered that it was exam week, so most of the students would be sweating over their exam papers. I looked at my watch. It was eleven thirty. I had half an hour before hoards of students would stream into the library to revise for the afternoon exam.

'Oh hell exams,' I murmured. I pulled my diary out of my bag. What day was it, Tuesday or Wednesday? Tuesday, thank God. Wednesday was the day that I was expected to invigilate an exam with the undergraduates. As a research student and a junior member of the faculty, I was expected to do things like that. When I complained to Isaac about him not having to do it, he said, 'So how the hell am I supposed to invigilate? I can't see! I'm blind.' He had a point.

✻

Isaac had asked me to photocopy page 391 of Ginsberg's *Legends of the Jews. Vol I* and read it out to him later. Isaac might not have been able to remember if he had his trousers on, but he was a wizard at remembering textual references. I laughed when I read it. It was a legend about Esau, Jacob's brother.

'In his vehemence of his rage against Jacob, Esau vowed that he would not slay him with bow and arrow, but he would bite him dead with his mouth, and suck his blood. But he was doomed to bitter disappointment, for Jacob's neck turned as hard as ivory, and in his helpless fury Esau could but gnash his teeth. The two brothers were like the ram and the wolf.'

✻✻✻

6.

When I returned to our apartment Isaac was sitting up in bed with the duvet wrapped around him, wearing his fur coat and his P.S.V. supporter's knitted hat. He looked like Scrooge waiting for a visit from "The Ghost of Christmas Future."

'So did you find it?' he asked.

'Yes, I found it, Isaac.'

'So what was it about?'

'You mean you don't know? It was about Mordecai, from the Book of Esther.'

'No, you bungler, that's page 391, volume four! I said volume one.'

'Oh, volume one, I am sorry. Can't you remember what it was about?'

'Of course I can remember. I wanted you to read it. It's about Esau...'

'Turning into a wolf,' I interrupted, 'and wanting to kill his brother by biting him in the neck.'

'Yes. So you did find it. Why do you have to be so devious?' Isaac moaned.

'Why do you?' I replied. 'Why didn't you just tell me the story instead of asking me to look it up in the library?'

'I won't be here forever, Johanna. You have to learn to do your own work. How was Eli?'

'Didn't you phone him, to apologise for not being at the meeting?'

'Why the hell should I need to do that?' he answered. 'I knew you would pop in and apologise on my behalf, just in case I had forgotten to phone. So I didn't need to phone, did I? You are just like Job.'

'Am I? In what way?' I asked.

'Well, Job was so self-righteous that he went to the temple to pray on behalf of his children, just in case they had omitted to do it for themselves.'

'I see. Well, it won't happen again, Izzy. I don't have the patience of Job. You can clean up your own mess in future.'

'Fine. Did Wise Owl ask about the paper?'

'Yes. Doesn't he always?'

'So what did you tell him?'

'I told him that it's practically finished. When are you going to start writing it, Isaac? The department hardly expects you to do more than is reasonable. They have been waiting nine years for it.'

'Only nine years? That's not so long. Why is everyone so impatient nowadays? Academics turn out papers every year and then revise them every year, until they eventually have to admit that it is all bunkum, and that they wrote them when they were much younger, and have changed their mind about it all. So why didn't they wait a while before committing themselves to paper? If Eli asks you again, tell him I am still thinking about it.'

'Tell him yourself, Isaac. One of these days they will throw you out, and then you will be sorry.'

'So let them throw me out. Do you really believe that they control my destiny, Johanna? My future has already been decided by forces far greater than a university faculty.'

His voice had changed. I wanted to ask him what he meant by that, but I didn't dare. Isaac had been different over the last three days. He had become more distant. Perhaps he was talking about the work that he had to do as a *Lamed-Vovnik*. I wanted to let him know that I had witnessed his sanctification on the plane but I didn't bring it up. We had a late lunch, and afterwards Isaac asked me to read out the stories in Genesis, the ones of the two brothers, Cain and Abel, Isaac and Ishmael, and Jacob and Esau. Then Isaac explained why the motif recurred. He told me that Genesis was part of Jewish mythology, not history.

'History started with the sons of Jacob, the twelve tribes of Israel. Before that the nation was only potential, and it was divided. Part of it was primitive and the other part was trying to be civilized. In the attempt to be civilized there was a rejection of the primitive nature, which is personified in the figures of Cain, Ishmael and Esau. But there was strength in these figures and they needed to be included, not exiled.'

'But Cain killed his brother Abel,' I said.

'Of course he did. But it was hardly his fault. He was in a rage, and it was quite right that he behaved the way that he did.'

'What do you mean, quite right? Whose fault was it? Was it Abel's fault?' I asked.

'No, it was God's fault, Johanna. He was an inexperienced father who also flew into a rage when things didn't go to plan. At that point he hadn't laid down any ground rules for his children. He simply liked Abel's offering, and didn't like Cain's offering. You know according to kabbalistic sources, the name Abel means a bag of wind, an inflation or something which has no substance.'

'What does the name Cain stand for?'

'It means a spear, a weapon, something which has metal, something substantial. Abel was just a compliant child, without any substance of his own – a false ego. Cain was the antagonistic child that got rejected. But he had substance.'

'So are you saying that the wolfman and Wilton are like Cain and Abel? That Wilton was like Abel, simply complying with his parents' wishes and not living his own life, and that the wolfman represented his opposite nature, a rebellious unlived part of himself.'

'Partly, yes, that's partly true, Johanna.'

'So what about the other twin brothers in Genesis, are they similar?'

'Well, they represent various attempts to heal the division, the split between the different aspects of human nature, the human and the animal, the compliant and the rebellious.'

'Alright, I understand all that. But apart from the general idea, how do you relate it to Wilton and the wolfman?' I asked. 'I can understand the connection to Esau, since he was mentioned in the notes that the ward nurses had made – but why Cain?'

'Cain was also there in the observation notes in the file that Wilton showed us. God had exiled Cain and put a mark on his head. Cain was in such distress at having been banished from ever seeing the Face of God again, that he cried out, "*My punishment is greater than I can bear. I shall be a fugitive and a wanderer on the earth, and anyone that meets me can kill me.*" Those are the words of Cain.' Isaac's voice sounded weary and he looked very tired.

'That's incredible,' I said. 'That's what the psychotic patient said. So the rantings of the wolfman were not meaningless?'

'Of course not, Johanna, let me tell you that…'

'No, you can explain the rest later, Izzy,' I interrupted. 'By the way, Eli told me to tell you that Professor Kemel's got the hump again and demands an apology. He has scholastic evidence to support his claims.'

Isaac laughed. I hadn't intended the pun, but Isaac was onto it as quick as a flash. 'Tell the old dromedary that he knows zilch about the Levant even though his ancestors have been driven through it since time immemorial. And ask how he is getting on with his oedema.'

'Tell him yourself,' I said. 'I didn't know that Professor Kemel suffered from water retention.'

'Yes, apparently it runs in the family,' he chuckled.

'Izzy you can be so cruel.' I noticed that Isaac had suddenly gone very pale. 'Go and have a sleep. You look tired. I'll probably visit my parents again this afternoon. We can talk again tonight.'

He did as I suggested and went back to bed. I didn't visit my parents. I rang them. I didn't want to leave Isaac alone. I sat in a chair by his bed and watched over him as he slept. At least I had discovered the reason why Isaac kept going on about Hittites recently; it was part of his feud with Professor Kemel.

*

Isaac slept right through the evening and he was still fast asleep in the morning, so I didn't wake him. I went into the university and invigilated the exam. When the exam was finished I gathered up the students' papers and left them with Lilith, the department secretary. Professor Kemel was just leaving the office as I was entering. He tutted and shook his head.

'What did he say, Lilith? What were you both talking about?' I asked.

Lilith looked a bit taken aback. 'Why do you want to know?'

'I need to know. Tell me!'

'Promise you won't tell anyone else.'

'Of course, it was about Isaac, wasn't it?'

'About Isaac?'

'Yes. I knew Weissel would say something about it. Oh, it's so embarrassing.'

'No. It was nothing to do with Isaac. Don't tell anybody yet, but Kemel wants to take me to Istanbul to meet his mother. I think he's going to ask me to marry him.'

'Oh dear, I am sorry.'

'Well, he's not that bad!' she shouted. 'He's younger than Isaac, and a lot better looking.'

'No, I didn't mean sorry about your engagement... never mind, sorry. Well done, congratulations and all that.' I started to leave the room.

'Leave it out Johanna,' she shouted after me. 'I'm not going to say yes. He'd have to be a real stunner to get me wearing a burkha.'

*

Isaac woke at about four in the afternoon and suggested that we go out for a walk before it got dark. He had been asleep for about twenty-four hours. Thank God he looked so much better. I had almost called the doctor to him. If he had looked any worse, I would have. Anyway, he seemed a lot better after his sleep and he was chattering away like his normal self as we walked through the park. It was cold in the park and we only had about an hour of daylight, so we walked quite fast to keep warm. We passed two of Toybe Rosenberg's daughters by the lake – Rachel and Sarah. They both blushed as they caught sight of us and started to giggle. I whispered to him that we were just about to pass them.

He tipped his fedora. 'How is your mother today, girls?' he asked. 'Has she recovered from the shock of seeing me without my clothes on?'

They giggled. 'She's fine, Professor Goldmund,' they said in unison.

'Good. I'm glad that she is none the worse for wear, after her experience. Now listen carefully. Please tell your mother that she is a precious dove, and if she liked what she saw last night, when Johanna decides to leave me for a younger man, I will be calling on her.'

'Izzy, what on earth has got into you?' I said.

Rachel and Sarah giggled and started to run home.

'Remember to tell her,' he shouted after them.

'We will, Professor Goldmund,' they shouted back.

*

Toybe Rosenberg's husband had died of a heart attack three years previously. At the time she was very distressed but also very close to being considered mentally ill. She would appear on her balcony late at night talking loudly to herself and sometimes wailing and shrieking and then it would turn into a strange laugh. For a period of about a month she came to visit Isaac about every two days, in the evenings, just when we should have been relaxing. She needed to talk to him. It's not so strange that she preferred to talk to him rather than her rabbi. Many people did. On those occasions I felt like a spare part. I could hardly listen in to what she wanted to confess to Isaac, and the apartment was too small for me not to hear. I used to go across to her apartment and play scrabble and snakes and ladders with her daughters, although they didn't really need babysitting; their mother was within earshot. The eldest, Rachel, was just turned thirteen, Sarah was ten, and Esther, the youngest, was eight. They were delightful to be with. They were so close to each other but also a bit subdued. They must have been terribly frightened about their mother's weird behaviour.

One night I had been out late, and I entered the apartment to find Isaac sitting in his chair. I expected to see Toybe sitting in the other chair as usual but she wasn't there.

'Thank God,' I exclaimed. 'Thank God she's not here and we can have the place to ourselves.'

Just as I said it, Toybe came out of the bathroom into the living room. We stood facing each other. I was about to apologize when she said, 'It's alright, Johanna, you have a right to feel like that. I would feel like that if the roles were reversed. But this is my last visit so I'm glad that you are here. I want to thank you for all that you have put up with, and for

93

caring for my daughters. Thanks to Isaac, I am better now.'
She kissed Isaac's brow and left.

'Izzy I'm sorry, I feel really guilty,' I said.

'Well, don't. That was her problem and now she doesn't feel guilty, so don't you start.'

'What did she feel guilty about?'

He tutted and said, 'You know better than to ask me that, Johanna.'

*

It had grown dark. We walked on in silence, through the park. I didn't tell Isaac that I was pregnant. I had told my mother, but that wasn't the same. If I had told Isaac before it was absolutely certain, then I don't think he could have coped with the disappointment of it not being true. So I thought I would wait a few days until I got further confirmation from Dr Diederik. Isaac was very quiet. There was something worrying him that he didn't want to talk about. I knew that his teasing of the Rosenberg girls was a smoke screen to hide whatever it was that was troubling him.

'There is something wrong, Izzy,' I said. 'Tell me what's bothering you.'

He sighed and asked me if the sky was clear and if I could see the stars. I told him that the whole dome of the sky was visible and the stars seemed nearer than usual.

'Why do you ask, Izzy?'

'You know that I have never seen the sky, Johanna. But I think that I have some idea what it is like. I think that it must be like millions of separate souls, like a diaspora of millions of shattered fragments of souls after the breaking of the vessels.'

'That is exactly what it is like, Izzy. How did you know?'

'I sense it, Johanna. Somehow I feel it. But how can you look at it? Doesn't it seem tragic? Doesn't it make you feel sad?'

'Yes, but it is also beautiful. That's your problem, Izzy, you always associate *tikun,* the restoration of the sparks, as being the most important experience of the Divine. As though the unity of God is the most spiritual condition. But the breathing out of the divine into an infinite number of individual existences is also extraordinarily beautiful. The multiplicity of life is also beautiful. Why can't you see that, Izzy?'

'Because I can't. I can't see. I thought you knew that. I need you to see it for me. You are my eyes, Johanna.'

'Oh, Izzy, I'm so sorry. I didn't think. I am so sorry, Izzy.'

I began to cry. I felt so stupid. I had never realized it before. The problem wasn't that Isaac had to feel for the corner of the bed, or use his stick to negotiate his way down the street, or guide his cups to his lips. The real problem was that he could never fully celebrate the creation of his God. That he needed other people to invite him to the celebration. That he was dependent on their ability to celebrate, and to share with him their experience. And that was why he felt so isolated at times, and in a strange sense so close to his God, because his God felt the same, because his God was only fully conscious of his own creation through the eyes of the creatures that he had created, the ones who were capable of self-conscious reflection. How desolate it must feel to be blind. How difficult it must feel to be Isaac.

*

It was good to be at home with him, and to relax at last. It had been a hectic few days in Ukraine and physically very demanding. I was excited about the news that I had received from Dr Diederik about my condition, but very upset about my father. The gravity of the news of my father's cancer was just beginning to dawn on me. I talked to Isaac about it before we went to bed. Isaac was very supportive. But he said something strange. He told me that I didn't need to worry about my father, because he would look after him for me. I asked him what he meant by that. But he just replied that he meant exactly what he had said. He told me that I would understand in time, and refused to say more. I think I knew what he meant by it, but I didn't want to think it.

*

'What are you doing, Johanna. Can't you sleep?' Isaac asked. 'Are you worrying about your father again?'

'Yes, I have been thinking about him, but I'm writing now. Am I disturbing you?'

'No, I can't sleep either. What time is it?'

'Ten past four. Are you alright?' I asked. 'You seemed a bit off-colour again today. I am beginning to worry about you.'

'Worry – what's to worry? I keep getting a little indigestion. I'll just get a glass of milk to settle my stomach.'

'I'll get it, Isaac,' I said as I leaped out of bed.

When I returned with the glass of milk he looked so much better. His colour had returned and there was a soft glow on his forehead.

***

7

We fell asleep and in the morning I brought him a cup of tea, climbed back into bed and snuggled up to him. Fortunately we didn't have to get up early. We made love of sorts. I wasn't really in the mood. I was too excited about my news, and couldn't take my mind off it. Isaac groaned a bit, and moaned, 'What's the point?' as he stomped into the kitchen to make breakfast. We were both silent eating breakfast. Then he asked me what I had done with the tape about his grandfather. He wanted to listen to it again. I told him that I had placed it in the university archive. He was obviously disappointed but he didn't make a fuss about it, which was unusual. I wanted to ask him all sorts of questions regarding Yehuda's ordeal, but it wasn't the right time.

*

We walked around the Madurodam at lunchtime. It was one of his favourite places, as well as one of mine. I would describe to him the thousands of models and scenes, perfect representations of famous Dutch places of interest but about two per cent the size of the actual ones. I had suggested we go there, because I knew that it would be teeming with small children and I thought it would be a good place to break my news. Isaac had been there many times. He couldn't see the children, but he delighted in the sound of their shrieks of laughter. It was, as I expected, teeming with hordes of children.

We were standing next to the model of the Portuguese synagogue in Amsterdam, when I said, 'You know when your grandfather suggested that you would want to tell his story to your own son. And you sort of suggested that you probably wouldn't have children.'

'Yes. I remember,' he said. 'What about it?'

'Don't be so shirty, Isaac. Have I touched a sore point again?'

He didn't reply.

'Well, you were wrong. I'm pregnant,' I announced and waited for his response. It didn't come straight away. I was surprised that such an intelligent man could have such difficulty with a fairly simple concept. He tugged at his beard a few times.

'You mean you are pregnant – as in pregnant – pregnant,' he enquired, in a low voice, not quite a whisper.

'Yes as in pregnant – pregnant. I am pregnant,' I shouted, 'Why are you whispering?'

He didn't answer. His arms shot up in the air. He squealed like a pig and did a dance on the spot, turning around, and jumping up in the air as though he was possessed by a *dybbuk*. We were the centre of attention. A few people seemed very concerned about him, but I calmed them down by rubbing my tummy and mouthing the word – pregnant. They smiled and walked away. Some children, not to be outdone, joined in the hysteria, and jumped up and down with him, but they settled down when they realized there was nothing particularly exciting happening. Apparently some teeny bopper pop star from England, Sid the Snake, was due to make an appearance and they thought that Isaac had spotted him. Eventually Isaac ran out of puff and calmed down. 'Thank you, Johanna,' he gasped. 'Thank you.'

'But it might not be a boy, Isaac. It might be a girl.'

'Who cares, we can tell our daughter Yehuda's story. A girl is good. A girl is very good. What do you take me for, a male chauvinist?'

'No, of course not, but Yehuda said that you should tell the story to your son.'

'Pshtt. Let's wait and see, Johanna,' he said calmly but breathless.

We took a taxi home, and Isaac was screaming at the taxi driver to go faster. I ran inside and jumped on the bed giggling, Isaac followed stumbling and still breathless. Then we had a pillow fight, which I always win for obvious reasons. Isaac was on the phone all day, squealing with delight, telling his friends and colleagues about his news. He was such a braggart. I have never seen him so full of himself, so happy, so ostentatiously joyful. It took him four hours to calm down. I ran to the deli and bought a bottle of wine, which I thought might sedate him. Eventually it worked and we lay on the bed purring like two cats that had just eaten the cream. We started to make love. In the middle of it he suggested that if the baby was a boy we should call him Aaron, and if it was a girl we should call her Aaron. I bit him and told him to concentrate on what we were doing.

✣

As soon as my back hit the bed and I lay there panting, he started rabbiting on about the baby again. Should I have it at home or which hospital would be best? Should **he** go to a Jewish school? Should we get **his** name down already? Then he got on to the subject of names, Aaron Nehemiah Goldmund, Rebecca Aaron Goldmund, Aaron Aristotle Goldmund.

'What do you think?' he asked.

I was about to suggest Aaron "the-side-of-caution" Goldmund, when I realized we hadn't. The curtains weren't closed and Toybe's three daughters were standing on the balcony giggling and clapping of all things, like they were at the theatre. They had a box seat and had seen everything. I felt like walking up to the window and taking a bow, but I slipped off the bed and crawled along the carpet, grabbing the bottom of the curtains and swishing them together. 'Can we change the subject now, Isaac?' I shouted, as I crawled back to bed and got under the duvet. (Why on earth I crawled back after I

99

had closed the curtains is anybody's guess. Perhaps I was trying to undo the mistake, like it would make a difference already!)

'What have I done?' Isaac asked.

'Nothing. I want to ask you something about your grandfather's story. What did he mean by the possibility of your animal soul and your spirit soul being there to help him? And couldn't he have written the note himself, meaning to leave it somewhere in Brody, and forgotten? The message could have said '*Come to the Kloiz in Brody when you are ready, Isaac Goldmund.*' What was it all about? I can understand that he hallucinated and that he interpreted the bear as trying to be helpful, but don't you agree that his mind would have been tremendously disturbed.'

'Which question would you like me to answer first, Johanna?'

'The message.'

'Yes, I thought so,' he muttered as he leaned over to his bedside bureau and opened a secret drawer that I hadn't known existed. He handed me a small piece of paper. I read it. It was in Hebrew and it was Isaac's writing. Isaac found it difficult to write but he was capable of leaving me short notes in a clumsy childlike hand. It was definitely Isaac's hand. I almost fainted. I felt dissociated from myself. I took a few minutes to re-establish contact.

'I'm sorry I doubted you and your grandfather, Isaac,' I said, 'but how is it possible?'

'I know how, Johanna, but I can't tell you. I have sworn to keep it a secret. If you like you can ask Professor Kemel, how Ibn Arabi could walk around the Kaaba at Mecca, and meet himself walking the other way as a five-year-old boy. It's very similar, and Kemel might not be sworn to silence. Isn't it enough for you to accept that it happened, without needing to know how and why?'

'Would it be enough for you, Isaac?'

He laughed and swore under his breath. 'Of course not, Johanna! Yet you can ask Wise Owl to believe your story about my alleged sanctification, without him needing to know how and why.'

'He told you? He promised he wouldn't tell anyone.'

'He didn't tell me, Johanna. I knew you would ask him. I knew you had experienced something on the plane, as I had. I could see you, Johanna. I saw your face and your body – only for about five seconds, but it was enough. God allowed me to see you for a brief moment. I saw the look of astonishment on your face, and I knew that you were seeing what I was feeling, *The Presence.*'

'So why were you so *kvetchy* then? Am I a disappointment to you?'

'On the contrary, you are delightful. I was annoyed with God for something else, as well as being grateful for that glimpse of you. I wasn't ready. But now I have come to terms with it. The news that you gave me today has changed all that. Now I am ready.'

I took hold of his hand and asked a question I had wanted to ask for years. 'Are you talking about your work as a *Lamed-Vovnik*? Don't refuse me this question Izzy.'

'Apparently I am a grumpy old man who walks around pretending he is a bear, according to you. But I think sometimes that my *neshamah* may be one of the thirty six. Sometimes I feel that my spirit has flown off somewhere else, and I'm left feeling tired and grumpy and dispirited for no apparent reason. So you see Johanna it has nothing to do with my human self. If anything it is in distinct contradiction to my human self, and to my animal soul. I am not in disguise. I am a mess of contradictions. You see, Johanna, my love of that fur coat is not because it is a disguise; it is a true connection between me and my grandfather. I wear it in remembrance of his ordeal and I wear it in honour of Grossmann. I know you think that it is a disguise, but it is my true nature. I appreciate that it is a little unusual to wear your animal soul on the outside and your human soul on the inside. But sometimes it is good to be constantly aware of the animal soul. It is instinctual and spontaneous, it carries no shame or guilt, it adapts, it survives and it has the energy that we need to achieve what we need to achieve. We are animals that have developed self awareness. But it comes at a price. It is not all good. Self consciousness brings with it shame and guilt, and sometimes too much suffering, as well as the light of knowledge. My grandfather was racked with guilt after the deaths of his wife and daughter.'

*

The phone rang. I answered it. It was Toybe from across the road. She sounded very perturbed. I couldn't get a word in for ages. She asked me what had been going on. She said that her daughters were delirious and kept pointing to our window, and that it was a criminal act to expose minors to such obscene behaviour. She went on for about five minutes and I could hardly understand what she was saying. Then she calmed down a bit and told me that it was only six at night, and that when her husband was alive they would only contemplate it two hours after the children were asleep, once a month, and only in the dark, through a sheet with a hole in it.

'Really,' I said, 'what's it like that way? Do you have to use your imagination a lot?'

'Don't be so impudent, Johanna. You have been behaving like Lilith.'

'What on earth has Lilith got to do with it?' I asked.

'You know, getting on top, sitting astride or whatever your name for it is.'

'Oh, I see, that Lilith, Adam's Lilith. I thought you meant Isaac's Lilith, the departmental secretary at the university. You had me worried for a minute.'

'Did I, well, you were behaving like dogs in the street. What have you got to say for yourself?'

'Oh, is it my turn now, Toybe? That's good of you.'

'Yes, please explain yourself.'

'Well, if you must know, we had just had a shower, which is why we were sort of naked. I had been giving Isaac a deep lumbar massage, because of his terrible sciatica, and it developed into a pillow fight.'

'A pillow fight?'

'Yes, Toybe, a pillow fight. What on earth did your daughters say we were doing? The trouble with pubescent girls is that their hormones get the better of them, as does their imagination. They like to indulge in sexual fantasies. Haven't they got anything better to do than titillate themselves with voyeuristic imaginings. Did I eavesdrop on you when you were revealing your most intimate secrets to Isaac?'

'Well, no. Oh dear, did Isaac tell you about my little affair?'

'Of course not, Toybe, and I don't want to know about it as long as it wasn't with him. I'm just saying that I didn't eavesdrop. So kindly tell your daughters to stop peering through my window and we will hear no more about it, is that clear?'

'Yes, Johanna, I'm sorry to have disturbed you.'

'I should think so too. Goodbye Toybe.'

I slammed the phone down. 'Shit. That was a close one, Izzy? That was lucky.'

'What was it all about? Since when did I have sciatica?' he asked.

'Since now, never mind — just put it down to a fairly good example of self consciousness giving rise to shame, or at least intense embarrassment.'

I looked around the apartment for the vodka bottle. We had run out. 'I'll never live it down,' I thought. I calmed down slowly and got back into bed.

'So where were we, Izzy?'

He didn't answer. I turned to him. He had fallen asleep and was just beginning to snore. He always snored after drinking wine. I covered him with the duvet and went into the kitchen to do some work. I couldn't concentrate when he was snoring. After about half an hour the snoring stopped, which was a bit unusual, it normally lasted for a couple of hours. I carried on working in the kitchen, struggling with the Jim Wilton saga, and went to bed around ten.

***

8

Isaac was dead. I could hardly believe it. He had just fallen asleep. When I joined him he was already cold. He was only fifty-eight years old. It was so sudden. I didn't suspect that there was anything seriously wrong with him. He just said that he felt tired. We had spent a wonderful day together, and I thought that he was tired because of the excitement of the day. I have never seen him happier than in those few hours, and I have never been happier, myself. Then all of a sudden he was dead. I didn't call the doctor or the rabbi straight away. They have a habit of taking the corpse before you can say goodbye. I wasn't going to have that.

I slept with Isaac that night, even though his spirit had departed. I clung to his arm like it was a log drifting out of the estuary at Sheveningen, into the cold sea; and I laid my head on the empty barrel of his chest and cried so much that his nightshirt was soaked. I kept trying to breathe in the scent of his body, as though it was the only thing left and that I had to keep it for him and not breathe out otherwise everything would be gone. He was so cold. I put an extra duvet over us. It's stupid isn't it? I thought it might help if I could keep him warm and then perhaps I would fall asleep and he would be all right in the morning. I didn't fall asleep. I kept awake. I lay awake in the dark all night dreading the light coming in the morning. I wanted it to be dark all the time, so nobody would know. I decided that he wasn't really dead until someone else knew about it. From about five in the morning I could hear people going to work and I didn't want them to know. I didn't want to phone the doctor. It was two in the afternoon when I phoned. I told the doctor and put the phone down. That was it. Now he was dead. Isn't it strange how we act? I even made Isaac a cup of tea in the morning. I always made the tea and brought it to him in bed and then he would get dressed and bless the day and say the *shahanith* and recite the *shema*.

✢

Then the phone calls started and they kept asking the same question. I wanted to answer no every time. No, he's not dead. They kept asking me to say that he was dead. How many times did they want me to say it? How many times did he have to die? Then they began to come around to the apartment, the friends that often came to his secret meetings. I just made tea and handed it around. I kept looking for him to give him a cup of tea. He wasn't there, my precious Isaac. They kept talking about him as though I didn't know him at all. They recounted all the stories that Isaac had told me so many times, and described how he danced – as though I didn't know him at all! The post mortem stated death by natural causes. He was only fifty-eight years old, he wasn't eighty! He had slipped away when he was at the height of his powers. What was natural about that? But the doctors said they could not find any other reason for his death, they were completely bemused by it. I knew that he had been taken from me for a reason, but I didn't say anything. Isaac wouldn't have wanted it.

I was torn apart by joy and despair pulling in different directions: the joy that we had just felt together about our child, and the despair that I felt because Isaac had died. It was too much for me. Fate should never be as twisted as that – to propel us so violently and so far beyond normal human experience into two opposite states of mind. It nearly destroyed me. For weeks I had to protect my child from the despair, the anger and the bitterness that shared the space inside me. But Isaac had died happy and I thanked God for that.

He had danced his final dance and now he could stand in front of the Face and see the sight that he often said was the

106

only sight he needed to see. For months I believed that he would come back from that vision, with his face aglow, like Elijah who saw and lived. But he did not return, except in my dreams. Many times he appeared in my dreams. Sometimes I would wake to suffer again the feelings of loss. But I do not complain about that so much now. Eventually his appearances in my dreams were more of a comfort than a suffering.

*

My parents attended the funeral along with hundreds of others. I knew some of them, but the vast majority of the mourners were unfamiliar to me. They say that the synagogue was packed. I can't remember. Some came from the far corners of the world and they all assembled at the *bet Knesset.* It's funny that Isaac always called it the *shul.*

I remember the day differently, as though I was alone in that huge house of God and there was only one voice that wailed and echoed around the walls, trying desperately to get out and fly upwards into the sky. And it was my voice. That is how I remember the day. Isaac was buried wearing his *tallith,* which I know was important, but I wanted so much to keep it for our son. I just wanted to cling on to something. Then came the period of *shiva,* which was not so difficult for me.

A week later there was a memorial service at the university and a study room was dedicated to Isaac's memory. Professor Weissel read a passage from the Book of Solomon. He kept glancing at me as he recited the verses.

*

My beloved is mine, and I am his; he feeds among the lilies. Until the day breaks and the shadows flee, turn, my beloved, and be like a roe or a young hart upon the mountains of Bether.
He who my soul loves, I sought by night on my bed; but found him not.

107

I will rise and go into the city streets and broad ways to seek him whom my soul loves. I sought him but found him not.

I said to the watchmen who walked through the city, 'Have you seen the one that my soul loves?' They told me little.

But I found him; I held him and would not let go, until I had brought him into my mother's house, into the room of she who conceived me.

＊

Professor Kemel was in floods of tears by this point and had to be helped to the lectern. He stood there gripping the lectern with both hands, shaking like a sapling in a gale, and eventually managed to read aloud a poem by Jalaludin Rumi, his favourite Persian poet.

＊

'I have again and again grown like grass;
I have experienced seven hundred and seventy moulds.
I died from minerality and became vegetable;
And from vegetiveness I died and became animal.
I died from animality and became man.
Then why fear disappearance through death?
Next time I shall die
Bringing forth wings and feathers like angels;
After that soaring higher than angels –
What you cannot imagine, I shall be that.

I was too overcome by grief to understand the deeper relevance of these two poems. It was not until much later that I realized that both readings referred to Isaac's absolute belief in *gilgul* and the passage of the soul. They were also chosen to comfort me, and they did.

＊

The university created a fellowship to be awarded each year for a period of five years in honour of Isaac. I was invited to apply to be the first recipient of the fellowship, presumably to give me some financial support whilst I finished my book on Simon Magus. How stupid, I thought, they have no idea whatsoever of the gifts that Isaac had already given me – as though I was not grateful enough to him. I was angry that they didn't realize!

After the memorial service, I went to the park in Den Haag where I had met Isaac for the first time. I placed some tulips and a Star of David on the bench where he would sit and tell me stories. I sat there for two hours. There were many more young people in the park than when I used to sleep there. They were all drunk or drugged, walking around like zombies in their private hell, but nobody bothered me. In my mind I traced the great tragedy of Isaac's family through Eastern Europe back to Israel, then to Lithuania, to Poland, Sweden and finally to Holland, to the park and the bench where I sat and hugged myself and kept warm the fragile spark of life inside me. In all of that former darkness of the *galut*, the *pogroms* and finally Belzec, there had always been a tiny light that had been kept alive, and now it was inside me. It was not just the stirrings of the child inside me, it was the *Nev Tamid* – the perpetual flame that burns before the altar, and I felt it inside me. It helped me to get through those dark days of my soul.

I returned to the apartment and read Rilke again. I thought of how Isaac had tasted the taste of death as a child and how it was all around him, and finally he had to swallow it. I read the lines from the end of the fourth elegy:

*

Who shows a child as he really is? Who sets him among the stars, and puts the measure of distance in his hand?

109

Who makes the child's death out of gray bread that gets hard?
Who leaves it there in his round mouth like the core of a lovely apple?
Murderers aren't hard to comprehend.
But this – to contain death, the whole of death, even before life has begun
To contain it so gently, and not to be angry, this is indescribable.

*

After the period of mourning was over, the members of Isaac's secret group asked if they could come to the apartment for one last meeting. When they arrived they noticed that I had set the chairs around in a circle and placed the two candles on the small table as usual. But they asked me where Isaac's chair was. I felt upset and suggested to them that I would rather they didn't sit in it. They explained it wasn't for sitting in. It was the empty chair. They needed it for their meeting. They would elect a new teacher from the group, and then the meetings would take place at another venue. They said that they would all miss me. I gave them Isaac's chair.

*

My father died six days after Isaac, and at my parents' house in Sheveningen there was also an empty chair. My father's passing had been totally overshadowed by Isaac's death. It was some months later that I eventually managed to grieve for my father. I felt guilty about it, but my mother and sisters understood, and did not attempt to open up this other wound, when I was suffering so much already.

*

Aaron was born seven months after Isaac's death. I had been to the hospital for a couple of scans, and knew that my baby would be a boy. My mother was at the birth and I could see the look of delight on her face when his tiny head

110

appeared. 'He's just like Isaac,' she screamed. I was shocked until I looked at Aaron. I thought she meant that Aaron was blind, but he wasn't. The next day I was allowed to go home, to the apartment where my mother was waiting for us. I walked carrying Aaron in my arms. It was not that far, and I wanted to show Aaron the bench in the park where his father and I had met. I sat on the bench for the last time and spoke to my child.

'We will not stay long, Aaron. We must walk on ahead, remembering how we came to be here and whose hopes we carry with us into the future. We must thank those who struggled to get us here. So much history died with Isaac; so much that you will not understand, Aaron. The world for you will be so different. You must be your own self and I must be careful not to form you into the image of Isaac, but I can be a small bridge to the past. I feel like your father felt – that sometimes people are in too much of a hurry to leave the past behind and to dismiss the old traditions as being unimportant. I will not forget you, Isaac, or your family. Until we meet at our *Sukkot*, the season of our rejoicing – Shalom, Isaac, Shalom.'

***

9

After Aaron was born my time was mainly taken up with tending to his physical needs, stimulating his curiosity for the world, encouraging his confidence and soothing his distress. It was difficult, but for a few months I resisted the impulse to withdraw into myself. I still lived in the old apartment. I didn't want to go back to live with my mother in Scheveningen. It would have been a negation of everything that Isaac and I had shared together. My mother visited every day and in that respect was a great help to me, and it was good for her to be with Aaron; but she was also another worry for me to bear. My father's death had affected her so badly. She used to be such a conversationalist. Before his death she would talk about anything and everything, but mostly everything. Now she had changed. Having a conversation with her was like pulling teeth. She would just nod and sigh.

If I asked her what she would like to do, she would say that she didn't mind.

'You choose, Johanna,' she would say.

I would ask her if she was alright, and she would just nod and look vacantly at the floor. Dr Diederik told me that she was suffering from reactive depression, and that her monosyllabic responses were a symptom of that. He said that sometimes people snap out of it and sometimes they don't. He told me that the best prescription he could give was to advise her to spend time with Aaron, whenever she could. It did the trick. Aaron pulled her out of her depression.

*

Then it was my turn to face the pain. I had considered that I had already grieved for the loss of Isaac and my father, but after that day in the synagogue I was somehow disconnected from my feelings, and when my father died some weeks later I was confused as to who it was that I missed so much. After my mother regained her interest in life I began to wander around the apartment with a strange feeling following behind me like a sad abandoned dog. It kept nudging me to let me know that it was still there. I tried to ignore it, but it wouldn't go away. This must have lasted for six months or so. Then one day it changed.

The depth of my loss hadn't hit me until the day when the fragile glass globe slipped from my hands and shattered into thousands of pieces on the kitchen floor. The globe had been an object that Isaac loved to hold when he sat by the fire and prayed. He would sit with his head bowed, and turn the globe in his hands, as though it was an eye through which he could see the world. I knew why he did it. He was meditating on the restoration of the vessels, on *Tikun*.

I regularly dusted the globe and sometimes I washed it carefully in warm soapy water. That day I had been washing it, when I reached for a towel and felt the globe slip from my grasp. Suddenly I felt hollow, and a sense of unpardonable guilt consumed me, as though I had miscarried, and the child that had once been warm and secure inside me was dead. There seemed to be an eternity between the globe slipping from my hands and the sound of the glass crashing onto the floor. My heart dropped with the globe, and it was only when I heard the breaking of the glass that I knew that both were broken.

Perhaps my imagination had placed Isaac's soul in that globe, and the globe had contained my hope that he would return; that he had to return to retrieve this valuable possession. Now it was broken I knew that he would never return to me.

*

Wilma once told me that after her mother died she couldn't grieve for her because she couldn't accept that she was dead. Then, some years later she had a dream that had

113

been a recurring dream of seeing her mother dead in the morgue. The dream had never really troubled her too much before. Only this time a man appeared in the dream. He was taking a caged parrot to be incinerated. Wilma said that suddenly this dream had broken the spell and that she had woken distraught with the knowledge that her mother was really dead. Her mother had owned a parrot and on the day of her death the window had been open and the parrot had flown off. Wilma had kept the window open, in case the parrot might return, but it never did. The parrot had carried her hope that maybe her mother would come back, but she never did. In the dream the parrot had been cremated, and Wilma had to face the reality that her mother was never going to return. Then, she said, all her feelings escaped from where she had hidden them.

*

I knelt amongst the shards of glass, collecting the tiny fragments and placing them into a cereal bowl, thinking that I could repair the globe and that I would be able to put the pieces back together and everything would be as it was. My knees and shins were bleeding, and when my mother returned with the shopping she found me lying on the carpet in the bedroom crying hysterically and holding a pair of scissors in my hand. I had cut off all of my hair. It took her three hours to remove the splinters of glass from my legs. I remember trying to lick my shins, like I was an animal tending my own wounds. My mother didn't call Dr Diederik. I think she felt that I might have started to self harm, and that it wasn't an accident at all. She wouldn't have wanted anyone to know. She held me in her arms and I told her that my world had been shattered and that my life felt like a shipwreck, and the only thing that I could cling to, the only fragment of my former life that kept me afloat was Aaron.

She held me tight and said, 'I know Johanna, I know.'

After that day I would often walk to the harbour and watch the tide coming in, hoping that the sea might return some portion of the past, some fragment of the world that had contained me. I would comb the beach and pick up small pieces of wood, beer cans and even plastic spoons, and inspect them to see if they had once been part of my life, and after picking them up I couldn't throw them away, in case I unwittingly let go of something crucial, something of Isaac's or something that my father had once used or owned.

The apartment became crammed with boxes and tea chests full of the rubbish that I had collected. In the evenings, when Aaron was asleep, I would tip out one of the boxes onto the carpet and sift through the debris trying to decide what I could throw away, and trying to piece together odd bits of wood, as though they all belonged to the same jigsaw and couldn't be part of something else, of someone else's life. I would stick pieces together and paint them. Occasionally a visitor to the apartment would comment on them and ask if I had taken up sculpture as a hobby. My mother knew what I was doing and she would try to persuade me to throw some of it away, but I couldn't. Sometimes she would visit when I was out shopping and get rid of the stuff that was unhygienic and dangerous for Aaron to be around. I knew that she did it, but we didn't talk about it.

The weird assemblages stood like sentinel gods in my apartment, which began to resemble a sepulchre. Dr Diederik visited a few times because my mother had said that she was worried about me. He took an interest in what I was doing and said that I should continue and that perhaps I needed to do it. He asked me if I was washing and cooking and doing all the necessary things around the house, and if I was looking after Aaron; and he seemed quite satisfied that I was, and told my mother not to worry too much about me.

*

I was in limbo between two worlds. My soul had gone off searching for Isaac, whilst my mind attended to the day to day issues reasonably well. But I had no world to belong to anymore. The world that Isaac and I had inhabited was no more. We had lived in a time bubble, amidst the chaotic world around us. The vessel had broken, Isaac had moved on, and I had been jettisoned into a future that I didn't want, and which didn't suit me, and in which I felt desperately alone. Like the *Lamed-Vovniks*, my mind wandered in the bleakness of night, at the edge of the world, searching for fragments of my former self.

If it had happened ten years previously I wouldn't have survived it. I would have taken the easy way out and followed the pull of my soul and left the world to be with Isaac. But Isaac had taught me how precious my life was and that it had a purpose, even though I might not be able to see it or know it yet.

*

Gradually I returned to the world. I had been in mourning for nearly two years. The university had given me leave of absence, so I still had my lecturing position there. I went back to work part time, whilst my mother looked after Aaron. I somehow managed to finish my book on Simon Magus and Helen. I still didn't have the heart to work on Wilton's story; there would be so many descriptions of his meeting with Isaac in Ukraine, and I wasn't ready to deal with it. Also I didn't see the point of it any more. Isaac was dead and I had only been doing it for him. It seemed a particularly futile task, but I managed to fill a few pages in my notebook with details of how Wilton had become more and more preoccupied with the patient whom he called the wolfman. I read it through a few times and considered ditching the whole thing there and then.

Despite my reticence I didn't give up completely. I suppose I felt that I had to prove to Isaac and to myself that at least I had tried. I have often embarked on projects and known more or less from the onset that they were destined to come to nothing, yet against my better judgment something, probably obstinacy or, more likely, pride would possess me, and I couldn't simply abandon the venture. But this particular project seemed like the labour of Sisyphus. I felt that I was walking up sand dunes carrying a burden that I had been stupid to take up in the first place, and I was continually slipping back down again. Why couldn't Isaac have asked me to write about him instead of Wilton? That would have been easier. At least I knew something about Isaac and his past.

Then I recalled what Isaac had said a few weeks after I moved into the apartment and when I had despaired of ever achieving my ambition to be accepted as a student at the university.

'Johanna, when the going gets tough, sometimes it is because you are walking down the wrong road, but sometimes you are walking down the right road and the devil is placing obstacles in your path. If you were on the wrong road he would leave you to it. There would be no reason for him to impede your progress. The problem is how do you decide which of the two options is correct.'

'Yes, how do you know?' I had asked.

'You don't. I have mainly tended to favour the second of the two options, but perhaps that is because I don't like to admit defeat.'

Well, that was true. Isaac was the Jewish version of St Jude, a sucker for lost causes, but he was right at that time. I persevered with my studies. I got over my despair, and despite the difficulties, it turned out to be the right road. I got accepted by the university.

Still, writing about Wilton was a completely different venture, for which I suspected I had little aptitude. I often wished that Isaac was here to help me with the story.

✻

A few days before he died Isaac had told me not to be too concerned with how Wilton had been when we had met him in Ukraine, but to look at what he was to become.

'Understand that the spark needs to rise,' he said. 'Understand his animal soul, and you will understand his transformation and his becoming. Be patient, but most of all, be tolerant. Remember Yehuda's story. The passage of the soul is long and hard, and this task will be difficult enough for you, as it was for Wilton. You will enter a world where you would rather not be.'

What had he meant by that? Was he being particularly melodramatic or just obscure? Was I supposed to be Sophia descending into matter, or Psyche, destined to become the bride of the demonic Eros? I had hardly lived in an ivory tower like Rapunzel. I knew how to let my hair down, and I had more than enough experience of the seamier side of life. I had worked at the harbour gutting fish. I had scrubbed the tables in the fishermen's café. I had slept rough for nearly three years before I met Isaac. Granted, I didn't have as difficult a childhood as Isaac had, but I was hardly cosseted.

✻

Eventually I managed to complete the first two chapters on how Wilton had begun his pursuit of the patient that he called the wolfman, and how he had crossed the path of Dr Spencer's secretary, Liz Flannagan. In my account of those meetings I more or less kept to how Wilton had described it. I'm sure he elaborated the story a little – narcissistic people have a tendency to exaggerate their own part in an event. He was a broken man when I encountered him, but he still could not resist the temptation to embroider his story with details of his own importance, though it was also apparent that the Fates had taken it upon themselves to knock him off his perch. Still I felt sorry for what had happened to him as a child.

✢

Then I decided that I couldn't possibly fulfil my promise to Isaac. I simply didn't have the heart for it. I read through the chapters again and put the notebook into a box in the wardrobe. I wasn't in the mood to write about Wilton, and I still didn't know what it all meant and why Isaac had asked me to write it. At least I had tried. I suppose that I had come to the conclusion that Isaac had been wrong about the importance of Wilton's story. It was a difficult conclusion to arrive at, since I had always looked up to Isaac and wouldn't acknowledge that he was capable of making mistakes, at least not on important issues.

I regretted not having stood up for myself on the flight from L'Viv to Amsterdam. I should have had the nerve to oppose Isaac and simply refuse his request. It's easy to contend with someone when they are alive, but it's different when they are dead and can't argue back; and it feels like there is something of a tabu about contradicting the dead. I owed him so much. I felt indebted to him for all that he had done for me, for all his help when I could have so easily taken the path to self destruction.

Perhaps now I had to rebel against him, and this was a test for me, to be able to make my own decisions, and not be so compliant. I knew that he would understand the reasons for my reneging on my promise. Caring for his son was so much more important than fulfilling my promise.

✢

Three years passed so quickly. They were magical years watching Aaron grow and delight in the world. I had forgotten about the story. Then, when I was clearing out a box in the wardrobe that had been hidden by Isaac's fur coat, I stumbled upon the notebook. That night Isaac appeared in a dream. He was smiling but he also seemed to be disappointed with me. He looked at me, shook his head and said, 'You promised, Johanna.'

What did I say about the dead not being able to argue back?

*

After that dream, I felt that I had no option but to finish what I had started. I did a little research and eventually managed to trace Jim Wilton and a man who Isaac had suggested could assist me with the story. His name was Philip Grimes. Isaac had implied that he would be able to help me solve the enigma of the wolfman. Philip Grimes was a psychologist, and as fate would have it, he was also the man that Wilton had suspected of being the psychotic patient. It was quite bizarre and seemed wholly improbable at the time.

I contacted Philip Grimes and Jim Wilton, and they both said that they would be willing to help me with the story. I sent them the first two chapters, which they confirmed were a fairly accurate account of what had happened. Perhaps it had been a mistake sending them to Wilton, who considered that I had been a little hard on him even though I had practically quoted him verbatim. He said that he felt embarrassed about his lack of self-awareness at the time, nearly five years earlier.

*

It was then that I realized that something else had affected my writing, although I suppose, looking back it was fairly obvious. At the time that I wrote the first two chapters my feelings had been frozen because of what had happened to Isaac. I didn't have any empathy for Wilton and his predicament. I had written the chapters without any real feeling for what was happening to him. It was all a bit matter of fact, and, to be honest, I didn't particularly like Wilton when I first met him. But then I suppose I was confirming his mythology about himself. He considered himself to be unlovable, but actually he made himself unlikable. He went out of his way to be disliked, because he was frightened that being liked and liking somebody in return might lead to love, and that was too dangerous for him. So he took the safe route. He had been in love with a spectre for twenty-five years, someone who was unavailable, who had rejected him, and it stopped him committing himself to another woman. He felt that he had been haunted by numerous love affairs that had gone wrong and he felt cursed by the fact that a lasting relationship with a woman was something he might never achieve. He felt cheated by love.

I was also haunted by a love affair, but one that had fulfilled my expectations and had been taken from me. I felt cheated by death. I wondered if the pain was the same for both of us.

✻

Isaac once told me that sometimes people are not grieving for what they have lost. They are grieving for what they have never found. They need to grieve when their natural instinctual needs are not met by the outside world, and also when they eventually accept that their compensatory fantasies might never be fulfilled.

I understand now what he meant. I see it in Aaron's eyes – his search for a father. Aaron needs a father, and there have been quite a few men that have shown an interest in me since Isaac died, but I'm not ready yet. People have advised me that I should look for a new man. They don't say "a replacement for Isaac," but that's what it feels like, and he can't be replaced. He is irreplaceable and he is still around.

I still miss him terribly, and I miss his ability to cut through the dross and find the gold. I miss his insights into human nature and his sense of humour. But the quality in

Isaac that is irreplaceable is his touch. Most of all I miss him touching me. For Isaac touch was never a casual act. He used the sense of touch to investigate the world. Sometimes he could tell, just by touching me, what kind of mood I was in, or even what I was thinking. It was uncanny. He said that when he touched Jim Wilton he knew that Jim's pretentious manner was a camouflage that hid a deep wound in his soul.

Isacc also used touch to give something back to people. He had developed a whole new vocabulary of communication just by nuances of touch, and used it to tell people he liked them, loved them, was indifferent or disliked them. Sometimes his touch was meant to encourage, sometimes it was a warning, and sometimes a kind of healing.

*

Aaron is nearly five now and he takes after Isaac. He laughs so loudly. I observe him carefully, watching him decide whether or not he likes objects by touching them. But slowly and surely his sense of sight is taking over, and his ability to recognize things and talk about them is increasing, as though, once he has given them a name, he doesn't need to bother touching them again. He remembers how they felt.

I think that it is a pity to have to relinquish such an important sense, such a particularly human sense, perhaps equivalent to the sense of smell that many animals rely on. So I play a game every night with Aaron. We take it in turn to place objects in a bag and we are only allowed to touch them and not to peek. We have to guess what they are, but more importantly whether we like them or not. Aaron is so much better at the game than I am, and certainly better than Philip. When Philip came to stay with us, he would join in the game. He wasn't particularly good at it. He was too much in his head.

***

PHILIP GRIMES

Why Philip Grimes? Why him of all people? Can life get any stranger? I suppose that there are precedents for bit players in dramas to be plucked out of virtual oblivion and become eponymous heroes of another story, like Rosencrantz and Guildenstern, but it doesn't happen every day. It's not the sort of thing you would expect. Isaac had suggested that I contact Philip, since he might be able to help with my story about Wilton. It seemed an innocuous suggestion at the time. It seemed fairly reasonable. How was I to know that it was part of Isaac's game? How was I to know that the Blessed Grizzly had been up to his old tricks again?

*

I have been talking a lot more with Philip recently, and twice he has visited me in Den Haag. He has proved really useful, and has offered to proofread the chapters as they emerge. He hasn't commented too much on my writing, apart from saying that it is a little stiff in places. Aaron thinks that Philip is great, and I do too, but I am not so sure that he is the one. I think that he would like to be with me. He said that he really likes me, which for Philip is tantamount to saying that he adores me, and I can't imagine that he would go to so much trouble flying to Holland just to help me with my writing without an ulterior motive. He is quite attractive physically, and he is his own man. He was amused that he had been implicated in Wilton's story. I liked that. It was how Isaac would have reacted. Isaac had known Philip Grimes. In fact he had known him for a number of years, since that conference in Cambridge, when Isaac lost his breakfast over the side of the ship.

When we were in Ukraine, and Wilton mistook Isaac for Philip, Isaac was quite perplexed at first. I remember that he had been flummoxed as to why such an error should have occurred. He brooded about it for days, and then suddenly he started to laugh uncontrollably. He told me that he had been looking at it the wrong way round, as if it was a mistake.

'What if Wilton had been partially correct?' he said. 'What if the mix up between me and Philip Grimes had some other meaning? If I am Grimes then Grimes is supposed to be me. Perhaps we were supposed to exchange roles. Then it makes sense, because God doesn't do things like that just out of devilment.'

I didn't know what he meant at the time, but I have my suspicions about it now, because I know one person who used to do things simply out of devilment. It didn't take long before I began to suspect that Isaac had asked me to write about Wilton for a completely different reason from the one I had first imagined, and that Philip Grimes was not so incidental to the story. I suspected that Isaac might have been more interested in him than he was in Wilton, and that writing the story was a sprat to catch a mackerel.

Isaac had more or less introduced me to Philip. It may seem a little paranoid to think that before he died Isaac had directed me to the man who was supposed to replace him in my affections, and he had meant to do it, but that was what I was beginning to think. Now, after meeting Philip and having become quite fond of him, I began to suspect that Isaac had deliberately orchestrated my future. Yes I know it sounds absurd, but Isaac was a real trickster. He was capable of such Machiavellian subterfuge. He was a crafty old bear. I began to think that he had led me to Philip like Grossman had led Yehuda to his dead mate, and I felt sick with that thought. Surely it wasn't true?

I couldn't help thinking that Isaac was probably still around somewhere, in some form or other, performing his tasks as a *Lamed-Vovnik,* because he still entered my dreams. I began to imagine him looking down and smiling as the situation with Philip began to unfold. I was angry with him, and it affected my friendship with Philip. I phoned Philip and when I told him what I thought he said, 'I think Isaac would have accused you of being an imaginative girl, Johanna. But if your fantasy has some basis in fact, don't blame me, blame the matchmaker. And if you think that I am simply here to serve Isaac's plans then you had better think again.'

Philip was right. I apologized. He wasn't going to wrestle with my ghosts on my behalf. I had to do it myself.

***

Wilma came round that evening bringing her usual Greek gifts, two bottles of Cote de Rhone. It was a perfunctory gesture which usually ensured her entry into my apartment. I told her about Philip, and what I had said to him on the phone, and about the story that Isaac had asked me to write. She was intrigued. She asked me what the story was about. I said that it was nothing important, just a bit of fun. I didn't want her to read it, but she kept pestering me. Halfway through the second bottle of wine I weakened and allowed her to read it. She laughed quite a lot. It was a bit unnerving. I didn't know if it was the story that she found amusing or the quality of my writing.

'So what do think?' I asked.

'It's so-so,' she replied. 'I wouldn't buy it from the bookshop.'

'For Christ's sake, Wilma, it's not for publication. I'm not stupid.'

'Yes, I realize that, that's obvious.'

'What do you mean by that? What is obvious – that I'm not stupid or that it's not for publication?'

'Well, that it's not for publication. It's a bit dated. Literature has moved on since you did your school exams. And anyway you are only writing it in a vain attempt to hang on to Isaac. Why don't you let go of the past?'

I gave her an icy look. She took the hint and left.

✤

That did it. That was the challenge I needed. I started on the third chapter of Wilton's story. I would only work on it after Aaron had been put to bed and was asleep. I wasn't going to neglect him. The few hours each day that I could spend with him were far too precious, and apart from his attachment to my mother, I was the one from whom he demanded so much attention. Like Isaac he had an inquisitive nature, and when he realized that I was writing a story, he wanted to know all about it. I said that his father had asked me to write it, and that he could read it when he was older.

That night Isaac appeared in a dream. It was a strange dream, and later, after talking to Philip about it, I realized it was quite significant, and probably relevant to my writing. I named the dream *The Crow Woman*. I had written it out initially in my notebook, but as I was typing the dream, I remembered more of the details.

✤✤✤

The Crow Woman

Hoarfrost carpeted the land around my parents' house, and made the flat Dutch landscape appear as bleak as the frozen wastes of the tundra. The dawn sky was a thin watery grey. The elm and beech trees wove black lattice patterns silhouetted against the sky. A crow cawed its disapproval of my presence at the window, and a second crow circled high above the orchard and then settled on a branch.

'Birds of ill omen,' I thought, 'like Odin's ravens.'

A shotgun fired and cracked across the sky. The crows flew up a few feet, twisted in mid air, and floated back to the bough like tattered black parachutes.

The sun was beginning to seep through the grey sky but it had little effect on the frost. I dressed and walked out onto the grass, which crackled beneath my feet, leaving chiselled footprints on the white ground. I walked across to the orchard and noticed that there was a patch of ground where the carpet of frost had been scuffed. When I got closer I could see that it was made from a number of footprints that had crossed the width of the orchard. In the middle of the patch lay what appeared to be the jacket of an Inuit child. It was made of an animal skin. It had been frozen overnight and was not lying flat but gave the impression that there was a young child inside. I peered into the hole which should have housed a head and a shudder travelled down my spine. The crows circled above like vultures.

It seemed that a whole tribe of people had walked across the orchard. They were probably gypsies or travellers of some description. I followed the tracks and went through the gap in the hedge where the footprints had passed. I could see that they then went diagonally across a field and into a small copse of birch trees. I came to the edge of the field and was about to enter the wood when I noticed that a crow had been pinned to a wooden fence post. It was hanging limp but was not dead. It had obviously been wounded by gun shot pellets and had been pinned to the post as a warning to other crows. This sort of thing happens once in a while with stoats, weasels and crows. It is a barbaric practice.

The bird sensed that I was approaching it and revived. It panicked and, in trying to escape, whirled round and round in a frantic circle like a demented Catherine wheel. I managed to stop it whizzing round, and holding it in one hand, I freed its claw from the post, but realized immediately that I had broken a part of its claw. I opened my hand and the bird flew upwards into a tree.

I entered the wood. It was only a small wood, mainly brushwood and saplings. There was a distinct smell of wood smoke lingering amongst the trees and as I approached the centre of the wood I could see a fire and smoke rising from it. A few adults and one or two children stood around the fire staring at me. They did not seem to be gypsies but were travellers of some description, outcasts from society. There was an old grey pony tethered to a tree and a mound of animal skins under which I thought I detected the shape of a human figure. The people around the fire nodded to me as I approached. I nodded back. I had taken the Inuit jacket with me, and I held it up to the group. A woman stepped forward and took it from me. She bowed her head a few times, as though thanking me.

From another part of the wood a young man dressed in a bright green robe approached the camp. He had a spyglass in his hand and was looking for something or someone. He had the look of a prince from a fairy story. Though the small tribe of travellers was unusual, at least they were credible. The young man appeared to be distinctly out of place. His demeanour was dismissive and arrogant. He did not greet anyone, but acted as though they had no status, or in fact no existence. He looked across to the mound of animal skins. Someone distracted his attention by shouting, and he turned his attention away from the mound. After snooping around for a few minutes, occasionally putting the spyglass to his eye, he turned and left the camp. I was about to ask someone what was happening, when the woman who had thanked me for the jacket put her finger to her mouth, as though to warn me not to say anything. The group watched the young man disappear.

After a few minutes of silence something stirred under the mound of skins and Isaac emerged from under the pile. He looked weak and ill, but he managed a smile and beckoned me over to him. He lay half under the skins and I squatted beside him.

'He will bring the grey soldiers, if he knows that I am here,' he said. 'They will take us away and force us to conform to their rules. He is a traitor. He is a betrayer of our people.'

'Who is he?' I asked.

'He is one who likes to stand out from the crowd. You see he calls attention to us, and then we are discovered.'

'Who are these people?' I asked.

'We are the outsiders, though we have always lived close by. We are useful to people, and look after what they reject, sometimes part of a child or some aspect of a child, or a pet, like that pony over there that was neglected by its owner. We look after these things, and sometimes later people come to reclaim what they have thrown out and we hand it back to them. We foster their cast-offs. Now we must move further away, because the grey soldiers are coming.'

'You said a part of a child. What do you mean? How can you look after a part of a child?'

"Yes. It must seem odd to you. You see that child by the fire. He is not a whole child. He is only a part of a child, the part that the parents didn't like to bother with, that got exiled and didn't comply with their expectations. It has to live somewhere. It can't die. If it died then everyone would be grey.'

'What happened to the child who was clothed in the Eskimo suit?' I asked.

'He returned to himself. He was a frozen little mite, but we managed to keep him warm and alive in a makeshift suit made from a wolf pelt.'

'And the youth that looks like a prince?'

'That is the other part of the child, that calls attention to himself and leads the grey ones to us. We have to be careful of that. I am tired now, and it is time for you to leave us. Do not mention that we are here.'

I promised that I wouldn't. I left the camp and waved goodbye.

As I returned home, a woman appeared before me. She had sharp piercing eyes that seemed to be able to read my thoughts, and she had a crow perched on her arm. She held out her other hand towards me and I noticed that her hand was missing two fingers.

'Thank you for releasing me,' she said, and disappeared back into the wood.

***

I woke up from the dream in a strange mood that lasted for a couple of days. I felt upset, but I didn't know why. I sent the dream to Philip by email and asked him for his thoughts about it. He worked with dreams in his therapy sessions with clients. He replied immediately and told me that he didn't interpret dreams without knowing more about the dreamer and their own associations to the dream. He agreed that it was probably a significant dream, and that he would be prepared to discuss it with me, if an occasion presented itself. I felt at the time that he was being a little dismissive, but later I realized that it wasn't personal. It was simply his way of working. He did say one thing though. He suggested that since I had just finished the chapter on Wilton and the wolfman, that it appeared reasonably obvious that Wilton was the egotistical youth in the green cloak and Isaac was a sort of wolfman, hiding under the animal skins. But he added that it went much deeper than that.

I also thought that the dream had something to do with the writing. I recalled Isaac telling me once that an early name for the Hebrew tribes was '*habiri*' — the outsiders, the exiled ones.

✷

Even though I had been reticent about writing Wilton's story, I began to feel a little more optimistic about it. I had been in contact with John Spencer's secretary, Liz Flannagan — someone who might have appeared to be simply a pawn in the game, but who had so much spirit. I wanted to know more about her and about the other protagonists in this drama. I emailed Philip and told him that I was going to continue for the time being. Philip said that he thought it was a good idea, and that there would be time for reflection later, and it was probably best not to scrutinize things too much. He also said that he knew John Spencer, and that Isaac would have been fond of him, despite the fact that Spencer lived in a very different world to Isaac's. By this time three of the characters in the story had been emailing me with information about themselves, but mostly about the others. Liz was a goldmine of information about all of them, and she almost bit my hand off when I asked her to contribute. She sent tons of information, much of it defamatory and mostly unprintable, containing what appeared to be her complete repertoire of pranks and practical jokes. She begged me to include it all in my story. I wrote back saying that I would try to include some of it, and that her anecdotes concerning Dr Spencer and his wife would prove invaluable. Of course the people that I was writing about had changed a fair deal in the last five years, perhaps with the exception of John Spencer. He wasn't averse to change. He just didn't need to change. I felt quite sympathetic towards Spencer. After all he had tried to help Wilton, and Wilton had repaid his kindness by bedding his wife.

✷✷✷

2.

When I was nearly halfway through the fifth chapter of Wilton's story, Philip invited me to spend a few days with him in the north of Scotland, near the Inverpolly estate. He said that he would go fishing during the day and I could write or go fishing as well, and in the evenings he would help me with my writing. I wasn't so sure about going so far away and leaving Aaron with my mother. He was only five years old. I was also a little concerned that Philip might expect me to sleep with him. I wasn't going to jump into bed with him so quickly. He assured me that we would have separate bedrooms and that he had no such expectations or indeed no such inclinations. That was a bit of a downer, "no such inclinations." Of course it wasn't true. Women know when they are the object of a man's passion. At least Philip wasn't as obvious about it as Professor Kemel had been, and I thought that I could deal with it. Eventually I agreed to go. I flew from Amsterdam to Heathrow and then to Inverness. Philip picked me up at Inverness airport and we drove across to Achiltibuie, where we stayed in a small cottage on the coast overlooking the Summer Isles.

The mountains of Suilven, Canisp and Stac Pollaidh rose majestically behind us. I had never been anywhere like it before. The landscape is so old, evoking a time before humans were on the earth, and it is so stark yet beautiful. The mountains are like great stone dinosaurs slumbering on a plateau of rock, petrified guardians on the surface of an immense sarcophagus lid. On the second day of our trip, whilst Philip went off fishing, I was content to walk along the shore and take in the soulful mood of the place. He didn't catch any fish, but returned with stories of the ones that he had almost caught. His cheeks were marked with tiny pinpricks where the hooks had caught him.

On the first night he cooked venison with figs and roast potatoes. We sat by the log fire drinking malt whisky and cans of draught Guinness, and it reminded me of the time when Isaac and Yehuda had spent that evening together. We talked for a couple of hours about Wilton and Isaac, and I told him Yehuda's story, and asked Philip if he ever been through an ordeal like that. He replied that he had never undergone such a physical ordeal, not in that way, but that something strange had happened to him in his twenties, but he didn't want to talk about it.

I remembered the dream that I had emailed to Philip, which he had promised to interpret for me. It was like the stories that Isaac used to tell. I reminded Philip of the main images in the dream – the empty wolfskin, the crows, Isaac hiding under the animal skins, the crow woman who had lost two fingers, and the part children.

I asked Philip what he thought it was all about. He said that my dream was trying to show me the dynamic that often occurs when people experience trauma in their childhood. He asked me if I had suffered some trauma. I said that apart from my father being away a lot on the fishing boats and the realization that he was in danger, and that he might not return, I didn't remember anything like that.

'Why do you ask?' I said.

He sat forward in his chair. 'Well, you see, Johanna, when young children experience trauma, they can't deal with it, it is too horrific, it threatens their whole being, so the emotional part of the child is split off, put in a freezer, a box, a submarine, a space ship, a dungeon – somewhere separate and safe – or it is looked after by a figure in the unconscious. The other part of the child grows up, and often, in a compensatory way, develops precociously. The emotionally traumatized part is looked after internally by the instinctual part of the psyche, as though it were a feral child, like Romulus and Remus or Mowgli.'

'It's an interesting idea, Philip. How does that happen? How can the psyche of a child look after itself?'

'It dissociates the experience, and it appears to be a cure, but it is only temporary. You see, in the dream this tribe of outsiders is looking after the dissociated feelings and memories.'

'Alright, but why is it only temporary?'

'It's as though you have a serious wound in your leg and you apply a tourniquet to stop the bleeding, and it works for a while, but then the temporary cure becomes malignant. It threatens the organism. That's when the symptoms begin to erupt. Sometimes the problem can remain dormant for half a lifetime, and then the slumbering beast wakes up. The symptoms begin to show, symptoms that are really connected to an experience that happened years previously and they need to be reconnected to the event. Well, that's the theory, but it doesn't explain why you had the dream. Apart from the dream being set near your parents' house, and the old man looking like Isaac, do you have any personal associations to any part of the dream?'

'No, I don't think so?' I replied.

'What about the crow woman with the broken fingers?'

'No, I don't think that she has ...oh shit!' I felt odd, as though I was going to faint. I remembered that when I was five I had been looking after Susannah, my younger sister. We had walked through a hedge and across a field to a stile. There was a dead crow hanging from a post next to the stile. I was helping Susannah over the stile, when she slipped and broke her hand. She had to be taken to hospital. My mother was furious with me.'

'Yes, that will be one of them,' he said, 'and the other?'

'What do you mean, isn't that enough?'

'No. There were two crows at the start of the dream and the crow woman lost two fingers, which probably means there are two dark memories.'

I grimaced and began to feel angry, 'Yes, well, it happened again when I was sixteen. I was looking after Ruth, my youngest sister, at the swimming pool and she slipped and broke her leg. She was only eight years old. My mother was furious with me again, but this time I didn't have to take it. I left home. Neither of those incidents were my fault.'

'So why do you still feel guilty?' he asked.

'I don't.'

'I think you do.'

'Yes, well, it's late. We can talk about it in the morning.'

I said goodnight and went to my room. Philip looked a little disappointed, but he didn't say anything. I lay awake for a while thinking of Aaron and hoping that he was safe. I couldn't contact my mother on my mobile phone, there wasn't any signal. Philip had told me that there was a phone at the hotel a couple of miles down the road. I thought that it would be best to phone her in the morning.

*

I woke early and walked to the hotel to phone my mother. Aaron was safe and he told me that he had been to the zoo, and he was going to be a lion tamer when he grew up. When I told Philip about it he said that it was a noble profession for a five year old.

That day we drove to Lochinver and walked along a track to the foot of Suilven. I wanted to climb it but Philip said that we didn't have time and it would get dark soon. He hadn't talked much, and I asked him if there was something troubling him. He said that there wasn't, and that he didn't like to talk much when he was walking in the mountains. Actually, Philip was taciturn most of the time, even more than Isaac was.

When we were driving back, he asked me if I felt a little less guilty.

'Look, I told you last night. I don't feel guilty. Don't shrinks ever take a holiday from work?'

'Well, you asked me to interpret the dream, Johanna. You see, in the dream you release a part of yourself that is being punished, and she thanks you for releasing her. I suspect that you are supposed to work with children, with lost souls. That is why you were attracted to Isaac. He was a sort of shaman, who went searching for lost souls, but in the dream he is weary, and a woman appears – a crow woman. So this is your future work, not Isaac's. But previously you couldn't follow your destiny because you couldn't take the risk of damaging anyone. You still carried the guilt about your sisters, so you limited yourself to academic study.'

We were only half a mile from the cottage. I asked him to stop the car and I got out. 'I'm walking the rest of the way,' I shouted. 'Limited myself! Well thanks. You really are an arrogant pig, Philip. You assume too much. You are a bloody know-all.' I slammed the car door and stomped off down the road. The car overtook me and didn't stop. When I got back to the cottage the car keys were on the table and a note saying that he was walking to the hotel, and would I like to join him for a meal. I didn't. I was asleep when he got back from the hotel.

The next day I had calmed down and we drove to Ullapool and took a boat trip. I was telling Philip about my father and what a great sailor he had been. I wanted to see the gardens at Inverewe, but Philip said it was quite a long drive to get there. I think he wanted to have a couple of hours' fishing. We bought food for the evening. It was to be my last evening with Philip, although he was staying on for another week. We walked around Ullapool looking in the tourist shops and returned to the cottage. It was a warm afternoon so we sat out at the front of the cottage. Philip opened a bottle of red wine. He drank too much. He didn't get drunk, and that was the problem. He had such a tolerance for alcohol that he could drink far too much of it without it seemingly affecting him, but it must have been exacting a toll on his liver.

I made food in the evening whilst he went fishing. The meal was nearly finished when he ran into the cottage holding a three pound sea trout.

'Cook this, Johanna,' he pleaded.

'But I have just made meatloaf,' I protested. 'Still, it is a beautiful fish. We could have it for starters, congratulations.'

'Don't congratulate me,' he moaned, 'I didn't get one bite and I lost four flying condoms.'

'Philip, what are you talking about?'

He showed me a lure. It had a big hook and a rubber body. 'It's called a flying condom,' he said and shrugged his shoulders. 'I didn't invent the name, Johanna.'

'I didn't mean that. How did you catch the fish if you didn't get a bite?'

'I didn't catch it. I never do. I bought the fish in Ullapool this morning, when you were shopping for shortbread biscuits. I put it in the boot of the car, and forgot about it. It's just nicely thawed out now.'

He changed from his fishing clothes which stank to high heaven, and we sat down to our last dinner together. The following day he would drive me to Inverness, and I would fly back to Amsterdam. It had been a great weekend, despite our argument. And then I spoilt it.

I stood up and faced him. 'I want to ask you an important question, Philip, and I want you to tell me the truth. Apart from that time when you met Isaac at the Cambridge conference, did you meet him again after that?'

'Well, yes. Don't you recognize me from the room in Medzybiz? I was there the night you brought Wilton to the room.'

'No, I don't recognize you from that night. Did he ever talk to you about me?'

'Who, Wilton?'

'Don't be silly. Did Isaac talk to you about me?'

'All the time. He adored you, Johanna.'

'I mean, did he ever talk to you about you being with me?'

'Of course not. We have been through this before.'

'Then why are you helping me with my book?'

'Well, when you contacted me, I agreed to help you for Isaac's sake. But now I suppose it is also for your sake. Is that alright? Why do you ask? Do you think that you are caught up in some sinister plot? What have I done to you that you mistrust me so much? If it was some sinister plot, I would have been around long before now, huffing and puffing and blowing your house down. It's over five years since Isaac died. Have I got you here under false pretences? Has Little Red Riding Hood met her comeuppance? My, what big ears you have Grandma!'

'I'm sorry. It was a bit over the top. I didn't mean to insult you. You are very like Isaac in many ways, Philip, yet you are not him, and I know that you don't try to be like him. I respect that. I think Isaac wanted you to look after Aaron and me, but I can look after myself. Isaac shouldn't have done it.'

'Isaac isn't controlling you, Johanna, and you know that. You are so frightened of being controlled that you look for the slightest hint of it, as though you would be giving up your free will, giving up a part of yourself if you complied with someone else's wishes. Compliancy and rebellion are two sides of the same coin. If you are governed by only one of them then it is the same as being governed by the other. Neither is proof of having a choice. You can choose to comply or choose to rebel, but make sure it is a choice not a compulsion. I don't want to be with you unless you choose to be with me. It has nothing to do with Isaac anymore.'

I went to the bathroom. I suppose he had a right to be angry with me. He had been a perfect gentleman, and really kind. Why should I blame him for my own internal conflict?

When I returned to the main room he was pouring out two glasses of malt whisky. I said that I was going to go to bed early and that it had been a really hard day for me, and that I was tired. He gave me the same look of disappointment that he had given me on the first night.

'Have I offended you, Johanna?'

'No, but why don't you ask me?' I said.

'Ask you what?' he replied.

I sighed, and started to leave the room.

'I don't need to ask you,' he shouted after me, 'you know how I feel about you. I assume that you will sleep with me if you really want to, and if you don't want to, you won't. So it doesn't matter what I say to you about it. I don't want to persuade you to do anything you don't want to do.'

'Thank you Philip, but you look so sad when I go to bed.'

'I don't mean to,' he said, 'I'm really happy that you are here with me.'

He left the room and went into his bedroom to read. I washed the pots, locked the doors and went to bed. I could hear him shuffling around; then it went quiet. I fell asleep and woke up feeling sad and noticed that it was only five o' clock in the morning. I wondered if he was awake, as I opened the door to his room. He appeared to be fast asleep. I looked at him.

'Well, I have made my choice,' I said, 'and you are not going to like it – I can be a real bitch sometimes.' I took off my dressing gown and slipped into bed with him. I put my arms around him.

He purred with pleasure, and said, 'I know.'

I hit him with the pillow, and looked towards the open window. 'Thank you, Isaac,' I whispered in a voice too low for Philip to hear.

We made love and fell asleep again. It was midday when I surfaced and wandered into the kitchen. Philip was frying bacon and singing to himself.

'Good morning. Did you sleep well?' he asked.

'Yes,' I replied, 'but I had the most extraordinary dream.'

'About what?'

'I don't know. It wasn't really like my normal dreams. It started out in a most peculiar way, and it got stranger and stranger.'

'So tell it me,' he said and handed me a cup of coffee.

*

I told him what I could remember of the dream, and when I returned to Den Haag I remembered more of it, and I wrote it down as a story. I called it *'The Abyss'*. It was the second of two dreams that I considered had something to do with my writing about Isaac and Wilton, but more particularly about Benjamin Spencer who was the one responsible for pointing Wilton towards Brody. Benjamin's parents had died in a car crash when he was three, and he had been adopted by John Spencer's parents.

***

3.
The Abyss

I was returning home shortly after midnight. As I approached the apartment, I noticed that the remains of a vehicle were strewn across the width of the road. It didn't give the impression that a road accident had occurred. It was quite eerie. It was strange that nobody had come out of their houses. The damp air caressed the broken metal carcass with its slim misty fingers. The fragments of the vehicle were spaced out along the road like parts of a boat that had been broken in a storm, and had drifted gently in on the tide, to be deposited at random on the beach. Viewed from a distance you might have mistaken the metal fragments of the vehicle for erratic boulders left by a glacier, somehow aware that they were alien to the environment. The metal carcasses seemed to groan like the last low notes of a cello in a symphony by Sibelius. Then the sound became so low in pitch that it was beyond the scope of the human ear to detect, but the air was still troubled by the vibrations.

The fragments were parts of a car, perhaps dating back to the 1950s. They were painted blue, and the paintwork was in quite good condition, a few scratches and dents, but no signs of rust. I circled around them for a while, half expecting to see a sign affixed to one of the surfaces, 'POLICE AWARE'. There wasn't one, and if there had been it would have disturbed the ghostly effect of the scene, and perhaps then I would have entered my apartment and gone to bed. I wanted to enter, but something was preventing me, some unnatural force or will was pulling me to return down the road.

Perhaps I had missed something – a stricken cat in the road or a child that was lost and was timidly calling for help, afraid that it would call down the terrors of the night upon itself. Perhaps the sound that I sensed did not originate from nearby, but from a distant source, like the moan of a lonely seal that is far out to sea, and echoes around the cliffs on the seashore. I tried to follow the sound. I walked slowly back along the road. After about seventy yards, I turned into a street that I hadn't noticed until that night. I had lived in that apartment with Isaac for many years, yet I had never noticed that particular street before. It was diagonally opposite to the back of the apartment and so would have been visible from the kitchen window. But I don't recall ever having noticed it before.

I sensed that there was a path, a shortcut that led from this street back to my apartment, and I began to look for it. I had already stumbled up the driveways of a few houses, thinking that they were the beginning of the path, but they weren't. I remember wondering if I was sleepwalking, but by then I was walking briskly and almost running on occasions. I was beginning to despair of ever finding the path.

Previous to this moment it did not seem important that I might be lost and unable to find my way home. My anxiety calmed a little as I noticed a man walking towards me from across the street. I spoke first and asked him if he knew the whereabouts of a footpath. I explained that I had been looking for the beginning of it. He pointed out a break between two houses and informed me that the path started there. I walked towards it, just as he was asking me if I had seen a young boy in the street. I didn't stop, but mumbled that I hadn't seen anyone and rushed away. I was in no mood for a protracted conversation. I just wanted to get home as quickly as possible. I should have stopped to help the man look for the child, but I didn't offer assistance and I began to feel twinges of remorse as I started out on the path.

In the moonlight it was not difficult to see the path, but then the moon became covered by cloud and it became more and more difficult to keep to the path. Eventually I could see nothing in the blackness that surrounded me, not even the streetlights, and I heard nothing in the silence that accompanied the darkness. This deprivation of sense perception began to gnaw away at me, until it seemed to hold me tightly in its jaws. I stood frozen and rooted to the ground, which I felt might at any minute suddenly disappear. It was as though I was suspended above an abyss, which I could not see but of which I had an intense and fearful intuition. I experienced a foreboding that deep in the abyss the world was being eroded by an unknown force. Slowly and tentatively I turned around as though I was standing on the point of a needle. Then the path and the ground were illuminated as though it was daylight. I turned back again, and the darkness returned as intensely as before. Panic overtook me. I tiptoed the first few steps and then rushed back down the path the way that I had come. My legs tried to keep pace with the furious beating of my heart. Soon I was back in the street, slumped over a wall, waiting for and willing my breath and my senses to catch up with me.

*

It took some time before I recovered sufficiently to start walking back along the street, when I noticed two figures walking towards me. One of them was the man who had directed me towards the path. The other was a young boy, about seven years old. They greeted me and I began to walk with them down the street. I took little notice of their features as I walked alongside them. I was looking ahead, hoping that soon my own road would become visible. The street was much longer than I remembered it, but our conversation occupied my thoughts and took my mind away from the experience on the hill. I think my two temporary companions

143

were Jewish. We strayed onto the subject of Hasidism, about which the older man appeared to have a lot of knowledge. I was mentioning that I had a read a fair bit on the subject, when my two companions slowed to a halt and stood at the entrance to a small suburban house. I gathered that we had arrived at their destination and I bade them goodnight. The man gestured to me that I was welcome to enter the house. Since I had been enjoying their conversation and was intrigued as to their identity, I decided to accept their invitation.

I entered the house, which was a single-roomed dwelling. On the outside it appeared to be a normal suburban house. Inside it had the appearance of a hovel from a Polish shtetl. I had never seen a peasant hovel before, and had little interest in the history of domestic architecture, so I cannot say exactly with which place or period in time it was connected. The walls were of rough plaster, showing patches of brickwork where the plaster had crumbled away. The floor was uneven with large flagstones that had settled on poor foundations. A few rough wooden stools littered the room, half circling a sturdy wooden table that stood defiantly in the middle of the room. The people in the room appeared to be a family of sorts. There were about eight or nine people in all, two of whom I had already met. There were two children of approximately eight or nine years of age, two or possibly three middle aged adults and an old man and woman, who were most likely the grandparents. From their clothes and facial characteristics they seemed to be Hasidic Jews from the 18th century.

I was not surprised at the time to discover that inside the façade of a twentieth century middle class house there was a rude hovel, inhabited by Jewish peasants. Too many odd things had occurred that night, and at least this scene was refreshingly warm and welcoming. Of course, such islands from the past are not unknown. One thinks of the Amish settlements nestling amidst the advanced technological culture of the United States, which are as out of place as a Vermeer painting hung in a car factory. But this cultural backwater was less than half a mile from my house. I am surprised about it now, but in the dream I wasn't.

I was sitting in front of the old man and woman, speaking German. I had been talking to them for about half an hour, and had hardly noticed the others in the room. There was nothing unusual about this couple, apart from them being from another time. They seemed neither sinister nor saintly. They were what you would expect eighteenth century peasants to be like. They asked questions about normal everyday things. We were having a pleasant chat, and they treated me as though I was a neighbour of theirs, which technically I was, so I didn't pry into what on earth they were doing here, since, from their behaviour, it appeared that they had no sense of my being from a different world to the one from which they originated. If I appeared strange to them, they certainly gave no hint or indication of it.

*

After a while I became aware of two children giggling somewhere behind me, and I felt the lightest of touches on my back, accompanied by soft swishing noises. This went on for about five minutes, and their laughter got louder as the strokes on my back became stronger. I would have turned around earlier, but the couple that I had been talking to gave nothing away and seemed to be ignoring the children. I turned around to see what was happening. The two children wore impish grins on their faces, which managed to shine through the dirt and the purple stains that covered their skin. Both children were holding leafy branches which I thought might have been some sort of herb. They had been striking me on the back with these bunches of herbs, and were obviously enjoying their game. I assumed that I had been involved in

145

some quaint custom connected to the receiving of guests. I was about to ask about this, when the two children rushed to the corner of the room and returned holding a small bowl and a small canvas bag filled with berries. They set the objects in front of me and showed me what to do. The bag was full of juniper berries which I had to detach from the tiny stalks and then place in the bowl. I began to do this and they nodded approval, laughed and ran off back to the corner of the room. I looked questioningly at the old couple. The woman looked at me in a strange way and whispered, 'Rue and juniper, juniper and rue, Walpurgis night encloses you.'

I began to feel slightly anxious. I looked to my left and noticed that the man whom I had met in the street was addressing the child that had been lost, and remonstrating with him about something. The man was leaning against the wall and the child was sitting on a stool a few feet from him in the corner of the room. I had not had the opportunity previously of seeing both of them in the light before now. I was curious to know what they looked like. I had assumed that they were relatively normal human beings, and I was surprised to find different. The man leaning against the wall was blessed with the snout of a jackal. I say "blessed" because what I saw was not ugly or grotesque. He was the most handsome of creatures. His face was how you might imagine the Egyptian god Anubis to have looked, and his posture had the dignity and grace of a higher being, perhaps an angel. I felt that he was aware that I was staring at him, but he didn't look at me. Compared to this magnificent creature, humans appear gauche and uneasy with their physical form. It was difficult for me to take my gaze away from him, but I also wished to look at the boy. The boy seemed to have his head constantly bowed down and was nodding or shaking it in response to the words that the adult was saying. So I could only really see the top of his head. At least that is what I thought I was looking at.

At first the boy appeared to be defiant towards the jackal figure. He was agitated and was furiously shaking his head from side to side, but gradually he changed and was gently nodding acceptance. He climbed down from the stool and approached the old couple. He embraced the old woman and then approached the old man and offered him his hand to shake. The old man placed a hand on top of the boy's head and said a few words in Yiddish. The boy turned around to face the other people and myself. I then discovered that what I had assumed was the top of his head was in fact his face. It was covered by short bristles, like the pelt of a badger. Only his sharp dark brown eyes could just about be seen looking out from behind the hair. He stood silent and still. A warm glow seemed to descend from the ceiling and the faint scent of wood smoke drifted into the room. I sat quietly looking straight ahead at the boy. I thought I saw a single hair fall from his face and settle on the ground by his feet. I could not be sure. I renewed my concentration. This time I was sure another hair had fallen, then another and another.

It was reminiscent of seeing a young tree in autumn, beginning to shed its leaves on a frosty morning. You suddenly sense that a leaf has fallen or is about to fall. You watch and the tree appears to vibrate a little as though all of its limbs are aware of the impending loss. You notice a leaf on the ground and then begin to see other leaves gently falling and resting near it. The tree begins to shed more of its leaves, randomly at first, like the way musicians tune their instruments before a performance. Then as though a symphony has begun, a gentle cascade of leaves builds to a crescendo, until eventually the last leaf has fallen.

Gradually the face of the young boy began to shine through the moulting hair. A face of the most angelic beauty

147

was revealed as the pencil lines of hair were shed. It was a radiant face, so bright that eventually I could only witness the event through the reflected gaze of the other watchers. The room suddenly filled with light. The old man beckoned the jackal and whispered into his ear. The jackal led the boy out into the street, but the light from the boy's face seemed to linger much longer inside the room and only slowly faded away.

*

The room returned to normal and the old woman rose from her seat, picked up the bowl of juniper berries and began to sprinkle the berries onto the small mound of hair that lay on the floor. She took a broom and swept the pile of hair and berries out of the door. Once this was over, the others in the room began to converse again and the old man produced a bottle of gin, which he proudly placed on the table in front of himself. I sat there immobilized by the beauty of what had taken place. The old man smiled at me and asked me if I would take a glass of gin with him. I replied that it was a little early in the morning for alcohol. The old woman laughed and gave me a knowing look. She obviously knew that my habits were not as I had implied them to be. I blushed, and she smiled. I took the glass that was offered and soon we were all drinking and laughing together.

It was very early in the morning and I knew that it was still dark outside and that I should return home. I thanked the old couple for their hospitality and edged myself towards the door.

'Will you be going back by the path?' the old man asked.

I had not forgotten about my experience on the dark path, and I wasn't very pleased to be reminded of it. 'I think not,' I replied, 'I'm sure that it is better to go by the road.' I was hoping that he hadn't noticed my anxiety.

'You are quite wrong,' he said. 'The path is by far the best way to go. My son and my servant are waiting outside to accompany you, if you decide to take the path.'

'Thank you. In that case, I will return by the path,' I declared as I left the house and walked up the street with the two beings who had led me to the house.

*

Despite my former trepidation about taking the path, I knew that this time everything would be different. The gaping wound in the earth had been healed and the darkness was no longer a threat. I arrived home safely, and rushed to the kitchen window, from where I would be able to see the path, if in fact it existed. The path, the street and the peasant's house were not there. It was now daylight in the dream, and the sun seemed to hover directly above where the peasant house would have been, and in that exact spot, I thought that I detected a wisp of smoke rising upwards. I stood at the window for a while, then the doorbell rang. I opened the door, but there was nobody there. I noticed an old blue car slowly driving past my apartment. The sun was being reflected from a wing mirror and sent a beam of light towards me. A small arm hung out of the passenger window and appeared to wave to me.

***

Philip had been very quiet and deep in thought as I was relating the dream, and when I asked him what he thought about it, he just said that it was an amazing dream and that I should be thankful that I had been allowed to witness such a wondrous event.

'Yes, I know that, Philip,' I said, 'but was it what happened to John Spencer's brother, Benjamin?'

'I can't say,' he replied.

'Why not? You told me that Benjamin's parents had been killed in a car crash, and that he went through some strange mystical experience, met his ancestors and changed.'

'Did I?'

'Yes, Philip, you did. I was writing about it yesterday. But you refuse to tell me what happened to Benjamin, even though I suspect that you know about it.'

'So why are you asking me again? It could also have been about Isaac. It could have been about both of them.'

'Yes, but I had that dream after I had been writing about Benjamin. Can't you understand that? I just want it confirmed.'

'You also had the dream after you had made love to me.'

'Yes. But that doesn't have any relevance to the dream. Why did you say that?'

'Because sometimes when you get close to people you can pick up their stuff. Sometimes I will dream about my clients and the dreams will tell me something I hadn't been conscious of.'

'Are you saying that my dream was about you?'

'Yes, but it is also about Benjamin and Isaac, and Yehuda. You see, we have something in common.' He went into his bedroom.

'You mean that you were all kabbalists,' I shouted.

'Yes, but we also share something else. We were all in some way estranged from our ancestors; and we were all drawn to the Kloiz at Brody.' He returned holding an old photograph which he placed on the kitchen table. 'Did the two old people in your dream look something like these two?'

I looked at the photograph and almost fell off my chair. 'Yes, it's them,' I stammered. 'Who are they Philip?'

'They are my great grandfather and my great grandmother. They were called Wolfenden. They lived in Brody until 1885 when they emigrated to England. It was not until I met Isaac at the Cambridge conference that I had the slightest idea that some of my ancestors had been Eastern European Jews. I was sitting next to him one day, when he turned to me and said, "You are a Hasid." I realized that Isaac was blind and couldn't see my face. I explained to him that I was English and that I was attending the conference on Hasidic stories because I was interested in comparative religion and kabbalah, but that I wasn't Jewish. He laughed and said, "You are a Hasid, young man. Trace your ancestry and come to the Kloiz at Brody when you are prepared." I smiled. I wasn't going to argue with him, but I knew that he was wrong. Then I felt like I had been punched in the stomach. Something shifted inside of me. After the conference I was mildly curious about what Isaac had told me. I did a search on the internet and found out that my great grandparents on my father's side had in fact been Hasidic Jews from Brody. Later I found this old photograph of them in my father's photo album. So, Johanna, what do you think about that? Spooky, isn't it?'

I smiled. Isaac had done that sort of thing all the time. He would meet complete strangers and tell them something extraordinary about themselves. 'Yes,' I replied, 'it's spooky. But not so unusual.'

'No, I gathered that,' he said.

Then Philip told me that three years later he had contacted Isaac, and that Isaac had invited him to accompany him on his annual pilgrimage to Ukraine. Philip had accepted the invitation, and during the pilgrimage he had dreamed the same dream that I had dreamed that morning, and afterwards he had experienced a powerful mystical vision of a young woman dressed as a bride.

Philip was crying after he told me about his vision of the *Shekhinah*, and went outside for a walk. Whilst he was away, I sat looking out of the window wondering why Philip had said that the dream could have also been about Isaac. Then suddenly it dawned on me. I felt weak. I almost fainted. In the dream I had experienced what Isaac experienced every day of his life — the blackness, the abyss, the void. I had felt so frightened at that moment in the dream, when I could not see anything, when I could not trust the world anymore, and when I could not be certain that it was there. In the dream I was frightened of taking one more step forward. In the blackness, without sight, I could not trust that the world would support me. I was dependent on faith, and my faith had let me down, until I had experienced that wonderful event, when my faith was restored.

I realized that when he was a child, Isaac had experienced that sense of being abandoned because of his blindness, and Ben had experienced it because he had been abandoned when his parents died in a car crash. Yehuda was separated from his family during the war, and Philip's bloodline and culture had been kept a secret from him. They all shared in the exile of the *Shekhinah*. Their souls were searching for her and for their home.

***

4.

After I returned to Den Haag, Philip phoned every day, and came over for a weekend. My mother liked him and my sisters seemed quite impressed. Of course he is a fair bit older than me, but not as much as Isaac was. He was completely knocked out by Yehuda's library and spent hours on the Friday night rummaging through the shelves and ignoring Aaron and myself. He apologized after I had rather pointedly placed a copy of the *Zohar* under the duvet on my side of the bed and got the old futon out. On Saturday and Sunday he was more sociable, but I kept catching him giving sideways glances at the shelves. I couldn't blame him. It is an unusual library, and when I first went to live with Isaac, I couldn't resist it either.

*

Two weeks after his visit I went to stay at Philip's flat in Manchester. We went walking over Kinder Scout. It wasn't as majestic as the landscape around Ullapool, but it was beautiful in its own way, and I was quite surprised that there was such dramatic scenery once you got away from the conurbation. Philip had been born in a town north of Manchester, and we went to visit the area where he grew up, and then went further onto the moors at Saddleworth. It was only then that he told me about himself and his childhood. I had spent a fair bit of time with him and suddenly realized that I knew hardly anything about him, but then, like Isaac, he didn't particularly volunteer the information. You had to drill for it. He made me promise not to include too much about him in my writing. I said that I wouldn't, but asked him why. He just shrugged, and said that he preferred me not to.

On the Saturday evening we went to an Indian restaurant in Rusholme. He thought I might be impressed by the number of foreign restaurants so closely packed together. I reminded him that the Dutch were a maritime nation and that we had all that and more in Amsterdam.

*

We got back to his flat just before midnight and went to bed. Then the phone rang and Philip got out of bed and answered it. It was for me. It was my mother. I knew immediately that something had happened to Aaron otherwise she wouldn't have phoned so late. I got up and tried to dress myself with one hand whilst listening to her. I was rushing round the room, backwards and forwards, and screaming, and shouting 'No, no, no!' Where is he? What has happened? Which hospital? Is he alive? Mum, is he dead?'

Aaron was in a coma. I shouted at Philip to phone for a taxi to take me to the airport, but he just looked at me and told me that I wouldn't be able to get a flight until tomorrow. I sank down on the bed and buried my head in my hands and screamed. Philip took the phone and talked to my mother. He got the story from my mother. I couldn't remember what she had said just that he wasn't dead but in a coma. Philip put the phone down and sat next to me. He put his arm around me. I shouted at him that he was useless and to get me a taxi to the airport. He calmed me down and brought me a brandy and hot milk. Then he went onto the Internet and looked up the flights from Manchester to Amsterdam, and booked a last minute flight for seven fifteen in the morning. I wanted to go to the airport there and then, but he told me it was pointless and that he would drive me there in the morning, and that it was better for me to stay at his place until then. I paced up and down the room all night.

My mother had said that Aaron was unconscious and having epileptic seizures. They were doing everything they could and had done some tests. Dr Diederik was there with my mother. But I wasn't there and I should have been. I shouldn't have left him. My worst fears had come true. My mother had said that he had fallen off a swing in the park, that his foot had become caught in the chain and that he was swung upside down and had landed on his head.

It was the longest night of my life. I couldn't sleep, and I couldn't do anything except phone my mother every hour to see if his condition had got better or worse. In between the phone calls I kept shouting at Philip that it wouldn't have happened if I hadn't met him. He didn't say anything. I know it was really hurtful to take it out on him, but I just couldn't deal with the horror that filled my mind. I kept imagining myself at Aaron's funeral. I kept shouting at myself to stop it. Philip was concerned about me taking the journey on my own. He couldn't cancel his appointments so suddenly, and anyway there was nothing he could do about Aaron. He talked to the staff at the airport and a nurse came and gave me a sedative. They allowed me to take my luggage in the passenger compartment and arranged for a taxi to take me from Amsterdam to Den Haag.

✻

'Where is he?' I shouted.

'He's in the side room over there,' my mother replied.

I rushed into the room. He seemed so small and fragile. His face was red: there were beads of sweat on his forehead, and his hair was wringing wet. He was surrounded by machines that he was attached to by wires on his wrists and head. It was so awful to see him like that. The doctor came and explained that he was stable and that there was a very good chance that he would be alright. There was some bruising to his frontal lobes but they couldn't detect any serious damage and he hadn't had any convulsions for the last seven hours.

My mother picked up her clothes and bag and said that she was going home to have a sleep, and that she would come back in the evening. She walked out of the ward, and I shouted after her 'You are a stupid bitch! You were supposed to look after him.' She didn't turn around.

Dr Diederik came to visit in the afternoon. He said that I should talk to Aaron and read him stories to stimulate his brain. I told him the story of Yehuda and the bear. I stayed awake all of the next night. My mother visited again and I said that I was sorry and that it wasn't her fault. I had let him play on the swings as well, and it could just as well have been me looking after him when the accident occurred. We both cried. My mother said that she had shouted at me in the same way when I was looking after my sisters and they had been hurt. I told her that I remembered both occasions, but that it was all in the past, and not to worry.

*

Waiting and hoping that Aaron would wake up was so difficult. It was two days of hell. He was so helpless. I was so helpless. My knuckles were bleeding. I had to bite something. I couldn't stop myself. I think that I fell asleep on two or three occasions, but when I awoke, a young nurse was tending to him. I will always remember her smile. It was so tender and understanding, and so reassuring.

It was Tuesday at four in the afternoon when Aaron opened his eyes and looked at me. His face shone more than usual and there seemed to be a fragrance of columbine in the room, but there were no flowers to be seen. I looked at him through my tears. 'Where have you been Aaron? We have all been so worried about you.'

'I've been in the forest with Isaac and the animals, Mummy.'

'Have you now? Why do you say that?'

'Because that's where I've been.'

I smiled and thought that maybe my reading to him had got through, and that he had dreamed of the story that I had read aloud to him.

He looked around the room. 'Where are we, Mummy?'

'We are in hospital, Aaron. You had an accident and you have been sleeping for three days.'

'Can we go home now?'

'Soon,' I said.

✻

I phoned my mother and Philip, and they were both so relieved. Philip had already booked a flight for Thursday evening, and asked me if it was alright for him to come, or if I preferred to be on my own with Aaron. I told him that I would appreciate it if he came. I was so tired I could have slept for a week. Suddenly my body began to shake and I was overcome with relief. But I couldn't stop crying.

The doctors at the hospital insisted that Aaron stay at least another two days just in case he might relapse, though they said that he was functioning perfectly normally. I took him home on the Thursday night, just before Philip arrived. I asked Philip to look after Aaron and I went to bed and slept until four o clock on the Friday afternoon.

✻

When I woke I could smell something cooking. They had been shopping and were making a meal of sorts. It was a bit of a concoction, but I didn't mind. Aaron went to bed early and I sat up with Philip.

'So you are not the only writer in the family,' he said.

'I'm not a writer, I am a scholar,' I replied. 'But what do you mean?'

'Aaron has told me a great story, all about meeting his father in the forest and living with the animals. And I made a little appearance towards the end. I wrote it all down. Do you want to hear it?'

'Not now, Philip. Aaron told me about it. It's only fragments of the story that I was reading to him when he was in the coma.'

157

'I don't think so, Johanna.'

'Look I have had enough stories recently to last a lifetime.'

'Okay, so what do you want to do?'

'Do you really want to know?' I asked.

'Yes.'

'I want to go to bed.'

'But you have been asleep for over sixteen hours. You have only been up for four hours.'

'No I want to go to bed with you,' I said.

He didn't say anything. His eyes lit up. I've never seen a man get undressed so quickly.

He slept until twelve the next day wearing nothing but a silly grin. He snored a bit during the night, but nothing like Isaac used to snore. In the afternoon he reminded me of Aaron's story, but I didn't really want to hear it. We went walking and swimming. I didn't do any more on the book for another six weeks. I visited Philip again in Manchester, but this time Aaron went with me. Philip looked after him most of the time, taking him to the park and to two football matches. It gave me a rest. During the time that I had been to northern Scotland and Manchester, and when Philip had visited me in Holland, I hardly wrote anything at all. I only just managed to finish the fifth and sixth chapters.

***

5.

Wilma came round again, under the pretence of seeing if Aaron was better. She was at a loose end. She was always at a loose end, especially since her divorce. I didn't normally mind her coming round, but sometimes it was a bit of an intrusion. I had been working on the story and she commented that it was neanderthal to be using a pencil and notebook instead of a word processor. I explained that I had started the story on the flight back from Ukraine and I had sort of got used to working on it in that way. She offered to type it for me as I went along. Rather stupidly I agreed.

After she had volunteered to type the manuscript, Wilma considered that she was then entitled to comment on each and every part of the story. Apparently, according to her, as well as my obvious incompetence with the grammatical nuances of the English language (which she was regularly at pains to point out), I was also straying too far from the main thread of the story, or as she put it, I was losing the plot. In her professional judgment, I should have concentrated on the major theme of Wilton and the wolfman and not got sidetracked so much with the peregrinations of the minor characters. Well, that's her opinion. I admit that Dr Spencer, Dr Scott, Mary, Liz and Benjamin are somewhat incidental to Wilton's story, but I feel more drawn to write about them than about Wilton. I seem to have difficulty in developing his character, which is hardly surprising. He also had difficulty developing his character.

I'm afraid that I find Wilton a bit hollow, and, although he is the supposed hero of the saga, it's such a struggle to keep to his story. It's like writing a biography of somebody whose only significance is that he just happens to encounter other people who are more interesting than him and probably more important in the wider scheme of things. It's beginning to feel like the whole thing is a case of multiple-personality disorder, where the number one personality has no personality to speak of, but is demanding to be placed centre stage. To be honest I am tempted to scrap the whole thing and start again with a story about Cleopatra the cat, who had the misfortune to cross Wilton's path; and I might one day, if I ever get the hang of this writing lark, and if I am allowed some choice in the matter. It was bad enough that Isaac made the first decision about the story, but now Wilma and Philip have offered advice about what I should include and not include. And also, to make matters worse, the characters that I am writing about are beginning to insist on editorial rights. I wish I had never contacted them. Liz is the most vociferous of the pack. She sent me reams about her trip to Prague, and more or less demanded that I include everything. It's all getting out of hand.

*

'Are you sure?' Wilma asked as she closed the notebook. 'It doesn't make sense.'

'You mean Cleopatra, the cat that spouts philosophy?'

'No, I can just about swallow that as some alter ego of Mary's or even yours. I suppose it's a residue of Isaac's animistic approach to spirituality. It reminds me of his little animal game. The cat doesn't have to be credible even though it is completely unnecessary and it complicates the plot.'

'But it's the section that I enjoyed writing the most.'

'Yes, that's often the case. A writer has to be ruthless Johanna. Cut out whole sections if they overcomplicate things and don't move the story on.'

'Cut out the cat?'

'Yes. But also are you sure that Mary suddenly did a u-turn with her emotions and seduced Wilton in her own house, with her brother-in-law within earshot. Why would she do that? From what you have told me about her, it seems to be completely out of character.'

'It's not believable then?'

'Of course it's not. Are you sure Wilton didn't just make that bit up, when he told you about the incidents leading up to his arrival in Ukraine?'

'Well, I admit that Mary's behaviour that morning is difficult to explain. But men aren't the only ones capable of screwing up in a major way, although we prefer to think so.'

'Do we?'

'Yes, I think so, Wilma. It suits us to believe that women are the guardians of morality and social etiquette. It suits us to think we are all devotees of the goddess Hera, maintaining propriety and setting limits on what type of behaviour is allowed in the house. So I agree that it is particularly strange that Mary not only transgressed her own moral code, but did it in her own house. I agree it doesn't make sense, but Wilton assured me that it did happen.'

'Perhaps he lied about it.'

'No, I don't think so.'

'So what possessed her to act like that?'

'I'm not sure. I'm baffled by it. She hadn't fallen in love with him. She didn't pity him. She wasn't sexually frustrated in her marriage to John, and she wasn't trying to get pregnant. She acted completely out of character, and probably regretted it almost immediately, but perhaps she had felt liberated and later, when she went to Prague with Liz Flannagan, it was as though she had reclaimed a part of herself and rekindled her passion for life. She hadn't felt guilty about it, like Toybe had, just a little regretful.'

Wilma shot up from her chair. 'Toybe? Toybe Rosenberg, did she have an affair? I don't believe it. She would rather die than commit adultery.'

'Yes, well, she nearly did die. Her guilt was so great that she tried to commit suicide.'

'Oh, my God.'

'Look, keep it to yourself. I shouldn't have told you. Anyway we are not discussing Toybe. We are discussing Mary Spencer, who also acted out of character.'

*

Isaac would probably have put it down to spontaneity. He said that often people can be so guarded about making a mistake that they don't allow themselves to act spontaneously and that they have to think everything out before they act. Perhaps that was why Mary had suddenly felt so liberated, and why she felt drawn to Liz, who apparently never considered the consequences of any of her actions and was in a constant state of spontaneity. That's what made her so exciting to be with. You couldn't predict what she might do next, whereas Mary generally took the sensible route. But this time she hadn't. She had simply acted on impulse, and although she might have chosen a more worthwhile recipient of her sudden aberration, at least she was being spontaneous.'

*

I suppose Wilma was right about the cat. It was an indulgence which represented my own thoughts and feelings and had little to do with Wilton's story. I read the section again.

Mary wheeled the rubbish bin to the front gate, trailing a faint odour of trout down the drive. Cleopatra was warming herself on the lawn. Her nose twitched slightly, but she knew that there was little left of last night's meal which would account for the scent lingering on for so long – perhaps a few bones or a tiny sliver of skin, but nothing of any real substance. She had already polished it off, and she wasn't one to waste time or energy on ghosts from the past, on reviving yesterday's disembodied pleasures, or regurgitating sentimental memories over and over again, or even licking her whiskers.

'Learn and move on,' Cleopatra thought. She glanced across at Mary and gave her a disapproving look. 'Christ, what have you got yourself into now?' she mused. 'Now you've put the cat amongst the pigeons. You have probably put the poor bloke back twenty odd years – reviving his interest again – raising his hopes which had been flaccid for so long before you stirred them up with your pheromones. He is obviously still searching for his soul mate, and now he's probably fixated on you just like before. You should know better. Seventy per cent of the world's male population is constantly looking for their soul mate; the one who will fill the emptiness of their lives, who will wash away their sins, who will make them feel complete – and make them breakfast, dinner, and Sunday lunch with roast beef and two veg, and be their mother, lover and Soror Mystica, all rolled into one stunning package.

'It's a bit like the coming of the Messiah. It could be the basis for one of the greatest ever world religions, if only men might share their individual faith with other men, but they wouldn't want to share the beloved, so it probably wouldn't work collectively. Of course, every man has been duped by a number of pretenders, the odd girlfriend or the one that they married, but in the end these women always turn out to be impostors, false messiahs. It's odd to think that millions of men believe that one day the Messiah will arrive and when she does, then all will be different, not for the world but for their own individual existence. As though their soul is totally distinct from the world, and as long as they can be redeemed then to hell with anyone else.

'The amazing thing about the "soul mate cult" is that men are all looking for the promised one as being between eighteen and thirty years old, beautiful with a great body, and there simply aren't enough of that type to fulfil the demand,

so some of the men are going to have to go without. If only they could believe that the soul mate could just as well be an eighty year old bag woman with varicose veins, or even something in between, then they might all get one, and have a better case for establishing a credible religion.

Socrates tried to get it off the ground with his theory that humans were once joined like Siamese twins, but they got cut in half and are now searching the world for the other half. It didn't take off then in a big way. It wasn't such an attractive idea to women I suppose. Of course most men don't appear to have a soul, so naturally they want to claim ours, and then tell us that it was theirs originally, and that we ran off with it. Nice try, Socrates, or was it Plato? It was one of them. The other one believed that the souls of human beings entered into beans when they were in between lives. No, I tell a lie. That was Pythagoras. That man seemed to have an angle on practically everything. Still, I prefer his theory to the Siamese twin idea. That one must have been Plato's. Maybe it was the other way round. God does it matter?' She yawned and stretched herself. 'Still, it was interesting, living in those times, before rational science reduced matters of belief to a few basic equations. It was different then. You were allowed to believe in metempsychosis – that souls transmigrated and had a brief stopover as a bean. Nobody minded or persecuted you for it. You had a choice, unlike in medieval Europe when the Inquisition stopped you believing anything that they didn't believe. Was that life number four or five? I can't remember. Anyway I preferred number two life, living in Ancient Greece. I preferred being a flageolet than a flagellant. I also remember that in the Greek academies you were allowed to debate the nature of all sorts of things, and propound a variety of quirky truths, without being censored all the time. Here's a little titbit that I recollect from when I attended Pythagoras's academy:

Student: What is the most unquestioned proposition?
Pythagoras: That all men are depraved.

'*Obviously Pythagoras had his best thinking cap on when he gave that reply. Philosophy doesn't come much better than that. That is one hell of a proposition. I have been propositioned a fair few times in my lives by a number of Toms, and that is the best one that I have heard.*'

She peed on a clump of snowdrops and pattered round the back of the house to the cat flap.

✿

Wilma was right. Reluctantly I ditched the cat, but there was no way I was going to cut out the chapters on Liz and Mary. Or so I thought.

✿✿✿

Wilma uncorked another bottle of wine. 'So what happened with Mary and Wilton? You've sort of ignored their little affair. You set it up, give it a whole chapter, and then clam up about it.'

'To be honest, Wilma, I really don't know. I think they had second thoughts. I've cut most of it out.'

'Well, yes, I can understand that she had second thoughts. But you have written that he had been in love with her for twenty years or so. Then he meets her again two days after the consummation of his fantasy. She snubs him and apparently he is alright about it.'

'Yes, that would seem to be the case.'

'So how do you explain that?'

'Perhaps it didn't live up to his expectations. Perhaps she wasn't a good screw. Perhaps when he had eventually conquered a woman, that was it – there was not much point in going on having a relationship with her. Perhaps he is a Don Juan, and his obsession with her was connected to the fact that she hadn't previously succumbed to his charms. Perhaps his obsession was simply narcissistic pride, and he couldn't accept failure, who knows?'

'You are supposed to know, Johanna. You are the author.'

'Oh, really, I thought you were, how silly of me.'

✻

Two nights later she waltzed into my apartment again, totally uninvited, at eleven o'clock at night, smelling like a Dutch gin hall. She threw the notebook on the table, stumbled into the kitchen, opened the fridge, grabbed the open bottle of Chardonnay, and proceeded to inform me of my mistakes.

'I fail to see the relevance of that last chapter, Johanna,' she sniped, 'the one about Benjamin Spencer. In fact it is not only extremely irrelevant, it is also irreverent.'

'What do you mean?'

'You attempt to give us some sort of amateurish psychological justification for his behaviour – that he was autistic as a child, and that his autism was caused by some early psychological trauma. That won't go down too well with the medical establishment. It is a well known fact that autism is a neurological problem, and is caused by a faulty gene. You are completely out of your depth.'

'Am I?'

'Yes.'

'Are you having second thoughts, Wilma?'

'About what?'

'About typing the manuscript. About typing *my* manuscript!'

'Well, you know me, I don't like to interfere. It's just that I hate to see you making so many pointless errors. I care about you.'

166

'Yes, of course you do. I realize that, and I appreciate you concern. I would never accuse your of interfering; however I never said that Benjamin had autism as a child.'

'You did.'

'No, I said that he was almost diagnosed as having it. There is a difference.'

'Is there?'

'Yes. How do you like my Chardonnay?'

'Its fine – a touch bitter,' she mumbled, took a few swigs from the bottle, and keeled over on the sofa.

✻

If I had thought that her reason for descending on me at such a late hour was really to do with my writing, then I would have been upset. She had drunk herself into a state of antagonism with the world; and I was the only one prepared to act as an Aunt Sally. Her other friends had given up on her. They had taken her attacks on them as personal. She had fallen asleep before we got to the main reason for her visit, but I knew what it was. She had to get out of her apartment. It was too empty, too lonely for her, and although she secretly hoped that her husband would return and bring her daughter back with him, she knew that he wouldn't. I found a spare duvet and draped it over her.

In the morning she left before Aaron and I got up, and left a note saying sorry, and seven euros for the wine. Her contrition was much less verbose than her attack on me, which, I suppose, was a blessing of sorts. But it didn't last too long. A week later she phoned me.

✻

'You have blatantly ignored my advice again,' she screamed down the phone. 'In fact, you have quite deliberately done the exact opposite of what I advised.'

'Really?'

'Yes, Johanna, you are as obstinate and incorrigible as Isaac was.'

'Well thank you, I will take that as a compliment.'

'I hadn't envisaged it was going to become such a labyrinth of a novel. You have gone off at a tangent again, following Mary and Liz to Prague. Do you still expect me to type it all?'

'As you wish, Wilma, I'm not bothered either way. And anyway I promised Liz that I would include it. She sent me sixty pages about her week in Prague. At least I have managed to cut it down to ten pages. What's your problem?'

'Look, I'm only trying to help. Liz and Mary spending a week in Prague has nothing whatsoever to do with the story. It is pure indulgence. The story should follow a simple chronological pattern like *The Odyssey* or *Pilgrim's Progress*.'

'Should it, Wilma? A simple chronological pattern is not the only format for a story. I cite in my defence, as a precedent, you understand, *The Life and Opinions of Tristram Shandy*. If I wish to deviate from the line of cabbage planters, and indulge myself in a little more tangential sidetracking, I will. Is that clear?'

'Perfectly, I suppose you are going to weave Aaron's little dream into the story next.'

'What a good idea,' I replied. 'Thanks for reminding me.'

*

I should have asked Aaron about his dream, about his experience of being in a coma, but I didn't. I forgot all about it. Perhaps I felt that he had been through enough, and that the experience had been too traumatic for him, when actually it hadn't. I was defending myself, I suppose. I didn't want to go back there. Later, when Aaron told me the dream, I realized that it would have clarified so many problems for me. It would have even explained the reason for my difficulty in understanding why Isaac had asked me to write this story. But that wasn't my only confusion. I was also confused about my feelings for Philip. I enjoyed being with him, but then, when I was with him I felt that I was also with Isaac. There was something about Philip which reminded me so much of Isaac that sometimes I couldn't distinguish between the two of them. They had merged with each other.

I had to distance myself from Philip. I told him that I had too much work to do, and that I couldn't see him for a few months. He didn't argue about it. He told me to contact him when I felt like it. I stopped writing to him and phoning him.

I had got to the part in the story where Wilton was to meet Isaac and myself in Ukraine. Suddenly I was a character in the story that I was writing, which felt quite odd. I was forced to imagine myself back in time, when Isaac was still alive and we were still together. Perhaps that was the main reason for my withdrawal from Philip. I couldn't play both parts. It felt duplicitous. Philip knew me as the writer, not the character in love with Isaac.

*

Wilma didn't help, although she thought that she was helping at the time. She didn't like to interfere! She started to email Philip to tell him how I was and how the story was progressing, if one can call it progress. They kept their little communications a secret from me and when I found out I was furious with both of them, and I suspected that Wilma was muscling in on Philip. I told her what I thought and she laughed and said, 'You don't appear to want him, so what's the problem?'

'You can have him,' I replied, 'but why don't you both keep your noses out of my story? Why don't you write your own story, *Phil Grimes' Progress,* a linear account of unrequited love? How's that for an idea? Perhaps it will drag you both out of your slough of despondency, or in your case a trough of despondency – then you can marry him. Would you like that, Wilma? He would be an excellent drinking buddy for you.'

'Johanna, he loves you. Why won't you see him?

'I can't.'

'Why not, do you think that the problem will simply go away? Even after you have finished the book, Isaac will still be there in the background.'

'I know that. Look, I'm really confused about Philip. Can't you both allow me to be confused?'

✻

Despite what Wilma had said, I knew that I had a rival for Philip's affection, and that incredibly she viewed me as the rival, even though I was there first. Rivalry amongst women can be so covert, so devious and so venomous. Now I felt it stirring inside me like a small poisonous snake inching its way through my intestines. I felt sick. So that was her motive. That was why she was being so cruel about my writing, and so irritated with me. She was jealous, and now I was beginning to feel jealous of her, or at least threatened by her growing friendship with Philip.

It isn't that Wilma is predatory with men. It's more that she doesn't need to be. When she walks into a room it isn't just heads that are raised, or hearts that stir. I can't begin to describe how stunningly attractive she is. She is a sexual magnet and you wouldn't believe how many little missiles lock on to her at parties. Of course I didn't feel threatened by her when I was with Isaac, but her being around Philip is a different matter.

The next time she came over to the apartment I refused to talk about Philip. She kept mentioning him but I managed to steer the conversation away from the topic. We had another little flare up when she mentioned that they both considered that I wasn't very good at descriptive writing, and that since my ability to write dialogue was a little better, then perhaps I should be writing a play instead.

I calmed down eventually and we drank wine for the rest of the evening and talked about Isaac. After Wilma had left, I cried remembering the week that Isaac and I had spent together in Ukraine.

I kept Wilma at bay for a few weeks and managed to finish the story about Wilton, and I suppose that I had come to a better understanding of why Isaac had asked me to write it. Eventually I phoned Wilma and told her that I had finished the story.

'What story?' she said. 'Do you mean that jigsaw puzzle that you have been writing?'

'Yes,' I said, 'that's the one, why do you say that?'

'Well, Johanna, it is customary to tell the story first and then add the commentary afterwards – or in this case, considering it is a Jewish tale, the midrash.'

'Yes, I am aware of that. But the midrash has taken on more importance than the text. In fact the text has been whittled down to its bare bones. It's about a tenth of what I originally wrote. It's taken me three years to write what amounts to about thirty pages.'

'Well, you should have taken my advice from the start, Johanna.'

'Yes, perhaps. Anyway, I have limited the story about Wilton to what he told Isaac and me when he met us in Ukraine. So it's all from the horse's mouth, except what happened in the room in Medzybiz. Philip told me about that and I had to take his word for it.'

'Fine. Did you ditch the chapters on Liz and Mary, like I asked?'

'Yes, Wilma, I did, but not for the reason that you suggested.

∗∗∗

WILTON'S ORDEAL

The town of Brody is situated about seventy miles from the Slovak border in the region of Podolia that is now part of Ukraine. It lies approximately forty miles east of the city of L'Viv and about sixty miles west of Kiev. It is a fairly insignificant place and is rarely mentioned in guide books about Ukraine, save for references to the killing of Jews during the Shoah. But for Hasidic Jews it occupies an important place in their hearts, for it was where the founder of Hasidism, the Baal Shem Tov, lived and worked during his early life; and along with the town of Medzybiz, it has become a place of pilgrimage for those Hasids who still revere the memory of their founder. Isaac visited the town every year for the last fifteen years of his life, and each year he walked from Brody to Medzybiz. During those pilgrimages he collected stories about the Hasidic Jews of that region as part of his research for the university. I accompanied him for the last few years, and on our final trip, as well as Isaac collecting a few legends that appealed to him, we both became protagonists in a story which was unusual, to say the least.

*

For the people of Brody the sight of an Englishman entering the inn wearing a Jasper Littman bespoke suit was already an unusual occasion. The fact that he looked half demented and was also bereft of shoes was even more extraordinary and astonishing. It's difficult to compare but I guess for the run of the mill Ukrainian the experience was equivalent to an English socialite witnessing a red hot lump of extra-terrestrial magnetite plummeting from the sky and divoting itself into the bishop's croquet lawn right in the middle of the jam judging. It was not only unexpected, it was totally unpredictable, even for someone like Isaac.

Perhaps only two or three people had actually witnessed the stranger's sudden appearance, but within minutes of his arrival a crowd of on-lookers had congregated outside the inn and were peering in through the windows, relaying commentaries to those who couldn't get a decent view. It was not unusual for a few distraught individuals to hang around outside the inn hoping to speak to Isaac about their troubles, and he would always allow them to speak with him. So it was not so strange that the exterior of the building was a little congested. But when the human meteorite collided with Brody, he had more of an impact than you might expect. The sunlight that normally illuminated the interior of the inn was totally eclipsed by gawking faces to the extent that Sergei, the owner of the establishment – a man not particularly renowned for excessive displays of wastefulness – was persuaded to put on the lights in the bar, even though it was the middle of the day.

*

My own experience of Dr Wilton's arrival was not so apocalyptic, though it was fairly disagreeable. He was arrogant and aloof, peacocking his way to the bar, ignoring my presence completely and interrupting my conversation with Sergei. If I hadn't noticed that he was shoeless I might have been a bit more hostile towards him. I simply decided that he was crazy, and I considered it best not to provoke him. I waited a while for his opening gambit. I didn't have to wait long.

'I'm looking for a man called Philip Grimes,' he announced.

Sergei corrugated his brow into a well rehearsed professional frown. '*Probachte aleh ya neh rozomeeyu vahs,*' he explained.

'Well yes, that sounds very interesting,' the man replied, 'but please don't translate it all just now. I can't wait all day. Is he here or not? Just nod your head or shake it.'

Sergei frowned again, glanced at the ceiling and began to petition God's help, '*Yak trihvohah to do Bohah,*' he said.

The stranger misconstrued the meaning of Sergei's gesture. 'I see, so he's in his room, is he? Then would you be so good as to inform him that a gentleman from England is waiting for him downstairs, and requires his presence immediately?'

I didn't mean to laugh. It just came out. 'I'm afraid that Sergei doesn't understand English, especially your English,' I said.

'But the barman gestured that Grimes was upstairs.'

'No, actually he was seeking divine assistance. He can be a little wary of strangers. Can I help?'

'Are you English?'

'No. I am from Holland.'

'Oh, you are Dutch, are you? Well, I suppose that will have to do. So what did he say to me?'

'The first time he said that he was sorry, but he didn't understand you. The second time he said that in times of anxiety one turns to God. It's an old Ukrainian proverb.'

'I see. Well, now look, my dear, I am searching for a chap called Philip Grimes and I think that he might be staying in this flea-trap, since it appears to be the only...' He halted in mid-stream having glanced towards the corner of the room where Isaac was sitting. '...never mind, I think that I may have found him.'

He strutted across the room, seated himself opposite Isaac, placing his elbows on the table and addressing him in the manner of a headmaster chastising a schoolboy.

'Mr Grimes, I expect you assumed that you could evade the authorities by hiding away in this godforsaken place and that nobody would find you here; but you didn't reckon on me did you, Grimes?'

'No. I must admit, it is quite a surprise,' Isaac replied, turning his face in my direction and grinning like a schoolboy who appeared to enjoy being caught *in flagrante delicto.* 'Exactly what authority do you represent, if you don't mind me asking?'

'I am a British psychiatrist and I am here to take you back to England. It is imperative that your psychosis is checked as soon as possible. You are a great danger to yourself as well as to others. I'm sure you appreciate that.'

'Yes, yes, people have been telling me that for years. But I gather that you think that I am called Grimes, which is something of a novel slant on the general topic of my insanity.'

'Don't be so insolent. I know who you are Grimes. I am afraid that disguising yourself as an Amish settler with ringlets, adopting a phoney German accent and hiding behind sunglasses, doesn't fool me. I have read your little autobiography and I am aware that you have a smattering of German. Could you stop that infernal habit of tilting your head and tugging your beard when I am talking to you? It's rather irritating. Take your sunglasses off and look at me. I have gone to extraordinary lengths to help you. You cannot imagine the hell that I have just been through for you.'

Isaac continued to grin. 'Well, thank you Doctor. I would probably appreciate it better if I knew what on earth possessed you to go through hell for me, but actually I have also been there a few times, so I don't need to imagine. It's hardly a pleasant place, is it? Tell me, since I appear to be at a slight disadvantage, do you have a name?'

'My name is Dr Jim Wilton.'

Isaac started to mumble to himself. 'Wilton – I'm sure that I have heard that name before.'

'Really, you have actually heard of me?' he preened.

'No, I've simply heard of the name. I think that it's either a cheese or a carpet. I'm not quite sure which.'

'Don't mess with me, Grimes. I am not one to be messed with.'

∗

They were both creating quite a scene and Wilton appeared to be getting angrier the more Isaac grinned at him. I walked over to the table and sat down next to Isaac. It was strange that despite Wilton's confident and aggressive demeanour his eyes betrayed a look of intense fear. He was frightened to death of something, and it wasn't Isaac.

'Can I help?' I asked.

'Perhaps, if you are a friend of Mr. Grimes, you might persuade him that it is quite stupid of him to persist in this charade. He is in urgent need of medical treatment.'

'I am sorry, but the man you are talking to is not Philip Grimes. You appear to have made a mistake. He is called Isaac Goldmund.'

'Goldmund! Very clever Grimes. I am aware that Goldmund is one of your fantasy aliases. I have read the transcript of your sessions with Dr Scott. Are you going to remove those sunglasses or shall I remove them for you?'

'Dr Wilton, this is too much, you can't simply...'

'It is alright, Johanna,' Isaac interrupted, 'don't worry. Let the *goy* have his own way. Dr Wilton is obviously very tired and upset. The least I can do is to comply with his request.' Isaac turned his head towards the doctor. 'Tell me, Dr Wilton, does Philip Grimes have eyes?' he asked, as he removed his sunglasses.

∗

I entered the bedroom to see if he was awake. He was writhing about on the bed, talking to himself. I placed a hand on his cheek. It was wet, and at first I thought that he was running a fever, but I soon realized that he had been crying in his sleep. Then suddenly he grabbed my hand.

'Mary, thank heaven you are here. I have had a terrible nightmare. Where am I?'

'It's Johanna,' I whispered. 'My name is Johanna.'

He looked anxiously at me. 'Johanna? Where's Mary?'

'I'm sorry; I don't know who Mary is. Are you awake now, Doctor? My name is Johanna Klein. Do you not remember what happened downstairs? You fainted and fell onto the floor when Isaac removed his sunglasses. You seemed very groggy so we helped you up to this room. We thought that it was best for you to sleep for a while. You have been asleep for six hours, now, so Isaac sent me to see if you were awake. He would like you to join us for dinner. I have brought you a pair of his sandals, since you don't appear to have any shoes with you.'

He started to cry. I waited for a while, until he calmed down. 'What is wrong, Doctor? Why are you so upset?'

'That poor man had no eyes. He must have felt so humiliated by me. I'm sorry. I'm really sorry.'

I was amazed at this sudden transformation in Wilton's personality. The arrogant man that I had met earlier was now a little boy pleading for forgiveness.

'Are you crying for Isaac?' I asked.

'Yes and no. I have been crying a lot recently, for no reason really. I'm in a taxi or walking down a street and suddenly I find that I am crying. But that poor man without eyes really upset me. Is he alright?'

'Yes, Isaac is fine. He is more concerned about you. Please come down and join us. A meal has been prepared and Isaac is waiting for you.'

'I don't think so. Thank you anyway. I have made a complete fool of myself. I think that I had better leave now.

Please tell Isaac that I am very sorry for humiliating him the way I did.'

'No, Dr Wilton. I think that you should tell him yourself. Isaac is not upset. It is your own humiliation that you don't want to face, and you should not run away from it. Don't worry Isaac is a very kindly soul. He is not in the least concerned about your ridiculous accusations. But he is concerned about you. He would like to help you. Please come and join us for dinner.'

'But I have no socks. Where are my socks?'

'They are drying at the moment. I took the liberty of washing them for you. They were very wet and dirty. I would have brought you some clean socks but you don't appear to have any luggage with you.'

'No, I lost it.'

'That's all right, Dr Wilton. It is warm downstairs. You won't need socks. Just put on Isaac's sandals and come down soon. The bar is rather full at the moment since the whole town seems to have turned out to see the mysterious stranger who walks around without shoes, so we are eating in the back room. You will come won't you?'

Dr Wilton nodded his head.

✤

Isaac and Sergei were playing cards across the corner of the table. Sergei looked at me anxiously, but then he always looked worried, especially when Isaac was staying at the inn. 'Is he alright?' he asked

'I think so. He will be down in a minute.'

Sergei began to clear the cards off the table. 'Tell me, Johanna, there is something that has always puzzled me. Why does Isaac win at cards all the time?'

I laughed. 'Well, either he is very good at it, or you allow him to deal every hand.'

'Why would dealing help him? He's blind. He can't see.'

'Oh. Sergei, you are innocent. They are Braille cards. There are little pin pricks on the corners. He knows exactly what he has dealt you.'

Sergei cursed and stomped off into the kitchen. '*Skoopihy dvah rahzih plahtiht!*' he shouted back

'What did he say, Johanna?' Isaac asked. 'Why won't he speak Yiddish or German?'

'He said that the miser pays twice. It's an old Ukrainian proverb.'

'Why did he say that? What have you been telling him Johanna?'

'It's time that you learnt Ukrainian, Izzy. I told him that you cheat at poker. He wasn't aware that the little pinpricks on the corners of the cards had any significance. He thought that it was just an old pack of cards. Do you have to cheat all the time?'

'It's my only vice, Johanna, almost.'

'Well, it's no way for a *zaddik* to behave, cheating at cards.'

Isaac laughed. 'So I am supposed to be a *zaddik*, am I?'

'Of course you are a *zaddik*. Don't be so incorrigible.'

'Johanna, I have told you many times, if someone assumes that he is a *zaddik*, he can't possibly be one.'

'Yes, yes, I know. But I can say that you are one. That won't discount you, will it? Anyway, shush, I think the doctor is coming down the stairs.'

*

The door opened and he nervously entered the room wearing Isaac's sandals. He was like a little boy who had come downstairs in his father's shoes to ask for a glass of water. He walked over to the table and took hold of Isaac's hand, hesitated for a moment and then shook it.

'It's Dr Wilton,' he announced.

'Yes, I know. We have been introduced before, although you may not have caught my name. It's Isaac Goldmund.'

'Yes, I am aware of that now. Thank you for inviting me to dinner, Isaac. Please allow me to apologise for what I said earlier. It was deplorable of me. I hope that you will pardon my somewhat crass behaviour.'

Isaac smiled and patted Wilton's hand to reassure him. 'Think nothing of it, Dr Wilton. To tell you the truth you injected some excitement into a rather boring day. But if you really want to apologise then you must tell us why you are looking for Philip Grimes and why you have arrived here without shoes.'

'Oh. I see. Johanna has told you that I didn't have any shoes.'

'No. I could tell that you were not wearing shoes. My hearing is really quite good. I can also hear that she appears to have lent you my sandals.'

'Yes. Do you mind?'

'Of course he doesn't mind,' I interrupted. 'Would you like a drink, Doctor? They have got a stock of Urquelle Pilsner here.'

'Yes, please. By the way my name is Jim. Please call me Jim.'

I went through to the bar to get the beers. When I returned Isaac was thumping the table and laughing in a way that only he could.

*

'What's so funny?' I asked.

'The border guards took his shoes off him. He didn't have a visa. So they sold him a visa and confiscated his shoes and his luggage. You know what they are like at Vysne Nemecke.'

'That's not funny, Izzy.'

181

'Yes, it is. He offered them his Rolex watch which is worth a fortune, and they spat on it, threw it back to him, told him it was a fake and demanded that he give them his shoes; and this is the best part Johanna – they couldn't decide who should have them so they took one each. What are they going to do with one shoe each, hop?'

'Well I still don't think it's funny.'

'That's okay, Johanna,' Jim remarked, 'I think that it's quite amusing. From what Isaac has just told me those guards seem to be quite famous for taking things. Did you have anything confiscated by the authorities, Isaac?'

'Just my family, but that was a long time ago,' he replied. 'Excuse me; I must go to the toilet.' He got up from the table and shuffled towards the door.

'What did he mean by that?' Jim asked.

'It doesn't matter. It is not a very nice story.'

'Can't you tell me? How did he lose his family, Johanna?'

'You really want to know?'

'Yes.'

✳

After a few minutes the door creaked and Isaac came back into the room. He sat down at the table. 'So you are telling him the story of the destruction of my family. How far have you got, Johanna, Belzec?'

'Sweden.'

'Very good, Johanna, you are getting quicker at it. At least I have missed the grim bits.'

'I'm sorry,' Jim said, 'I asked her to tell me. I hope that you don't mind.'

'Not really,' Isaac replied.

Sergei came to the table with three bowls of soup and a slightly less worried frown. 'Borsch tah kasha yeezhah nahshah. Dobreh yeestih,' he announced proudly, snapping his heels together and bowing his head slightly, as if to imply that occasionally the aristocrat may stoop to serve the commoner, but that the commoner should never take it for granted. Sergei was a White Russian, a descendant of a Cossack who had served the last of the Tsars, and he would constantly remind us that his position as an inn keeper was temporary. He wore a long white apron that reached to his feet, so Isaac called him *The Cassock.*

'What did he say?' Isaac asked.

'The Cassock said that borsch and kasha are our food. Eat well.'

'That man has got it in for me. We have had borsch for the last three nights.'

'I thought we ordered prawn cocktail.' Wilton complained.

'You did,' I replied, 'but it's a bit hit-and-miss here. The menu is mostly ornamental.'

Jim started to eat his soup. He kept looking at me sideways and then looking at Isaac. It was quite bizarre. He obviously didn't dare ask me the next question that was on his mind, not with Isaac present. What am I doing with an old Jewish man twenty-five years my senior, who is blind and can't appreciate what a beautiful young woman I am? What is my relationship to him? Are we married? Is he my lover? Am I his social worker or his nurse?

Isaac broke the silence. 'She is my *Soror Mystica*, Dr Wilton. I found her in Tyre, working in a brothel.'

I laughed and Jim blushed.

'Stop it, Izzy. He's teasing you, Jim. I have never been anywhere near Tyre.'

Sergei entered and cleared the soup bowls from the table. He returned with three plates of *varenyky* – dumplings filled with cabbage.

'I'm afraid I didn't get the joke about the brothel.'

'You weren't supposed to, Jim,' I said, 'it was aimed at me. I wrote my thesis on a Gnostic heretic called Simon Magus, who went around with a young woman called Helen. She had been a prostitute in the city of Tyre. Their union symbolized the reunion of God and Sophia, the Divine Wisdom, which in the Jewish and Gnostic traditions is feminine.'

Jim looked at me as though I had been speaking a foreign language. There was an awkward silence until Isaac came to the rescue.

'Johanna, do you think you could inform Sergei that I am allowed to eat other things as well as dumplings and cabbage. We have had the same meal for the last three nights. Where the hell is the roast beef we ordered?' He turned to Jim. 'Dr Wilton, Johanna is an ex-student of mine who took advantage of my blindness and seduced me when I wasn't looking. Everyone tells me she is very beautiful, but I don't believe a word of it.'

I stuck out my tongue at Isaac. He returned the gesture and Jim looked astonished.

'How did you do that, Isaac?' Jim asked.

'Do what?'

'How did you know that she had stuck out her tongue? And before that, when I was wondering about her relationship to you — you answered a question that I was only thinking about asking.'

'I was just guessing. They were easy. I could have also guessed that the Cassock was going to serve me dumplings and cabbage. One gets used to the predictability of people. Now then, Dr Wilton, the deal was this — you were invited to eat with us so that we could hear your story about Philip Grimes, and why you are pursuing him. Up until now we have only heard the little tale concerning the loss of your shoes. So would you like to tell us your story?'

'Is that really necessary? Can't you predict it?'

I laughed louder and longer than was appropriate. It was good to see Isaac being challenged. But then he laughed louder and longer than I did.

'Touché, Jim,' Isaac said. 'Actually I am a little tired. I think I will go to bed early. You can tell me your story tomorrow. You may walk with us to Medzybiz, and if you do I assure you that you will find what you are looking for. Now, if you don't mind, I am going to bed. Have another beer with Johanna. I will see you both in the morning. We need to set off early, about seven. Goodnight, Dr Wilton.' Isaac walked slowly out of the room and belched. 'Mazeltov,' he shouted as he mounted the stairs.

*

'Jim, you look tired. Would you like another drink or would you prefer to go to bed? Isaac has booked a room for you.'

'Will you be there, wiping my face like before?'

'No. I will be down here drinking a beer.'

'In that case, Johanna, I will have a beer as well. On second thoughts, do they serve brandy? I would prefer a brandy.'

'They probably have some such thing. But I'm sure it's different to the brandy you normally drink. Do you want to risk it?' I asked.

He nodded.

When I returned with the drinks, he was hunched over the table and his body was shaking. He took the brandy, drank it and grimaced. 'I'm sorry,' he said, 'I've had a hell of a journey here. It was more than frightening, it was horrendous. I don't mean the little incident with the border guards. If I was at all superstitious I would say that I was assaulted by demonic spirits. It was that terrifying. There is a lot that I didn't tell Isaac. You see during the past few weeks I have been having weird thoughts and hallucinating. I suppose that I have been under a lot of stress. Perhaps I shouldn't have come here.'

'Well, it is a long drive from Prague. How long did it take you?'

'I'm not sure, about eighteen hours I think. I stopped for five hours and had a sleep between two and seven this morning, but it didn't help. I had awful nightmares and I saw three old hags sitting in the back seat of my car.'

'You mean in your dream?'

'No, unfortunately I was awake. It was whilst I was driving, before I stopped. They were talking to me. One looked like my mother and another resembled Mary's mother. The third one didn't have a head. The other two told me that I was going to die, and that their sister, the one without a head, was going to kill me. I didn't know at the time that I was hallucinating. It all seemed so real.'

He looked at me as if to ask me to comfort him, swish a long broom under the bed, open the wardrobe and tell him that it was only his imagination playing tricks on him.

'Look Jim, start from the beginning. What exactly happened?'

'Well, I flew over to Prague to find a psychotic patient who has escaped from a hospital in south London. The man is under the delusion that he has turned into a wolf, and I have convincing evidence to support the probability that he is around here somewhere.'

'I see, but why did you fly to Prague? Its miles away.'

'Yes, I know, but Mary was flying to Prague, so I thought that I might accompany her.'

'Who is Mary? You mentioned her before.'

'I'll tell you later. Anyway she was on a different flight, which was already fully booked, so I took a later flight. I exchanged a few words with her in the departure lounge and then she boarded her plane. I took the next flight and rented a car from the airport in Prague. I drove out of the airport, looking for the road to Brno. It was about ten o'clock at night. I kept seeing signposts, Praha Visovice, Praha Nusle, Praha something Mestro. I thought that I was driving around in circles. It seemed ages, but perhaps it was only fifteen minutes. I can't say for sure. I saw an old woman at the side of the road selling flowers. It seemed strange for her to be standing at the side of a busy road so late at night.'

'She was probably a Roma, Jim. Sometimes they park their caravans in the lay-bys.'

'Yes, probably, but she had a strange look on her face, as though she knew or had mistaken me for someone else. She looked as if she hated me. I got out of the car and pointed down the road and said Brno. She laughed and thrust some flowers at me. I kept asking for Brno and she kept thrusting flowers in my face and screaming at me to buy them, or so I assumed. She grabbed my arm. She wouldn't let go of it. So I pushed her and she fell. I didn't mean to hurt her. I ran back to the car and I could see her running and spitting at me and then she started to bang on the window of the car. I pressed the central door locking button and sped away as fast as I could. I drove around for another hour or so and eventually I saw a sign for Brno.

'It had turned foggy, and I was driving along the side of a river for about twenty miles. The fog crept onto the road and seemed to be clawing at the car trying to force me to stop, but I didn't stop. I don't know why I was so frightened to stop the car. I suppose I felt that the woman was still chasing me, even though I had driven miles away from the lay-by. I kept driving and then I felt a bump and I heard a horrible scream. It was then that I stopped and walked back along the road through the fog. I knew that I had hit something and I had to find out what it was. I know it seems silly now, but I thought that I had run over the flower seller. I saw something or somebody lying in the middle of the road. I approached it and realized that it was a vixen and that she was pregnant, because her flank was bulging. She wasn't dead but she was close to it. She looked at me, just one frightened eye looking at me. There was no sound apart from a soft panting. I couldn't bear to look at her so I walked away. But I had to go back. I got a tyre lever from the boot of the car and I killed her. I had to. Have you ever witnessed an animal die, Johanna? I mean, when you are so close to it, that you can see your own reflection in its eyes, when your own fear is being reflected back to you?'

I was horrified by the image that Jim had just drawn – a pregnant vixen dying in the road, but I understood why he had to kill her. 'Yes,' I said. 'I once watched my own dog die. It was confused and bewildered that it couldn't fight or run away – that its instincts didn't work anymore. It was unable to react. It just lay there. It wasn't shock or pain that it displayed, but total bewilderment in the face of a question that it was incapable of understanding. Its eyes expressed the fear of something that was absolutely unknown to it, and for which it was completely unprepared. I wanted to explain to my dog that it was dying. I wanted to help it to understand what was happening to it, but of course I couldn't. I think that was what hurt the most. I cursed God for not having prepared my dog for death. But also I could not tear myself away from watching it die. It's difficult to resist the look of an animal that is about to die, and it is impossible to forget.'

'Yes. That's exactly how I felt. I had to wait until that look had left its eyes. I couldn't leave before the fox had died. Then I ran back to the car, and drove away as fast as I could. I suddenly felt cold as though the angel of death had walked right through my body. I had to find a reason for this awful feeling. I imagined that I wasn't alone and that someone or something was sitting behind me. I imagined that some threatening presence had climbed into the rear seat of the car, whilst I had been watching the fox die. I didn't dare to look. I glanced in the rear view mirror and saw what I thought were the headlights of two cars behind me. I drove faster but they didn't change, they didn't get smaller. So I drove slower and they didn't get bigger. Then I stopped and the lights stayed the same and I realized that it was two pairs of eyes staring at me from the back seat of the car. I didn't look around. I felt an icy chill on the back of my neck. I was frozen with fear, like the fox. I didn't know what was happening.

'Then a voice said, "*You are a mistake. You shouldn't be alive.*" It sounded like my mother's voice. A second voice said, "*You are an abomination. You should be dead.*" That was the voice of Mary's mother. I turned around and I saw that they were both sat in the back of the car and sitting between them was an old woman without a head and a hissing noise came from her open neck and small red and black snakes came out of the wound. Mary's mother had a carrot in her hand and she stuck it into her mouth and pushed it in and out as though she was performing fellatio, and my mother screeched at me. I don't know what she said, it was unintelligible. She was holding a scalpel.

At first I panicked, but then I thought that I can stop this happening. So I turned on the radio and a strange voice came out of the radio and told me to kill myself. But a gentle voice told me not to do it. That was the voice that had been speaking to me before this; sometimes once or twice a day for about four days. It was a woman's voice, and was so caring and tender. Then someone or something howled. It howled such a lonely and painful howl.'

He began to beat his head on the table and he started to whine like a dog. He was dripping with sweat. I stroked his head for a while and he calmed down a little. Sergei entered the room and looked decidedly worried. I gestured to him to bring more brandy. Everything had gone quiet in the inn. The singing and the conversations that came from the bar had suddenly ceased. Sergei returned with a bottle of brandy and poured some out for Jim. He drank a little and continued his account of the journey.

'It was such a painful howl, Johanna, and I realized that it was coming from my own body. I put my arms around myself and I rocked myself to sleep.'

'It's alright, Dr Wilton,' I said, 'you don't have to continue.'

'I have to, Johanna, I won't be able to do it again ever. I have to tell you it all. I must have been asleep, because it seemed that I was no longer in the car. I was behind bars and two dark figures were copulating in the corner of the room and my mother came in and started to hit them with a piece of wood, and they ran away, and she came over to the bars and she struck me on the head with the piece of wood and she screamed and screamed at me to be dead. I lay on the floor. I saw a body hanging from the ceiling and I froze in terror. I couldn't move at all. Then I must have woken up because I realized that I was still sitting in the car, and I heard a great thundering noise and what I thought was the sound of the devil's horn, and I opened my eyes to see a great juggernaut of a lorry just miss the car. Then some music came on the radio. It was *The Song to the Moon* by Dvorak.' It was very soothing. God! That's it. That's it. It's over. It's finished.' He drank some more brandy and stared at me, as though he wanted me to explain it all and make it all go away.

'And then you drove here?' I asked.

'I must have, Johanna. I must have driven on automatic pilot. The only other bit I remember was the incident with the Ukrainian border guards. I think that they thought that they were intimidating me. It's quite ironic really. I had just been through hell and I had been assaulted by demons, and the guards thought that they could frighten me. I didn't really care what they did to me or what they took from me. I was just relieved to see human beings again because I knew, despite their intimidation, that I was safe.'

✻

I suppose most people would consider the story Jim told me to be a strange event but I wasn't in the least surprised about it. I had seen other people who had sought Isaac's help show the same look of horror in their eyes, and all had similar stories to tell of being pursued by demons, although I must admit that none of them looked as terrified as he did. His body didn't stop shaking for over twenty minutes and the look in his eyes was that of a man who had gazed on the face of evil. He was truly petrified.

'It's over now, Jim,' I said, 'Don't worry. Isaac will help you. I shouldn't really tell you this, but when Isaac retires to his room early, he doesn't go there to sleep. He will be praying for you. He usually stays awake all night, and I am not allowed to enter the room. You must believe me, Jim, the worst is over.'

'I'm sorry,' he said, 'I find that hard to believe. I am not a religious person.'

'That is of no consequence, he will still succeed. He will intercede on your behalf. As Isaac often says the issue is not that you believe in God, but that God believes in you.'

'Isn't that blasphemy?'

'No. I think that you had better sleep now. We have a long walk in the morning. You will be coming with us, won't you?'

Jim nodded, said goodnight and walked up the stairs to his room. I settled into a chair in the corner of the room. It was going to be another uncomfortable night. On this sort of occasion I was forbidden to enter Isaac's room, and I did not wish to enter it. I didn't know what demons Isaac was wrestling with, but judging by how frightened Jim looked, I knew that they were not insignificant. I preferred a wobbly wooden chair to what was about to happen in Isaac's room.

Sergei sat with me for a while. We had a couple of beers. He looked worried. I think that he was frightened of going to bed as well, and he hadn't even heard Jim's story. I asked him why he always looked so anxious. He replied that he was very fond of Isaac, but he wondered if there was anywhere else that Isaac could perform his exorcisms, since the public liability insurance for the inn didn't cover assaults by *dybbuks* and the like. Sergei had a point. I said that I would have a word with Isaac about it in the morning.

***

2.

The next morning Isaac entered the breakfast room early looking like he had been wrestling crocodiles all night. Since Wilton was still asleep, I took the opportunity to tell him about Sergei's concern and about Wilton's description of his journey to Brody – the Romany flower seller, the fox, the three women in the car and Jim howling after he had told me the story. Isaac listened and nodded a few times.

'Yes,' he said, 'they were furious with him and also with me for trying to protect him. Fortunately they've gone now. So what do you reckon it was all about, Johanna?' he asked.

'Well he obviously has a problem with women. I don't know – perhaps his mother didn't want him, or something like that.'

'Yes, well done, you have guessed it. You see Jim was born illegitimate, although he still isn't aware of the circumstances surrounding his birth. His mother was a Jewish servant girl who was raped by his father. She was allowed to stay in the house and have the baby on condition that she kept quiet about the rape, but then when Jim was three years old the father tried to seduce her again, and the wife discovered them having intercourse in the corner of the nursery next to Jim's playpen. The young girl was so ashamed that she hanged herself from a light fitting in the ceiling. The friends and neighbours thought that Jim was the legitimate son of his parents and that the girl who committed suicide was his nanny. His parents kept *shtum* about the truth of what had happened and maintained the veneer of respectability, but the wife, Jessica, who Jim still thinks is his biological mother, hated him and once she tried to kill him with his father's cricket bat. She was a surgeon, who specialized in abortions, and so wasn't averse to killing children. Fortunately his father had some positive feelings for him and felt some degree of responsibility towards him. He placed Jim in a boarding school, mainly to protect him from his wife's hatred. Jim grew up thinking that his mother despised him, but he didn't know about his real mother, and he still doesn't.'

'God, that's awful. How do you know all that, Izzy?'

Isaac grunted something inaudible, but I had a pretty good idea how he had found out about Jim's past. During the night when the inn was quiet, I had heard him invoking the *Messengers*. He only did it on extremely rare occasions, since it placed such a strain on him. The messengers would have told him the facts about Jim's childhood.

During the time I knew Isaac, I only felt the presence of the *messengers* three times; twice in our apartment in Den Haag and that night in Brody. I have never been allowed to see them or hear them, but I have felt their formidable presence. I can only describe it as an electro-magnetic charge that grips the space in which they manifest themselves and everything within it so that one feels unable to move or think. It is a highly charged suspended animation like that between a lightning flash and the resultant thunderclap – only the thunderclap never arrives. Then gradually the space returns to normal.

'I see. So you have been talking to the three messengers again,' I said. 'You promised me that you wouldn't. The last time you invoked them you finished up nearly having a seizure.'

He shrugged. 'What else was I supposed to do? I had to find out from somewhere. Wilton has no conception what his early life was like, or the reason why he has been drawn to this place. He is Jewish by matrilineal descent, and his mother's family came from Ukraine. I had to find out why the demons wanted him dead. He is searching for the soul of his real mother, Johanna, although he doesn't know that yet, and they are trying to obstruct him in his purpose.'

'Is his mother in limbo?' I asked.

'Yes, you could say that. Let's just say that she is stuck between the worlds and she needs to move on, but she refuses to move on until Jim knows the truth about himself.

'So the Furies, the three women in the car, appear in order to thwart his future progress and not as retribution for the past actions of his father?'

'Both. But there are three causes, Johanna.'

'You said three, but you have only mentioned two causes.'

'Do you really think that he is totally innocent of any involvement in his own dire predicament, Johanna? The Furies are the avenging goddesses, like Lilith, and the Erynyes – the angry ones. He must have done something to attract the heavy brigade. He has obviously offended women in some way. We will find out in time. We will talk about it later. I can hear him coming down the stairs.'

✻

We breakfasted early at seven o'clock. We had scrambled eggs and dry rye bread, with weak tea. Sergei was quite surly and kept looking at Jim and shaking his head. Isaac was in a good mood and asked me to enquire of Sergei why we weren't having dumplings and cabbage for breakfast. I didn't ask. We had stretched Sergei's patience far enough, and it would only have worried him further. I thought it better to stretch out the kinks in my back, so I ate my breakfast standing by the side of the table.

'Well, Jim, I assume that Johanna has inspired you to come to Medzybiz with us.'

'Inspired me, Isaac?'

'Yes, Dr Wilton. I am under no illusion that if I did not have an attractive female companion you would not be travelling with me.'

'Stop being so fractious, Izzy,' I said.

'You are a bit sensitive this morning, Johanna. Didn't you get any sleep?'

'No, I didn't, what with you stomping about above my head all night, invoking this and that.'

'What should I be doing stomping around? I was sound asleep. It must have been Sergei's *dybbuk* that was making all the noise.'

I smiled. I knew that Isaac wasn't telling the truth.

'Did you sleep well, Dr Wilton?' Isaac asked.

'Yes, thank you, like a baby.'

Isaac nodded knowingly. 'So you will be ready for our little walk, then?'

'Well, yes, of course. But we can go by car. I can drive you to Medzybiz, instead of us all having to walk.'

'Dr Wilton,' Isaac said sternly, 'we are not walking there because we cannot get there by easier means. We are walking to Medzybiz because that is our reason for going there. '*To Kotsk one does not travel. To Kotsk one may only walk.*' And the same can be said about Medzybiz.'

'I don't understand,' Jim said, and looked towards me for support.

'Izzy, now you are being *kvetchy*. How should Jim know why we are going there? You haven't told him. He was only trying to be helpful. He doesn't know the Hasidic tradition. What does he know about *Halikhah*?'

'Yes. You are right, Johanna. I do apologise, Dr Wilton. I have had a rather troublesome night. I will explain it to you later, perhaps. Have you got the rucksacks packed, Johanna?'

'Yes, and Sergei has made us some sandwiches.'

'Good then let's be on our way.' Isaac stood up and reached for my arm. Jim followed, still sporting his pinstriped suit and Isaac's old sandals. At least he was wearing clean socks. Sergei looked immensely relieved to see us all depart. He was actually smiling, which was a first for him. Some of the Jewish population of the town had already lined the road and were waving goodbye to us as we passed.

Dr Wilton stopped suddenly. 'I'm afraid that I have forgotten to pay for my room and board.'

'It's been taken care of, Jim,' I explained.

'But I can't possibly allow you to pay for me.'

'We haven't. They have,' I said as I pointed to the people waving to us. They do it for Isaac, Jim. They would be insulted if they thought that a friend of ours had paid for himself. So please don't worry.'

'Oh. I see,' he said. But he didn't.

We walked for a few hours along the verge of the road. Isaac was singing and whistling back to the birds that greeted us along the way. I saw a few storks and a buzzard, and told Isaac about them and of course he asked me to make a note of my sightings. Wilton didn't seem to notice them at all. He was engrossed in his own thoughts most of the time. Or perhaps he was focused on walking. Still he was managing quite well for a man who was obviously not used to walking long distances. That was before he asked us how far it was.

'A hundred and forty kilometres, that's almost ninety miles! Just a minute, are you telling me that I am expected to walk ninety miles in one day?'

'No, five days,' Isaac replied. 'We normally arrive for the evening meal on the fifth day, which will be the Sabbath.'

'You mean you do this often?'

'No, of course not,' I said, 'just once a year.'

'I can't do that. I am sorry. I would love to come with you, but I really can't walk all that way and then walk back again. My suit would be ruined.'

'Don't be silly, Isaac remarked. 'We are not walking back, we are returning by bus. Johanna, haven't you explained anything to him?'

Wilton sat down on a rock and folded his arms. After a few minutes an old man from Brody cycled past. Isaac called out to him and he cycled back to us. I went to sit on the rock with Wilton whilst Isaac talked to the cyclist. Eventually the man put his bicycle down by the side of the road and walked off laughing.

'Come on, Jim,' Isaac called out, 'I have got you a bicycle. I presume that you are capable of cycling to Medzybiz or would that be too difficult?'

'How the hell did he manage to make that man part with his bicycle?' Jim whispered. 'Did he pay him?'

'No,' I answered. 'The man is happy to lend it to us. Now he will be famous in the town, and everyone will respect him.'

'That's a damned weird town, if you ask me. A man gets conned out of his bicycle and they honour him?'

'Yes, but he wasn't conned, Jim. Come on. Let's get going. It's a bit silly you cycling along with us. Why don't you go on ahead for about ten miles and wait for us? We are staying the night at the village of Kobzarivka, which is about eighteen miles from here, and it is a straight road so you can't get lost.'

I laughed quietly to myself as I watched Wilton attempt to master the bicycle. He looked quite absurd, wobbling down the road in his pinstriped grey suit and Isaac's bright green sandals.

*

'Is he out of our view yet?' Isaac asked.

'Yes, he's nearly out of sight, Izzy. It's only your sandals that are still visible, why?'

'I thought that we could go into a field and lie down for a while, Johanna. You know, play around a little.'

'You are impossible, Izzy.' It would have been nice, but we certainly wouldn't have completed the day's journey if I had let him have his way. Isaac sat on the stone stroking the grass. We waited for a few minutes and then I heard the creaking of a rusty chain.

'Good,' said Isaac. 'Perhaps his *Halikhah* is not ruined.'

I looked up to see the unmistakable figure of Dr Wilton returning.

He approached us and dismounted. 'I have been thinking,' he said. 'If you can both walk to Medzybyz, then so can I.'

Isaac had a grin on his face as broad as a crescent moon. 'Just leave the bicycle by the side of the road. It will be found by its rightful owner.'

✽

We continued on our journey. After about fifty yards I thought I detected the sound of whistling behind me. I turned to see the owner of the bicycle ride away on it laughing. Dr Wilton did not hear what was happening behind his back and I didn't have the heart to tell him that Isaac had once again correctly assessed "the predictability of people." I smiled. We walked a further five miles and stopped for a rest. It was then that Isaac asked Wilton to tell us why he had come to Ukraine and why he was so particularly intent on finding Philip Grimes.

'Start from the beginning, Jim,' Isaac said, 'and don't leave anything out. I want to know all of the details of how you came to be here in Ukraine and why you are chasing Philip Grimes.'

✽

Jim began by recounting what had happened almost a week earlier when he received a hand-written message that had been delivered to his club. The message informed Jim of the whereabouts of a patient who was suffering from a lycanthropic psychosis. He considered it to be a stroke of luck at the time since he was doing some research on that very topic and was short of case material. He took a taxi to the hospital named in the message and entered the office of Dr John Spencer, who fortuitously happened to be an old friend from his time at Cambridge. Naturally, since they already knew each other, Jim had assumed that the message had been sent by Dr Spencer.

Jim explained what had happened when he met his colleague, and how Dr Spencer had been surprised by Jim's sudden appearance at the hospital and informed him that he hadn't asked anyone to give him a message. So the message was still a bit of a mystery. Who had sent it if it wasn't Spencer? Apparently, according to Jim, Spencer was prevaricating, and trying to put him off the scent, and Spencer's secretary, Liz Flannagan, who had mistaken Jim for an undertaker, was also interrupting the proceedings with her practical jokes.

*

Isaac laughed about the antics of the secretary. But Jim didn't see it like that and he became incensed that Isaac wasn't taking his story seriously enough.

'I don't like being the butt of peoples' jokes, Isaac. I felt like giving her a piece of my mind, but I was more concerned about meeting the patient.'

'Yes, I can imagine,' Isaac said. 'But can't you see the funny side of it?'

'Not really, the woman was most offensive.'

'Like you were to me last night, and I managed not to take offence.'

Wilton blushed and started to apologise again but Isaac asked him to continue his story.

Jim explained that he had begun to feel anxious, and suspected that something had happened to the patient, since Spencer seemed to be employing delaying tactics. He confronted Spencer about it and was mortified to learn that the patient had escaped and that Spencer's registrar had contacted the police and that they hoped to apprehend the patient, but apparently there was little chance of finding him. Then Spencer suggested sarcastically that they should contact every psychiatric department in the country to ask if they had admitted a wolfman recently and issue a public appeal on television: *Does your husband regurgitate his food for the children? Does he scratch his ear with his foot? When you count sheep at bedtime, are there any missing?*

✻

Isaac was giggling so much that he almost wet himself and had to go and pee against a tree, so we took a timely break from Jim's story. I hadn't found it as amusing as Isaac had. I was trying to get my head round the fact that people can actually suffer prolonged delusions that they are wolves. It was, to say the least, difficult to believe.

'Well, Jim,' Isaac shouted, 'I suppose that's one way of finding out if someone is a werewolf. You shouldn't have got so upset about losing him. We are not far from Transylvania here. The forests are teeming with werewolves and vampires. They are ten a penny in this neck of the woods. You don't fancy doing some research on people who think that they are bats, do you?'

Jim's face suddenly reddened and I thought he was going to physically attack Isaac. It was fairly obvious that he suffered from labile mood swings.

'Stop taunting him, Isaac,' I called out. 'Don't be so insensitive.'

Isaac was still laughing. He had never known the meaning of retreat. 'Tell me, Jim,' he said, buttoning his fly, 'do you suffer from grandiose rages?'

'Absolutely not,' Jim replied.

'Oh, I see,' said Isaac, 'well, let me put it another way. Do other people suffer from your grandiose rages?'

I looked at Jim, and I was sure that he was going to explode. But gradually his expression changed and a wry smile crept across his face. He nodded his head. 'Yes, all the time, Isaac. What timely perceptions you make. Actually, now you mention it, I remember that I fell into a complete rage in Spencer's office. You could say that I went ballistic.'

'Oh, why was that?' Isaac asked.

'It was quite innocuous really. All Spencer said was that he appreciated that my research was important, but the wolfman wasn't my patient, he was his. Then he said, "Be reasonable, Jim," which sort of set me off, especially after he had made that satirical remark about the television appeal.'

Jim stopped and looked at Isaac. 'I don't like being the butt of peoples' jokes, Isaac.'

'No, I gathered that, Jim,' Isaac said. 'You mentioned it before. I am sure that your research is very important, and I do apologise for my insensitivity earlier. So what happened then?'

'Well, then he invited me to dinner and to stay at his house for the night. He said that his wife, Mary, would be thrilled to meet me again after all this time. I wasn't so sure. I had once been in love with Mary and it had been a messy affair. I didn't even know if John knew about it. Anyway I thought that it was decent of him to invite me to his home, so I accepted and…'

'Just a minute, Jim,' I interrupted, 'are you saying that you had an affair with Spencer's wife?'

'No, I was in love with her, Johanna. We were nearly engaged to be married. We were at university together, before she met John and …'

'I see. Was that the Mary you kept talking about last night – the one that you mistook me for?'

'That's correct, Johanna.'

'So that must have been strange meeting her again. How did you feel about it, Jim?'

'I'm trying to tell you, but you keep interrupting me.'

'Sorry. Please continue.'

*

Jim told us that Spencer left the hospital under the pretence of having to visit a patient in another hospital. It was then that Jim picked up the photograph of Mary which was on Spencer's desk and heard a strange voice talking to him. He described how he had suddenly become upset and didn't know why he was crying so much. According to Jim he fell asleep and dreamed of his childhood in Tenby. He began to reminisce about his early years and how his mother had been so cold towards him.

I wanted to explain to him that Jessica wasn't his mother. I was so tempted to tell him what Isaac had told me that morning in Brody, so that he could understand why she had been like that with him, and why she could never be pleased by what he did or didn't do. I wanted to tell him that it wasn't his fault. I could hardly bear to see the bewilderment in his eyes – the same look that he had described when he told me about the fox that he had killed, and couldn't bear witnessing its suffering. Isaac sensed that I was on the verge of spilling the beans. He knew I was no good at keeping secrets. He gripped my hand tightly. 'Go on, doctor,' he said, 'Why did you suddenly feel upset?'

'Well, I realized that I had been fairly successful, but that I wasn't happy, and I thought that Spencer seemed more content with life. But then Spencer had Mary. Perhaps that was the problem. Was I still upset about not having married Mary? I was, but it went deeper than that. I simply wasn't happy, and the strange thing was that I didn't know it! That was the most remarkable thing. I suddenly became acutely aware of the fact that I had been desperately unhappy for years, and I hadn't dared to think it.

'Anyway to return to the events of last week – I was reading the file on the wolfman when the secretary appeared in the doorway. She told me that the police had just phoned about somebody of the patient's description who had been questioned at Heathrow. He was carrying a rucksack and fishing rods, and was on his way to Ukraine. They had released him because he had been a complete nuisance and had been asking more questions than they had. The suspect was a man called Philip Grimes, who told the police that he was a psychologist and claimed to be something of an expert on lycanthropy. Apparently he was a little annoyed by the fact that he had been arrested, but he didn't act crazy, so they let him go. Well, that's what John's secretary told me. I thought that the police were probably right about the man. There must have been a battalion of teachers, social workers and psychotherapists that looked like the description of the wolfman, all wearing beards, fleece tops and scruffy shoes. I certainly wasn't considering tracking one to Ukraine. It would have been more than likely another wild goose chase, which is somewhat ironic since that is exactly what I have done. Still I didn't imagine at that time that the man boarding the plane was the escaped patient. I didn't think anymore about it until that evening when the man's name cropped up again.'

✻

Jim had talked for about half an hour and it was time to make tracks again. We continued on our journey and after a while he took a turn at leading Isaac by the arm, while I walked ahead. I could hear Isaac asking him about the voice and I heard Isaac saying that it could have been the *Shekhinah*. Then Isaac started to explain to Jim why we were walking and that *Halikhah* is a means of progression on the spiritual path, from gradation to gradation, and should be done with a joyous heart, for it is an expression of love. He told Jim of the exile of the *Shekhinah* and of the "feet of the *Shekhinah*" that journeyed from town to town, and the *zaddikim* who accompanied her in her homeless state. He told him that often people think that they are travelling on business, but that the real purpose of the journey is that there is a spark that needs to be elevated and it can only be elevated by the person of whose soul it is a fragment, and not by anyone else. So, in walking, the Hasid is seeking the forgotten fragments of his own soul.

I do not know what Jim thought about Isaac's beliefs, but there was more of a bounce in Jim's steps, and the conversation took his mind off the pain in his feet. Isaac did not reveal to him the sacred sexual significance of the feet and the shoes, as told by Cordovero, and the metaphor of the *zaddik* as the cobbler.

*

That night Wilton confided in me that he and Mary had almost got engaged and that he had never made love to her because she was one of his special angels. I reminded him that he didn't believe in angels, and he replied that he believed in the mortal ones but not the celestial type. He told me that there had never been any girls at the schools that he attended, and that he hadn't learnt how to relate to women as friends, as colleagues, or as competitors. By the time he reached university he arrived with a limited and split experience of women. Apart from having a mother of sorts, and several nannies, he had learnt about women from two distinctly different sources – from the angelic little girls at his local church up until the time that he was seven, and after that from the sticky magazines that were passed around the dorm at school. He explained that he had difficulty seeing women as ordinary human beings and that he saw them as either goddesses or harlots. I felt like saying, 'Yes, you and thousands of other men,' but I didn't. I suppose that Jim's belief that he possessed a unique pathology was a vestige of his need to feel special, and I could hardly rob him of that possession. He had already had his luggage and his shoes confiscated.

*

We stopped for the night in Kobzarivka. We had walked thirty kilometres that day and had arrived at the village at ten o'clock. For the last two hours of our journey it had rained heavily and when we arrived at Jacob's house, we were soaked and bedraggled. Jacob was an old friend of Isaac's who used to go on the pilgrimage, but was now too frail for such a long trek. He made us some soup which we ate in silence. We were far too tired to talk any more. Wilton finished the soup, mumbled goodnight and hobbled to his room.

'Leave your wet clothes outside the room, Jim' I called after him. 'I will hang them up to dry.'

Isaac looked tired, and no wonder. He hadn't slept the night before.

'How are you feeling, Isaac?' I asked.

'It gets harder, Johanna. Fifteen years ago it seemed a lot easier than today. Do you think that I might be getting old?'

'You mean like the rest of us?' Jacob said. 'Now that would be an admission.'

3.

The next morning we breakfasted at nine and set off again on our journey. Jacob and Isaac hugged each other and Isaac whispered something that made Jacob cry. I guess that he told him that it would be his last visit, and I reckon that Isaac already knew that he was going to die soon, but I can't be sure.

Jim looked a lot better and wasn't limping anymore. The weather was much milder. The sun was shining most of the time and we made good progress. The road from Kobzarivka to Lozy was quite winding, but it was much less busy than the main road from Ternopil, and the footpath was wide enough for us to walk three abreast, so Isaac asked Wilton to continue with his story as we walked.

*

'Where did I get to yesterday, Isaac?' he asked.

'You were about to go to dinner at Dr Spencer's, and meet Mary again. Is that where you met Benjamin?'

Wilton's face suddenly turned pale. 'How do you know about Benjamin Spencer? I haven't mentioned him.'

'No, that is true, Jim. But I had an inkling that Benjamin was going to crop up when you accused me of being Philip Grimes. Your predicament carries Benjamin's hallmark. I know that he has a brother who is a psychiatrist and I assume that there aren't many psychiatrists living in London called Spencer. So Benjamin tricked you into coming to Ukraine, did he?'

'What on earth do you mean? Do you actually know Benjamin Spencer?'

'Yes, I visit him when I am in London, although I have never met John and Mary. It's a small world, Jim. Don't look so shocked. Continue with your story. You were about to tell us about your dinner with John and Mary.'

'Just a minute, Isaac, I am beginning to smell a rat. Tell me, do you know Philip Grimes as well?'

'Yes, of course,' Isaac replied. 'I have known him for about ten years.'

'You know him,' Jim shouted, 'but you didn't say anything when I asked about him.'

Isaac smiled. 'You didn't ask me if I knew him. You asked me if I was him, and I told you that I wasn't. What are you getting so angry about?'

Wilton sat down beside the road, holding his face in his hands. It was as though someone had hit him over the head with a lump hammer.

'Come on, Jim, don't worry about Isaac,' I said. 'He can be a bit heavy-handed sometimes. We really want to know about the rest of your story.'

'Yes, well, I am beginning to think that I am the only one who doesn't know what is going on. This is just one coincidence too many. I feel that I have been set up, and that you are both part of a conspiracy against me.'

'Well, I assure you that we are not, or at least I'm not. I haven't the faintest idea what is going on. I sympathise with you, Jim, I really do. This sort of thing happens all the time when Isaac is around. I have been in your position many times. Isaac doesn't mean to upset you. It's just that he sees connections that others can't see. Please carry on with your story. I want to know about your meeting with Mary.'

It took a few minutes for me to persuade Jim to continue with his story. Eventually he did.

*

He described how he had taken a taxi to their house and arrived promptly at eight. Mary answered the door, and she was obviously nervous. He gave her some flowers and a bottle of red wine, held her hand for a few seconds more than was necessary, and rather foolishly sat on her cat, which was asleep on the sofa until he sat on it. He apologized to Mary and enquired about the health of her parents, and whether or not they were still alive. She said that her father's health was at rock bottom since he died eight years ago and didn't seem to be getting any better, but that her mother was fine and active. She was still hard at it with her weavings. He then admitted to having made an insensitive remark about her mother being a spider weaving webs, and that he always felt she wanted to eat him alive, and that she was the reason why they never got married.

Mary became incensed by his comments and said that her mother had nothing to do with them breaking up. She told him that he was insecure and didn't feel safe with the love of only one woman, and that he needed the security of feeling that other women loved him, just in case she left him, and that ironically it was his own insecurity that drove her into leaving him, not her mother. She couldn't live with his infidelity.

✳

'Was that true?' I asked.

'I suppose it was,' Jim said, 'although I hadn't seen it like that. I had used her mother's antagonism towards me as a vindication for my failure to win her. It was easier. When I met her parents for the first time I felt intimidated by them, but it was probably my own sense of guilt that affected me. Perhaps I felt that they could see through my self-assured exterior and could perceive what a jerk I was, or perhaps they had somehow guessed about my womanizing. I was going to ask Mary to marry me and to ask her father for permission. I never did. I decided that it would be futile. Anyway, that's enough of that.'

Jim then described how he had sat down to dinner with them and how John had asked him if he had managed to read the file on the wolfman. Mary went to bed early, saying that she had a migraine, and when Jim began to reveal to John his radical new theory on the causes of mental illness, and how the lack of carotene in the diet was the primary cause of personality disorders, for some reason John suddenly announced that he was tired and needed to go to bed.

It was then that he began to suspect that Spencer had been keeping something from him. He had never known John to behave so nervously.

*

'Then Spencer let slip that his brother, Benjamin had a friend called Philip Grimes who knew a fair bit about lycanthropy, and who had been visiting during that day. Well, as you can imagine, Johanna, I was bowled over. It was too much of a coincidence. Was he toying with me? I began to see the connection. I began to suspect that Spencer had actually known the patient, and had probably helped him to escape. More than likely he had been harbouring him as a guest in his own house. That's why he had been so nervous earlier when I arrived at his office. That was why he left the office at midday to ensure that Grimes had left his house. At least I now knew the identity of the wolfman. I knew the man's name and where he was likely to be found, although Ukraine is a fairly large country and I would need to be more exact about the actual destination that the wolfman was heading towards, if I was to catch him. Spencer didn't know about the phone call from the police, so he wasn't aware that I knew where Grimes was headed. He probably thought that he had got away with it. But I knew different. I decided that I would need to question Benjamin Spencer about it.'

***

4.

Over breakfast Jim explained what had happened that morning at the Spencers' house. How Mary, contrary to his expectations, especially considering how angry she had been the night before, had slipped into bed with him, and had seduced him after her husband had left for work. He talked about it as though he had got one over on John. I wondered if he had any feelings for other people. He said that he felt a little guilty about it, but I wondered if he was capable of remorse. He quickly moved on to tell us of his meeting with Dr Scott.

He had made an appointment with a dermatologist in Harley Street, and had taken a taxi to her consulting rooms. He sat in the waiting room touching his cheek and hoping that the rash was still there.

✻

'There's nothing more embarrassing than arriving at the doctor's surgery to find the symptom has disappeared, especially if you are a doctor,' Jim explained.

'I don't know about that, Jim,' Isaac interrupted. 'Once I turned up to give a lecture to a hundred or so students, having forgotten to put on my trousers. I couldn't understand why there was a lot more giggling than was usual. I imagined that some students had been eating space cake. Nobody said a word to me, and it wasn't until I got home and tripped over the trousers on the floor that I realized what had happened. Anyway, no matter, please continue with your story, Jim.'

✻

'Well, after a mild altercation with the consultant's receptionist, who considered herself to be a doctor as well, Dr Scott informed me that it was only metal rash. I remarked that I thought it might have been *lupus*, and she told me that it was a ridiculous idea and completely wide of the mark.

'I was about to leave when she asked me if anything was worrying me. I told her about my pursuit of the escaped patient and she seemed very interested and informed me that one of her clients had written about lycanthropy, a gentleman called Philip Grimes who had published an article about it in the Observer the previous Sunday. I almost fell off the chair.'

Isaac laughed. 'I suppose you thought that she was in on this conspiracy against you,' he said.

'No, I didn't know then that it was a conspiracy,' Jim replied and scowled at Isaac. 'Then she asked me to tell her a little more about the psychotic patient, so I told her that on Sunday morning he was found in Regent's Park Zoo, in a Burmese python cage, holding the python and howling like a wolf. Then you wouldn't believe what she said next. She said, "Dear me, it's the third largest snake in the world, you know. It can grow up to twenty feet long. Was it alright? Who was this nasty man who traumatised the python?"

'Can you credit it? She was more concerned about the bloody snake. I said that I thought the patient was probably Philip Grimes and she said that it was highly unlikely since he was in Czechoslovakia, researching something about a Hasidic rabbi, called Israel Besht, who had an encounter with a werewolf. That's what the patient was raving about, Isaac. Israel Besht! Everywhere I went Grimes seemed to have been there, one step ahead of me. It was most strange.

'Dr Scott assured me that it was highly unlikely that Philip Grimes had suffered such a severe psychosis, and she asked if my quest might be about something else. She explained that the wolfman might have simply been a carrot to tempt an ass, and inferred that perhaps destiny was leading me on a journey so that I might change in some way, and that perhaps I was really pursuing my future self, and the man with the lycanthropy wasn't really that important, except that he represented my shadow self.'

'How did you react to that? Did you believe her, Jim?' I asked.

'Of course not, the woman was a druid. She even asked me about my dreams as though they had any bearing on anything. Anyway she helped me more than she knew. The filing cabinet in the office was open, and whilst the receptionist was dealing with my prescription, I found the file on Philip Grimes and took it. Later that afternoon I read the file and it confirmed my theory about the identity of the escaped patient. It was all there in black and white, I saw it for myself.'

Isaac laughed again. 'Did you, Jim? Well, sometimes people see only what they want to see.'

✵

I began to pick some wild flowers by the roadside. Isaac and Jim walked past engrossed in their conversation.

'So if the *zaddikim* journey in search of love, why is that so different from the rest of the human race? Aren't we all in search of love?'

'There is a slight but important difference, Jim,' Isaac replied. 'Most people are searching to receive love. The *zaddikim* search to give it.'

I caught them up and handed them both a small bunch of flowers. 'Lighten up, Izzy,' I said. 'We have a heck of a long way to go, and plenty of time for all that.'

I think Dr Wilton was quite pleased with my interruption. We rested for a while and left Isaac peeing against a tree.

'Tell me, Johanna. Why do you do this walk once a year?' Jim asked. 'What is so special about it?'

'I have only done it for the last five years, Jim. Isaac has done it for fifteen years. The other ten years he walked with a friend from Utrecht, and Jacob joined them on the way.'

'But why from Brody to Medzybiz?'

213

'When Isaac's grandfather's father came from Germany to live in the Carpathian mountains, he was coming home. He was a Hasidic *Rav*, you know a rabbi, and his father and grandfathers before him. They were all Hasidic rabbis stretching back to the beginning of the new Hasidism. Some of Isaac's ancestors were members of the Kloiz of Brody.'

'What was that?'

'It was a small sect of mystics who studied Kabbalah and who practised some of the Sephardic rituals, which weren't normally allowed within Ashkenazi custom. They wore white gowns on the Sabbath and also on feast days. Anyway, after the *herem* by the *kahal* of Brody in 1772...'

'I am sorry; you are going to have to translate that.'

'That was an attempt to excommunicate the Hasidim.'

'Oh. I see, go on.'

'Well, quite a number of them, including Isaac's ancestors, emigrated to Safed in Galilee in the late 1770s, as part of the Erets Israel movement. It was a sort of Zionist movement. Eventually Joseph, Isaac's ancestor, somehow finished up living in Augsburg. Don't ask me how. It all got sort of complicated after Erets Israel.'

'I am not sure how all this relates to my question. Did he walk all the way, or something?'

'No, Jim,' I laughed. 'I suppose I am being a bit long-winded. The point is that Isaac's ancestor returned to his roots, to the town of Brody, and Isaac comes here once a year to honour him and his grandfather, Yehuda, who walked six hundred kilometres to freedom, and of course to honour the Baal Shem Tov.'

'But why walk to Medzybiz?'

'Oh, yes, I'm sorry. Your question was why walk from Brody to Medzybiz? Well, the Baal Shem Tov, Israel ben Elizier, lived in Brody and then moved to Medzybiz, so we are walking there to see the Baal Shem Tov. And also the second most important Hasid, Rabbi Nachmann is buried there. It has become a place of pilgrimage for Hasids around the world. Most go there in August and September, but it can be very crowded and quite difficult to find accommodation at that time of year. So Isaac and his cronies go there in March.'

*

'Is this it?' Isaac shouted. 'Am I engaged to Thisbe? Am I supposed to take root and marry this tree, or is somebody going to help me back to the road?'

Jim ran over and led Isaac back to the road and we continued our conversation.

'But why did you say that we were going to see the Baal Shem Tov?' Jim asked. 'Benjamin told me that he died over two hundred years ago.'

'Israel ben Elizier is dead,' replied Isaac. 'The Baal Shem Tov is a title. It means Master of the Holy Name. Tomorrow we are to meet the new Baal Shem Tov. That is why we are walking to Medzybiz, Jim. Why are you walking to Medzybiz?'

'Well, I was hoping to catch Philip Grimes.'

Isaac roared with laughter. 'You will have more chance of catching a snowball in hell. Philip Grimes is not the wolf man. Of course there is a slim chance that you might just meet the wolfman. Whether you catch him or not is another matter.'

We arrived at the village of Lozy and stayed there for the night, in a small peasant farmhouse.

***

On the third day we walked from Lozy to a village called Kurovecka, where we joined the main road. For most of the way we walked past Ukrainian farms and waved to the farmers perched on the front of their horse drawn carts. A few of them stopped to bid us good day and ask where we were going. Two of them offered us a lift, and were quite insulted when we didn't accept their kind offers. Along the roadside the cherry trees had not begun to blossom yet, but there was already a variety of spring flowers sprouting from underneath the hedgerows. We passed a couple of old women selling garlic and herbs, and Jim made a point of buying from them. He must have felt guilty about the flower seller he had snubbed in Prague.

Once we passed some children wearing the traditional Ukrainian costume, beautifully embroidered skirts and blouses. On another occasion, Jim was astonished when I pointed out to him a stork's nest perched on top of a telegraph pole. He didn't believe us at first that it was a stork's nest, but then we saw one of the storks raise its head above the side of the nest, stand up and take off into the air. It was a wonderful sight. It was a glorious spring morning and I wanted to enjoy the walk in silence, but Isaac wanted Jim to finish his story. Isaac listened in silence whilst Jim recounted the meeting with Ben Spencer, who had informed him about the Besht, and the town of Brody. I knew something about Benjamin, since Isaac had talked about him quite a bit.

I knew that Benjamin had joined the Spencer family when John was thirteen years old. Ben was five at the time. From the onset Benjamin had displayed behaviour that was diagnosed as autistic. For the remaining five years that John lived at home, before escaping to university, he witnessed the distress that such a condition creates. Mary Spencer believed that it was this experience that prompted John to opt for psychiatry. Even at the age of thirteen John had more of an insight into what was wrong with Ben than his parents and the psychologists that visited the house from time to time. When John and Mary married, Ben came to live with them. He wasn't a problem for them. He lived like a hermit in his small bedroom and read most of the time. Wilton was already aware that Philip Grimes had stayed in the house two days earlier as a guest of Benjamin, but he wasn't going to take the head on approach and confront Benjamin with that fact. In any case during the conversation Benjamin volunteered the information that Jim needed, that Philip Grimes could be found in the towns of Brody or Medzybiz.

*

'That's your man,' Isaac cried out, 'the kabbalist, Benjamin. He's your man. Benjamin is a ravenous wolf, in the morning devouring the prey, and at evening dividing the spoil.'

'What are you saying?'

'It's from Genesis, the naming of the tribes of Israel. The wolfman is Benjamin Spencer, Dr Spencer's younger brother.'

'But that's nonsense, Isaac. He was a very quiet and learned man and he was very helpful to me.'

'Yes, I know,' Isaac replied. 'He must have got through it. He must have got through the ordeal. Good for Benjamin, he has discovered the Name. Look, Jim, Benjamin wanted you to come here for a reason. Not the one that you thought, but another reason.'

'You mean all that stuff he told me about the Besht and the village of Brody was a lie.'

'No. It was all true.'

'I'm sorry, Isaac. How did you arrive at Benjamin being the wolfman? And why do you discount Philip Grimes?'

217

'You missed Philip Grimes' psychosis by about eight years. There are some similarities. He obviously had an encounter with his wolf nature. He didn't get so far as to know the Secret Name, but at least he survived the ordeal. I can't tell you anymore now, Jim. You will have to be patient.'

'I'm sorry, but I can't accept that. Why can't you tell me now?'

'Because, Jim, tonight you won't believe me, but on Friday you will. So I will tell you on Friday.'

*

We had travelled sixty-three miles in three days, and Jim was on his last legs. I don't know how he did it, but on the fourth day of our journey he seemed to have a surge of energy. He was skipping down the road, all the way to Chemel'nyc'kyi, a reasonably large town where we managed to get rooms in a small hotel. Probably Jim's renewed vigour was instigated by Isaac informing him that there was a bar in the town and he would be able to get his alcohol fix.

***

6

On the fifth day we set off knowing that it was the last day and that it was also the shortest section of the trek, so Isaac and I were in good spirits. Jim had a bit of a hangover. Isaac was wearing the white robe that his grandfather had given him. It had been passed down through the generations of his family. It was the original robe that had been worn by his ancestors at the Kloiz of Brody. It was still in quite good condition, since it had only been worn a few times every year. I was wearing denim shorts and Jim was still in his suit. Isaac had offered him a change of clothes, but Jim had insisted on wearing his suit.

'How far are we off Medzybiz now?' Jim asked.

'About six miles,' I replied. 'We have just passed the village of Masivci. Can you manage it?'

'I'll try. At least it's not raining. Do you have any idea how surreal we must look to everybody?' He blurted, as though he had only just realized.

'Yes, Jim, I do. We are only a trumpet short of being the opening scene of a Fellini film.'

'Juliet and the Spirits, is that the one?'

'I think so,' I replied.

We had been walking abreast of each other, but at Isaac's instigation we adopted single file and strode down the road singing and trumpeting like elephants. I led, then Jim followed with an exaggerated limp and his hands on my waist and Isaac was at the back with his hand on Jim's shoulder. It was a merging of the Fellini scene, the conga and Breugel's painting of the blind leading the blind. It didn't seem to matter too much what we looked like, we had been getting funny looks as it was. Since we were in such good spirits, the time went fast and the distance to Medzybiz was getting shorter and shorter.

'Where are we now?' asked Isaac.

'Nearly there,' I said. 'It's just over the brow of the next hill.'

'Good. We are going to make it to Medzybiz in time,' he said.

We climbed the hill and there was a small grassy clearing by the side of the road. From there we could see the town below us. We ate bread and cheese and shared a bottle of cheap red wine. Jim winced after his first sip, but still managed to drink more than his fair share.

'You know, I had a strange dream last night,' he said. 'It was quite extraordinary. I don't normally remember dreams. Dr Scott must have hexed me. I remember it quite distinctly. It was very vivid.'

'You must tell us the dream, Jim,' I said. 'Isaac would like to hear it. The Hasidim have been interpreting dreams for two centuries, and before that they were also important to the kabbalists. In the bible, Joseph and Daniel were dream interpreters.'

'I thought Freud started the interpretation of dreams,' Jim said.

Isaac groaned. 'Freud!' he shouted. 'Good God. The man had no idea whatsoever about the meaning of dreams.'

'Izzy, if you are ready to get off that high horse, Jim is going to tell us a dream. Why do you get so heated about it all?'

'Passion, Johanna. There is nothing wrong with passion. Okay, I'm ready, Jim. Go for it.'

✻

Jim had dreamed that he was a cobbler working in Prague with a beautiful wife as his companion. The workroom was filled with light and his wife was knitting socks. There were two pairs of small socks on the table. Jim told us that it was the most wonderful dream that he had ever had. But when he awoke he felt sad because he realized that it was only a dream.

Isaac told him that the dream would come true, except that he wouldn't be living in Prague, but somewhere in England, and that he would be married and have two more children. Jim scoffed at him and told him that it was impossible. I chatted with Jim as we walked. Isaac was silent for most of the time. He had got the hump. He didn't like it when his insights were rejected, but I found it quite amusing. Isaac could be a little overbearing at times. Even though he probably was a *zaddik*, he still had to master his anger when his ideas were rebuffed or rejected. He walked along mumbling in German so Jim couldn't understand. '*Schuster, Schuster, mein Freund ist ein Schuster, der mir nicht glaubt.*'

'What did he say to you?' Jim whispered.

'He said that his friend is a cobbler who doesn't believe him.'

'That's right, Jim,' Isaac shouted from behind us, 'a doubting cobbler. Now then, Dr Wilton, is there any more of your story to tell, or have we heard it all?'

'No, there is still a little more. After the consultation with Dr Scott, I met my daughter, Veronica. She had come to the club to look for me. She asked me why I hadn't gone to the funeral. I asked her what funeral, and she said that it was the funeral of my secretary, Jane. Apparently she had hanged herself. Then Veronica told me that I had been missing for over a week, and asked me where I had been. Now it was beginning to make sense to me – the confusion and the strange feelings. I had suffered an amnesic fugue. Slowly I began to remember. It was all coming back to me. I had been in Wales, staying in bed and breakfast houses in Tenby. I don't know what possessed me to go there. I felt very lonely. I just kept walking along the beach at Tenby and Saundersfoot. Then I remembered that I had been searching for one of my nannies. She had been very loving towards me. It was such a shock seeing her hanging like that, above my playpen. It was awful.'

'Jim, do you know what you just said?' I asked.

'What, Johanna? What did I say?'

'You implied that it was your nanny who hanged herself, not Jane.'

'Did I? How odd,' he said as tears rolled down his cheeks.

I wanted to tell him what Isaac had found out. I wanted to explain it to him – that it was his mother who had hanged herself above his play pen, and that he had dissociated from the memory. Isaac gripped my hand tightly, and whispered to me not to say anything just yet.

***

7

We arrived at Medzybiz at about seven thirty and were welcomed by a number of Isaac's friends. There were others present whom I did not really know, though I remembered some of the faces from the previous years' visits. In all there must have been twenty people who had arrived for the special meeting. Dr Wilton made a beeline for the bar, and had already downed a couple of brandies and half a bottle of Pilsner before we joined him. Isaac explained to Jim that he wouldn't be able to attend the meeting, but that he could stay in the bar area and have a meal with me. I wasn't allowed to attend the meeting either. It was not because I was a woman. Unlike some modern Hasidim, the members of the group allowed women to be a part of all ritual worship. It was because I wasn't a Hasid that I could not attend the meeting. Jim asked Isaac to ask his friends if they had come across a man called Philip Grimes. Isaac smiled and assured him that he would make discreet enquiries.

Isaac went with the other group members to the small room above the bar. The noise from the room was unbelievable. There was singing and great roars of laughter, and when the dancing started, Jim was concerned that the ceiling above our heads was going to give way and suggested that we sit by the wall. After about half an hour I detected that there was only one person dancing and the others were clapping in unison and singing for the dancer. I knew that it was Isaac's solo performance. He only danced like that when in a state of religious fervour, either privately or at these special meetings. They say that at such times it was as though he could see everything. He danced around people, missing them by half an inch, but never touching them. His feet moved with the speed and agility of a stoat.

*

'What an extraordinary rhythm,' Jim remarked.

'It's Isaac, Jim, he's dancing.'

After ten minutes the others joined in again and the noise increased.

'Are you telling me that this is a religious ceremony? It sounds like a stag night at a rugby club.'

'Well, it's not, Jim.'

'That dance lasted for at least ten minutes, and you say that it was Isaac dancing, after walking almost ninety miles?'

'Yes. That is what I am saying.'

'Who the devil is he, Rasputin?'

'Oh, he would love that. I must tell him that.'

'And the dancing, singing and shouting is a form of worship?' Jim asked.

'Yes, particularly the dancing. It is not enough to concentrate one's mind on God. Why should God only be worshipped with the mind, why not the body? The *nefesh*, the animal soul, must also find expression.'

'It would make a Pentecostal choir seem like the Quakers.'

'I know. I'll tell him that too, he will take it as a compliment. They are certainly not Quietists.'

'Can anybody join in?'

'Well, you are supposed to believe in God, Jim. And that sort of rules you out, doesn't it?'

'Yes. I suppose so. But I think that I could be persuaded. It sounds a hell of a lot better than the Carton Club, and also they appear to manage it without the brandy.'

'Yes. But they are full of real spirit, Jim.'

Dr Wilton looked at me as though a great big penny had dropped and had hit him on the head. Then he was deep in thought. I left him for a while and took a walk outside the inn. The noise of the meeting was less harsh from where I stood. I walked for a while but I could still hear it. It was a clear night and the stars were sharp and in focus. An owl hooted from across the street and was answered by two others. It was strange. The rest of the town was completely silent. The lights were on in some of the houses, but it seemed to me, or at least I imagined, that the occupants were all sitting quietly listening to the noise that came from the inn, and somehow being comforted by it, though few of them nowadays are Jewish. It was different sixty years ago. Then perhaps forty per cent of the town was Jewish, and there were also Poles and other nationalities as well as Ukrainians living there. The Ukrainians were used to upheaval. They were used to going to sleep, and waking up in the morning to discover that they now lived in another country.

There is a saying amongst the Ukrainians, 'Who was born in Austria, married in Poland, had children when in Germany, died in the Soviet Union and is buried in Ukraine, and has never ever left his village? The answer is a Ukrainian. So perhaps they were used to sitting in the dark at night listening to the noise of tanks rolling into the town, and were now happy to hear the noise of festivities at the inn instead.

*

When I returned, Jim was still deep in thought. 'Would you like another drink?' I asked.

'Not for me, thank you,' he replied.

The noise from the room above abated and I detected a single voice speaking, but not what was being said. A few minutes later we heard the door open and the sound of footsteps on the stairs. One of Isaac's friends approached our table, and addressed Dr Wilton. 'The Baal Shem would like you to join us.'

Jim looked at me with an anxious look on his face. He turned to the man and said, 'Please thank the Baal Shem, but I really couldn't.'

The man smiled and said, 'Isaac says that you should join us. The Baal Shem has some news about Philip Grimes.'

Jim's jaw dropped. 'About Philip Grimes,' he stuttered.

'Indeed,' said the man. 'The Baal Shem can help you resolve this problem of yours. Will you come with me?'

Jim looked at me again, and I nodded encouragement. He gingerly got up from the table and followed the man up the stairs. From below I could hear the company of Hasidim welcome him.

✻

When Jim entered the room the Hasidim stood up and greeted him. Gradually they allowed him passageway through their midst and eventually he stood before a man who was sitting on a rough wooden chair.

'We meet again, so soon after our last meeting, Dr Wilton. I am afraid that I do not have any tea to offer you this time.'

Jim looked petrified. 'Benjamin? Benjamin Spencer, is that you?'

'Indeed it is. So you remember me, Jim?'

'Well, yes, of course I do. But where is the Baal Shem Tov.'

'You are talking to him. Didn't Isaac tell you that Baal Shem Tov is a title?'

'Yes. He did.'

'So there you are. It is my title.'

'But I left you in London. How on earth did you get here?'

'Well, I left you in London. How did you get here?'

'I flew.'

'So did I.'

'What, on British Airways?'

'No, not exactly, Jim. I see that you have lost your shoes. What a pity. They really were fine shoes.

'The border guards…'

'It's alright, Jim. I know. Isaac told me.' He smiled, and his smile went right through Jim, who felt a violent thump in his stomach as though something had been released. He felt relieved, but he did not know what he was relieved about.

'Now then,' said Benjamin, 'I am going to tell you something, and you are going to accept that what I am telling you is the truth. Philip Grimes is not the wolfman.

Wilton looked slightly shocked, but I think he had already arrived at the conclusion that Philip Grimes was not the wolfman. 'But why didn't you tell me that in London. You would have saved me the journey,' he stammered.

'Firstly, would you have believed me then?'

'Yes, well, no, probably not.'

'So there you are, it would not have made any difference. But you believe me now?'

'Yes, I suppose so. I am not sure.'

'Well, you should believe me. Secondly, was it such a wasted journey? Have you not benefited by spending five days enjoying the company of Isaac and Johanna? Do you not feel better for that experience?'

'Yes. Yes, of course I do. I have really enjoyed their company. I even enjoyed the walk. It was not so hard, and I feel stronger for it.'

'You see, Jim, when you are doing the right thing for yourself, you gain in energy and peace of mind, no matter how hard the task. So now what? Are you going to take me back to the hospital in order to complete your research?'

'My research?'

'Yes, your research into lycanthropy and carotene deficiency. You see I am the patient that you have been pursuing. I am the wolfman. It was I who sent you the message to come and find me, and I pretended to be the police when I phoned the hospital to let you know about

Philip Grimes. You see I needed you to come here to Medzybiz, but I knew you wouldn't come without being offered a fairly large carrot.'

'So was Dr Scott in on it too?'

'Who on earth is Dr Scott?'

'She knew Grimes, and she had a file on him, which I managed to read. It confirmed my view that Grimes was the wolfman.'

'No, Jim, I assure you that it was a complete coincidence. It had nothing to do with my plan, but it obviously helped.'

'I see. So what is so important about me being here in this town?'

'Isaac will explain that to you tonight. It's better that you hear it in private. I can only tell you that you will not be angry when you hear the reason why I have drawn you here. It will be a great relief for you.'

Benjamin smiled and Jim looked nervous. There was a long silence and the other Hasidim muttered to each other while Benjamin sat and looked Jim in the eye.

'To tell you the truth, Benjamin, for over seven years now I have been getting more and more disgruntled with my work as a psychiatrist. In fact I never wanted to do it in the first place. So I couldn't care a fig for my research.'

'Is that a fact, Jim?'

'Yes. I don't know what on earth made me so obsessed about the wolfman patient in the first place. Actually, I don't want to be a psychiatrist anymore. Do you know that? It's quite extraordinary hearing myself saying that, but it's true.'

'I believe you, Jim,' Benjamin said. 'What would you like to be instead?'

'This might sound daft. But I want to be a cobbler. You know, a master craftsman who makes fine shoes. I love fine shoes, I always have. I always wanted to make a pair of good quality shoes.'

'It is a noble profession, Jim. It is honest work,' Benjamin remarked.

A man at the back shouted, '*Robotah neh vovk; v lees neh vtehcheh!*'

Benjamin and a few of the Hasidim laughed.

'It's a Ukrainian proverb, Jim,' Benjamin said. 'Work isn't a wolf; it won't run away into the forest.'

'What on earth does that mean?'

'I haven't the faintest idea, Jim. Still, working as a cobbler you would be making a worthy contribution to society. Now are you sure that you have got the name right? You do mean Cobbler and not Kabbalah.'

Jim blushed and everyone laughed.

'Do they all understand what we are saying?'

'Some of them understand what we are both saying,' Benjamin replied, 'and the others only understand when I am speaking.'

'I am not with you, Benjamin. We are both speaking English.'

'Yes, but you are only speaking English. When I speak English, those who don't understand English hear what I am saying in their own language. By the look on your face, Jim, you appear to doubt my sanity again. As I was saying, to be a cobbler is a worthy occupation for a man. You should read Moses Cordovero on the *zaddik* as the cobbler. And also Jakob Boehme. Have you read anything about Jakob Boehme?'

'No, who is he?'

'A sixteenth century German mystic who was known as the gentle shoemaker and sometimes as the inspired shoemaker. For a few years he sold gloves in the city of Prague. He was a great man. It's a pity that he wasn't Jewish. He wrote a wonderful book, *Signatura Rerum*. He said that if a man's sound and spirit, out of his signature and similitude, imprints his similitude into mine, then I may understand him really and fundamentally, be it either spoken or written, if he has the hammer to strike my bell.' Does that make any sense to you?'

'No. It's complete gobbledegook as far as I am concerned. Are you talking about how some of these people can understand you, though they don't understand English?'

'Yes.'

'I thought so. It is still a bit difficult to believe.'

'Never mind, Jim, it's hardly worth fighting about. Will you be coming to join us next year? You can bring some of the shoes that you make. We are always in need of good shoes. We tend to walk a lot.'

'Well, yes, I would like to come again, but...'

'It's alright, Jim. You are one of us, now, though you still have a lot to learn. You may stay for the closing ceremony if you wish.'

Benjamin recited a few lines that Jim didn't understand, and the group recited them as well. Then Benjamin snuffed out two candles that were placed on a small table at the side of the room. This done the members of the group began to talk amongst themselves before leaving the room and going downstairs. Jim, Benjamin and Isaac were the last to leave, and Jim helped to guide Isaac down the stairs. When he looked around, Benjamin had disappeared.

✡

We walked through the dark streets of the town of Medzybiz. The stars were still clearly visible in the sky, but the owls had ceased calling to each other. We arrived at the door of a small house at the edge of town. Isaac felt above the door jamb and handed me a key. I opened the door and led Isaac into the house. A fire had been left burning, but it was nearly out. Still the house was warm and not too damp. I found some candles and lit them. Jim warmed himself by the embers of the fire.

'You will have to sleep down here, Jim. There is a small bed in the corner of the room and a few blankets.'

'That's fine, Johanna. The way that I feel at the moment, I could sleep anywhere.'

'Good, sleep well, Jim. God bless you,' I said.

He looked at me with a deep sadness in his eyes, as if he was pleading with me to stay, perhaps to read a story or sing to him, and to hold the candle until he was asleep. I smiled and left the room. Isaac stayed downstairs for another hour. It was then that Isaac told Jim the truth about his parents and about his real mother whom he had called Nanna, the one who hanged herself. He told him that Benjamin had arranged for his soul to be brought here to this house in Medzybyz, because it was the home of his great grandparents, and that his soul had found what it had been searching for, and would be at peace in the morning.

***

8

I woke early. Jim was already up. He had relit the fire and had made himself a cup of coffee. He looked at me strangely.

'Is Isaac still asleep?' he asked.

'Yes. I think we should let him sleep a little longer. We have plenty of time. The bus for Brody leaves at eight. Is there something the matter, Jim? You seem perplexed.'

'I am,' he said. 'I don't know how to say this. I just want to say thank you for what you did for me last night.'

I laughed nervously. 'You mean what Isaac and the Baal Shem did for you.'

'No, I mean what you did for me, Johanna.'

'I didn't do anything.'

'Yes. I thought you might disclaim any knowledge of what happened.'

'I am afraid that I do not understand what you are saying, Jim. Perhaps you should tell me what you think occurred.' I sat down next to him and he stared into the fire. He began to explain.

'I fell asleep quite quickly. I didn't toss and turn as I normally do and I wasn't tormented by the usual dreams. Suddenly I knew that I was fully awake, but my eyes were closed. I felt something brush my brow, like the fluttering of the wings of a small bird. It didn't alarm me. It was warm and soft and I felt that my face was being bathed in a soft light. I opened my eyes. There was a light in the corner of the room. It gradually moved closer to me until I could see a figure standing at the foot of my bed. It was you. You smiled at me and I felt the light from your eyes seep through the whole of my body as though it was liquid honey. You kept smiling at me and you said, "Jim, you are alright. Go to sleep." After that, you remained still and silent. I couldn't speak, but I kept looking to see if you were still there, and you were. Each time

I opened my eyes, you were standing at the foot of my bed smiling at me and lighting up the room. When I awoke this morning it was just getting light. I could not see you but I felt your presence, and then it gradually faded. But it did not upset me that you were not there. I have never experienced a feeling like that before last night, and I will probably never feel it again. I just want to say thank you.'

*

We sat in silence for a few minutes. Sometimes silence is full of anxiety, of nervous embarrassment; sometimes it is empty and cold; but sometimes it is magical and mysterious and is almost unbearable.

Jim was still sitting staring into the fire.

'It was not me, Jim,' I said. 'It would be a dreadful mistake to think that it was me.'

'Yes. I think I know that. But she looked like you. I also know that it wasn't a dream. It was a vision, and more than a vision, because all my senses were involved in it. I know who it was.'

'You do? Who do you think it was?' I asked.

'It was the *Shekhinah*, God's bride.'

'Yes,' I replied. 'It was her. Her scent still lingered in the room when I entered.'

Jim began to cry. He looked at me. 'Why?' he asked.

'I do not know" I replied. 'You probably think that you don't deserve it, and you are probably right. You have received the blessing of the *Shekhinah*, not for what you have already done, but for what you must do in the future. It is a gift that you must earn after it has been given.'

I turned to see Isaac standing in the doorway. He was smiling and nodding his head.

'You see, some things cannot be owned and controlled,' he said. 'You have to let go, Jim. You have to let go of the image of Mary that you carry around with you, but most importantly of your need to rationalize everything. Accept wisdom when she comes to you, and do not be bitter when she doesn't. Work and hope that your efforts are making some small contribution to the Great Work. See the *Shekhinah* in all women. She is the joyfulness of being alive, a joy that can revive the weary man, soften his rigidity and allow him to be part of the dance, to be part of the feast. When did you first hear her voice? Sometimes she speaks to the inner mind, before she appears to the senses.'

'The voice, so that's who it was. It was that Wednesday when I was at the hospital – then a few times before I arrived in Prague. Then when the other voice told me to kill myself, she stopped me doing it. Finally I saw her and she spoke to me. She said that I would be alright.'

'Good,' said Isaac. 'I want to tell you something. When she is not amongst us, sometimes it is hard. But we must remember that she is everywhere. We should respect the *Shekhinah* when she is manifest within the world in other forms. Be kind to Veronica, your daughter. Remember that.'

'*Krahshch odihn rahz pobachitih, neezh sto rahz pochootih,*' I said.

They both looked at me.

'It's an old Ukrainian proverb,' I explained. 'It is better to see something once, than hear about it a hundred times.'

✳

We left the house, locked the door, and replaced the key. We walked in silence through the town, and caught the bus from Medzybiz to Brody. I sat next to Isaac, and Jim sat on his own, at least until the stop at Ternopil, when he was joined by a woman and two children, and had to have one of the children sit on his knee. I explained that it was a Ukrainian custom and he said that he wasn't at all surprised. Isaac meditated and Jim fell asleep for the remainder of the journey. We arrived back at Brody at ten, and Jim explained that he had to rush, because his flight left Prague at ten that evening, and he thought that it was touch and go whether he would get to the airport on time. We said goodbye. Jim thanked us for our hospitality, but added that he had heard enough Ukrainian proverbs to last him a lifetime, and that he wouldn't be at all upset if he didn't hear another one, ever again. He gave me his business card and said that it was a pity that he didn't know anything about me; and would I write to him sometime.

And that's where it all started, when Isaac and I took a taxi to L'Viv airport to board the plane for Amsterdam. That is when Isaac asked me to write the story about Jim Wilton. It was a few days before Isaac died, or as he would say, "moved on."

✳✳✳

AARON'S DREAM

I had completed the story about Jim Wilton, although I have not included the full version here, simply what we learned on the pilgrimage. I had traced the events from the day that Wilton arrived at the hospital to the day that he returned from Ukraine, intent on changing his life. I had understood something of his background, and the reasons why he had become the person that he was. I had finished the story as far as Isaac had known about it, up until a week before he died; and perhaps the rest of it, the chapters on Liz and Mary, were not so important. At least, Wilma had considered my writing about them to be superfluous. Anyway now I had more time to reflect on what was significant and what was not.

I suppose that what had happened to Jim in Ukraine was the real issue that Isaac wanted me to explore. Had I written enough about Jim's vision of the *Shekhinah*? I remembered the discussion that I had had with Professor Weissel, when I had just begun the writing, and when I was disturbed by the experience of seeing Isaac beatified. I had accused Weissel of cynicism, of not being awed by the miraculous. I remember saying to him, 'You have the unfortunate ability to make the miraculous appear somewhat commonplace. I was going to say uncanny ability, but that would have been something of a contradiction. And he had replied, 'Indeed, Johanna. Don't judge me too harshly. I know that you consider me to be an old cynic. But cynicism doesn't come with age – it comes with over-exposure.'

Had I been guilty of the same cynicism, especially in my judgment of Wilton? Had I been overexposed to the miraculous in my own life with Isaac and in my studies in Gnosticism, to the extent that I took the miraculous to be commonplace, and perhaps disregarded the commonplace as being of little significance? I had seen the stars in the night sky so often, yet I was less enthralled with the experience than Isaac was, and he had never seen them. He could only guess what they were like. I had written about Wilton's experience of the presence of the *Shekhinah* in his room that night as commonplace, without understanding the extraordinary impact that it must have had on him. But how could I have described that? How was I to know that his life would be changed by his ordeal? Was it because it was Wilton who had been chosen? I had never felt the same about Isaac's experience and the incident with his grandfather, Yehuda. They had become legendary figures for me. But who was I to judge or know what was to become of Wilton, or Philip, or even John Spencer? Perhaps that was why Isaac had asked me to write about Wilton. I was being weaned off my *magus*. I had become so besotted with my own holy man that I could not see the millions of ways that the divine presents itself to us. I could not see the world in a grain of sand, or the creator in the reflected light off a tin plate. I was in love with the messenger, not the one who had sent the message.

*

I felt guilty about leaving Philip in the lurch. I didn't know if he understood why I had to distance myself from him. I wondered if he had decided not to wait for me. Perhaps I had missed my opportunity to move on in my own life. I phoned Philip to tell him that I had finished the story and to explain what I had realized. He wasn't there and I had to leave a message on his answer machine. I told him that I did love him and that I was sorry for cutting myself off so completely from him and I asked if he would ring me when he got back. I had lots more to tell him.

I felt more involved with the story. I went back over it and began to see connections that I hadn't seen before. I realized that people had to accept change and that I had been stuck in the past with Isaac, even though he had moved on. I was still unsure of the significance of the wolfman, but I knew at least that it represented some resistance to moving on, some sort of regressive movement back to animal nature, which had to be lived out and tamed before it could move ahead again.

*

That evening, after I had put Aaron to bed, I recalled the time that I had spent with Philip in the Inverpolly estate in Scotland, when he told me that I was avoiding my own destiny because of having made mistakes in the past, and that I was fearful of repeating those mistakes. I remembered how furious I had been with him when he said that to me. But I never told him that I had always secretly wanted to be a child therapist. So why was I so angry with him? What he had said was true. I would have accepted it if it had come from Isaac. But it hadn't, and that was the problem. I took it as an affront to Isaac and to myself, that someone else could see something that we could not see. After all we were Simon Magus and Helen, living in the certainty that between us we held the truth about life.

I telephoned Philip again but there was no answer, and his mobile was switched off. It was unusual for Philip to be away on Thursday, when he normally saw clients on that day.

I was tired and ready for bed, when Wilma turned up at the door again with a bottle of wine.

*

'I would love to talk with you, Wilma, but I'm really knackered. I've just finished the story about Wilton and I'm just about to go to bed.'

'But I need to talk to you. It's very important.'

'Go on, you have twenty seconds.'

'It's about Philip.'

'What about him?'

'He's here. He has been staying with me for the last three days.'

I slammed the door in her face. I had been friends with Wilma for twelve years. It was an outrage.

'It wasn't like that, Johanna,' she shouted through the keyhole. 'It's not what you think.'

'Did he sleep with you or not?'

'Of course not.'

'What do you mean of course not? He's been in your apartment for three days. That must be something of a record if you didn't get him into your bed.'

'He didn't want to sleep with me,' she shouted.

'So you asked him to?'

'No, well yes, does it matter?'

I opened the door. 'Come in,' I said. 'Aaron is asleep, so you only have to sit in this chair for ten minutes, just in case he wakes up. Do remember whose child he is. Now give me the keys to your apartment, and don't even think of phoning your place to warn him that I am on my way.'

I left and walked the two hundred yards to Wilma's apartment, keeping to the side of the street where Philip would not be able to see me.

*

If anyone was a wolf, it was Wilma. Her voracity was unnatural, it went beyond greed. It was a compulsive hunger for ownership of anything or anyone that took her fancy. It wasn't just food or drink or men. If she sniffed out that something might be available, she had to own it, because somehow her experience of life could not be validated unless it was turned into a possession. So anything that wasn't obviously claimed by someone else, that wasn't battened down, or written on with an indelible marker pen, was up for grabs — and, boy, could she grab! She had no conception of the meaning of waiting or queuing, and she had the tenacity of a fishwife from Rotterdam at a rummage sale, with the elbows to match.

The tragedy was that her compulsive behaviour caused her to lose the two most important people in her life – her husband and her daughter. He filed for divorce on the grounds of her infidelity, citing e-bay, Ikea and numerous drinking establishments as co-respondents. On the conclusion of the divorce her daughter chose to live with the one parent who, in her prior experience, had partially attended to her needs.

*

I entered the building, took the lift to the third floor, and let myself into the room. Philip heard the door open but didn't turn around. He was sitting by the window looking down onto the street.

'Is Johanna alright?' he asked. 'How did she take everything?'

'I'm over the moon, Philip. What do you expect.'

He turned and looked at me contritely. I could tell that he had been crying.

'Oh, it's you, Johanna.'

'Yes, were you expecting Jezebel?'

'You mean Wilma.'

'Who else – get your things together, you're leaving.'

'Where to?'

'To my place. I have been informed by Wilma that you have managed to resist temptation up until now, but I am also aware that few men could continue to resist the sexual allure of that succubus who calls herself my friend. So get ready. I haven't got all night.'

We walked back to my apartment. Wilma mumbled an apology and ran out of the door. We drank her wine. I considered it a justifiable penalty for her behaviour. We stayed up for a while and Philip read the final draft of Wilton's story.

*

'So what do you reckon?' I asked.

'About what?

'About the story and what I have just said.'

'Yes, its fine, Johanna. I'm pleased that you have finished it. You have cut out all the bits with Liz and Mary though. I quite liked the chapter about their trip to Prague, when Liz got thrown out of the museum for taking photos of the whale penis.'

'Yes, I liked that bit, but Wilma persuaded me that it was confusing. But there is still something troubling me about Wilton. Why should Benjamin have taken such an interest in him, and conjured up such a scheme to get him to Ukraine? He didn't know him.'

'Didn't Isaac tell you? I'm sorry, Johanna, I thought you knew.'

'Knew what?'

'That Jim is Benjamin's cousin. He hadn't met him until that morning in Spencer's house, but he did know of him. Jim's mother was Benjamin's mother's sister. Benjamin was trying to get Jim to know the truth about his background.'

'So why didn't he just tell him?'

Philip smiled. 'Well, you should ask Benjamin that question.'

'I think I would rather not know. I might have to rewrite the story.'

'So what now?' Philip asked.

'I am going to train to be a child psychotherapist.'

'Good, is there a training group in Holland?'

'Of course there is, but I think that I might apply to the Tavistock Institute in London. Aaron is about to start school. But we can find a school in England, although I don't want to live in London or Manchester. I thought we could settle down in a small village near Manchester. You would have to work your client sessions around my trips to London, so you could look after Aaron whilst I was away.'

'Really?'

'Yes, you started all this. Of course it would be better if we got married.'

'Better for whom?'

'Better for both of us; you aren't married are you?'

'No, not at the moment.'

'Well there we are. There's nothing to stop us.'

'What if I don't want to? What if I have other plans for the future?'

'Don't be silly, Philip.'

***

A few months ago Aaron and I moved to England to live with Philip in a cottage near Clitheroe. We were married in the village church and everyone came to the wedding – my mother and my sisters and Wilma, John and Mary Spencer, Jim Wilton and Liz Flannagan, and even Benjamin came. Everything went quite smoothly apart from when Wilma caught the bouquet – who else? As a consequence, the other bridesmaid, Philip's niece, Anna, caught an elbow in the face, and had to lie down for a couple of hours.

The wedding meal was venison with figs and roast potatoes. Liz showed me the engagement ring that Jim had given her, and Jim simply said that the strangest things can happen. Philip overheard him and laughed. Jim Wilton was a changed man. He seemed so relaxed and content.

We didn't go away for the honeymoon; the reception at Whitewell cost enough. Philip took ten days off work and we used the time to go walking in the Forest of Bowland and the Dunsop Valley. Philip had a few days' fishing at Stocks Reservoir near Slaidburn and took Aaron with him and started to teach him how to fish. It was a case of the blind leading the blind. Anyway it gave me some space to myself for a couple of days. Thank God the writing was finished and I could get back to normality.

The next month I enrolled at the Tavistock Institute.

*

Aaron started school a few weeks ago. He has managed to learn English very easily since we only speak English in the house. He was really enjoying living in the country and attending the village school and then one day he came home upset. He told me that he didn't want to live in England and that he wanted to go back to Holland and live with my mother. He was crying and he told me how the teacher and the other children had laughed at him when he told them the story of his father and the animals. It was difficult to understand what had occurred but I gathered that the teacher had asked all the children to tell a story about their father and that when it came to Aaron's turn, they called him a liar and laughed at him.

I was incensed. I almost walked into the school there and then. Eventually I calmed down. I realized that it was Aaron's battle, not mine. He was almost seven years old and he had to learn how to deal with his own problems. I could support him, but I couldn't fight his fights for him.

'What story did you tell them?' I asked.

'The one in my dream.'

'What dream? When did you have a dream about Philip?'

'No, not Philip, it was about Isaac, my father.'

'Isaac?'

'Yes. I told you about it, but you didn't want to hear it.'

'When was that?'

'When I hurt my head, and I was in hospital; and you said you had been reading me a story when I didn't wake up. You didn't want to hear my story because you said that it was probably your story jumbled up. I told it in class, and they laughed at me and they said that I was a liar.'

'The children in your class called you a liar?'

'Yes, and Mr. Roberts laughed too and said I was making it up or I had seen it on the television. He said that it was probably an episode of Doctor Who. And then the class laughed at me again. But it happened. I saw my father and he looked like your picture of him.'

'What was he doing, what did he say?'

'He said that Philip would look after me.'

'Is that all?'

'No, but you didn't want to hear my story before.'

244

'Can you tell it to me now, Aaron? I really want to hear about it now. I promise that I won't laugh, and I know that you are not a liar. Tell me the story, Aaron, please. Tell me what you saw in your dream.'

✻

'I was hot and my head hurt so much, and I was walking through a forest and it got hotter and hotter and I was tired, and there were lots of animals running around, and they were angry because it was so hot. I saw wolves and bears and lions. I saw elephants and camels, and lots of other smaller animals – squirrels, cats and rabbits. They were all angry and I was afraid of them, so I climbed a tree. Then I saw the fire. It was all around us. The forest was burning and the animals couldn't escape. The fire got nearer and nearer, and I was frightened and my head hurt, and I tried to scream but I couldn't. Then I saw a man walking through the fire towards me.'

'Was that Isaac?'

'No, he was a very old man with white hair and a white beard. He looked like Isaac but he was a lot older, and he carried a long pole and he wore a big bear coat, like the one that Isaac had.'

'Yehuda. Was it Yehuda?'

'He didn't say his name. He walked towards me and told me to jump into his arms. I did and he caught me. And the animals stopped being angry and we sat on the floor and some wolves came up to us and they licked our feet. Then I saw the fire wasn't there any more. And then this man walked through the forest carrying me, and all the animals followed us. They weren't angry anymore or frightened. The man said that my father had sent him to help me, and that soon I would see my father. He said that Isaac had gone on in front to interfere for me.'

'You mean intercede? Did he say intercede?'

'What does that mean?'

'It means to help, to speak for you.'

'Yes, he said that my father was going to help me. We walked a long way. Then we were out of the forest, and the animals had gone. And there was a long train, like a long snake. The train was full of people and it stopped near a hill. The old man said that the hill was too steep for the train, so all the people had to get out and walk up the hill. And the old man said that they were going to meet God. And my head still hurt a lot. And we stood looking at the people walking up the hill, but they were going a long way around the hill.'

'Like a spiral, Aaron?'

'What's that?' he asked.

I drew a spiral on his hand with my finger.

'Yes, like that. Then the lady got out of the train. She had a white dress, like you had in the church with Philip.'

'A wedding dress?'

'Yes. And then the old man carried me over to her, and told me that she was the Bride of the Serpent, and that she was very important. She was talking to my father and some other men. They all had long poles like the old man; and Isaac had a long pole.'

'How many men, Aaron, were there thirty six?'

'I don't know, there were lots. And the lady was talking to Isaac, and the old man said that Isaac was interfering.'

'Interceding, Aaron.'

'Yes. And she held my hand. Then she put my hand into Isaac's hand and she smiled and got back on the train, and the old man was crying and Isaac was crying. Then I saw seven children, a bit older than me, with white clothes and a long orange scarf that was wrapped around them, and someone fastened the scarf to the train, and the children danced around in a circle and as they danced they pulled the train up the hill. And I wanted to go up the hill, because Isaac said that the lady was going to marry God, and I wanted to be there to see it. But Isaac told me that I would see it later, because every morning she arrives on a train with lots of people and every morning she marries God, and then returns to the world. I asked Isaac if everyone would get to go to the wedding, and he said yes, everyone would go eventually and that I would go and see it, but not yet. He said that it wasn't the right time for me.

Then Isaac took me away and we walked a long way until we met Philip, and Isaac said that Philip would look after me.'

✻

I was crying and Aaron looked concerned.

'Then I woke up in the hospital, and you were there and the lady that I saw in the dream, she was there in the room.'

'But there was no-one else in the room at the hospital.'

'Yes, there was. There was a nurse.'

'The nurse, you mean the young one that smiled, was that her?'

'Yes.'

I could hardly believe it. I remembered the young nurse who had taken such good care of Aaron when he was in a coma. She had the most radiant smile. It couldn't have been. It simply couldn't. Then I had a sudden thought. I had kept the clothes that Aaron had been wearing when he had his accident. My mother had returned them in a small case. I was sure that I still had the case. I found the trousers that he had been wearing. I phoned my mother.

'It's not funny,' I shouted.

'What isn't?'

'This label you stitched to Aaron's trousers. It wasn't there before.'

'Which trousers?'

'The ones he was wearing when he got admitted to hospital. You have stitched a label on the inside of them.'

'I haven't done anything of the sort, I never touched them. They had some blood on them. The young nurse took them to be washed. I just brought the case of clothes to your apartment. I never even looked in the case. What's the problem? They are probably too small for him now.'

I knew that she was telling the truth. Why was this happening, just when I had decided to live in the mundane world again? I had married Philip and I was starting a new life with him.

'What is the matter, Johanna?' my mother asked. 'What on earth is the matter?'

'It's the label. It's in Hebrew.'

'What does it say?'

'It says – *Aaron Goldmund, son of Isaac Goldmund.*'

'Well, that's true. Why are you getting so hysterical about it?'

'Just a minute there is a note in the pocket.'

I read the note – *Join me at the Kloiz in Brody, when you are ready.*

'What does the note say, Johanna,' my mother asked.

'It doesn't matter, Mum. It's just a laundry note.'

*

Isaac appeared that night in my sleep. He stood there holding a birch staff in his right hand. He was larger than I remembered. He was not like a ghost or a shadowy spectre, but a mature and healthy man, with his barrel chest filled with pride. He was wearing his *tallith* over a long white robe and had his *teffellin* strapped to his arms and forehead. He had Aaron's eyes, deep brown laughing eyes. They were identical but deeper and there was some sorrow mingled with the joy that they expressed. He beamed at me and his forehead glowed around the *teffellin*, like there was a candle inside it; and like Aaron's face had shone when he had awoken from the coma.

He spoke to me and said that it would be his last visit. He told me that tolerance and compassion were the most holy virtues, and that is why he had asked me to write about Wilton – to learn toleration, and to see the Bride of God at work in the world. He asked me not to dismiss the commonplace, and not to judge anyone until I had walked a mile in their shoes. Then he laughed, and said, 'Or until they have walked ninety miles in your sandals.'

Isaac told me that he had to move on now, and accompany the *Shekhinah* in her work. Someone was standing behind him, but I couldn't make out who it was. In the morning I realized who it was.

The fragrance of columbine still lingered in the room.

✿✿✿✿✿✿